GOING DOWN
FOR THE COUNT

GOING DOWN FOR THE COUNT

by

Cage Thunder

A Division of Bold Strokes Books

2013

GOING DOWN FOR THE COUNT

ISBN 13: 978-1-60282-962-6

THIS TRADE PAPERBACK ORIGINAL IS PUBLISHED BY
BOLD STROKES BOOKS, INC.
P.O. BOX 249
VALLEY FALLS, NY 12185

FIRST EDITION: NOVEMBER 2013

CREDITS
EDITOR: RUTH STERNGLANTZ
PRODUCTION DESIGN: STACIA SEAMAN
COVER ART BY MIKE SMARRO (MIKESMARRO.COM)
COVER DESIGN BY SHERI (GRAPHICARTIST2020@HOTMAIL.COM)

Acknowledgments

This book would have been impossible to write without the assistance of everyone at BGEast: Stephen Driscoll, Stuart Wamsley, Rob Tocci, and Jon Thornhill. I also have to give a shout out to some of the wrestlers at BGEast, who made doing the research a lot of fun, gave me some amazing memories, and who I can call friends: Mitch Colby, Jobe Zander, Brendon Byers, Scott Williams, Cole Cassidy, Maxx Thunder, Rafe Sanchez, Billy Lodi, Lon Dumont, Bud Orton, Doc Holliday, and so many, many others. Everyone I've met through BGEast, frankly, has been pretty amazing.

The wrestling bloggers, Joe Marohl (Ringside at Skull Island) and Bard (Sidelineland.com) were also an enormous help, with their blog posts and reviews of wrestling matches, wrestlers, and websites. It was great getting their perspectives on the world of gay wrestling videos and the homoeroticism of professional wrestling in general.

There are any number of wrestlers I have met over the years that deserve a shout out as well—so many that I can't name them all, so alas, guys, know that I owe you a debt I may never be able to repay.

I do have to single out Alex and his partner Bud for thanks, however. Alex was a wonderful introduction to the world of gay pro wrestling, and over the years he and Bud have become really good friends. I wish you guys hadn't moved to Texas!

In my day-to-day life, I have a support group that I couldn't write without: Julie, Lee, Pat, Michael, John and Michael, Jean and Gillian, Josh, the evil Mark, Brandon, Alex, Drew, Lauren, Aaron,

Jamal, David, Kosta, Stan and Janet, Beth, and so many, many others I am sure I am forgetting (and will be hearing from).

Peter, aka Mighty Mike Armstrong—thanks for being such a great guy and so much fun to spend time with.

I have to thank Mike Smarro (mikesmarro.com) for the amazing cover art. You're a great guy, Mike, and the photo shoot was a blast.

I would be remiss if I didn't mention my evil stepsister, Marc Scharphorn—who always makes me laugh. It's okay, Marc— you're pretty.

Everyone behind the scenes at Bold Strokes Books—Radclyffe, Sandy, Ruth, Stacia, Cindy, Connie, Shelley, Lynda—are amazing people that make the production/publishing side of being an author an absolute joy.

And of course, Paul, who just rolls his eyes every time I come up with a harebrained idea for a book. Thanks, boo, the last eighteen years have been extraordinary.

This is for the wrestlers at BGEast, who welcomed me into the family, but especially for Steve, Stuart, and Robbie.

PROLOGUE

I stood before the door to room 322 with my hand poised to knock and sighed. I couldn't believe I was doing this. Yet another hotel hallway—this time a Wyndham in San Diego—and I was disgusted with my childish compulsions. *Turn around, get back in the car, and get the hell out of here, what do you care if you never see him again? It's not like he's going to see you and suddenly fall madly in love with you. And why do you care? Why do you care what he thinks? Why do you still drop everything and come running the minute he snaps his fingers?*

I'd sworn the last time I wouldn't do this again, for Christ's sake, no matter what he said, no matter how much he begged—which he hadn't done, actually. No, it had been the usual friendly e-mail out of the blue, like it hadn't been two years since the last time I'd seen him, like nothing had ever gone wrong between us in the first place, like there was no history or hurt. And instead of deleting the e-mail like any sane person would have, no, I wrote back and one thing led to another and—sure enough—we wound up making plans like we always did. And here I was, once again telling myself this was definitely going to be the last time.

But God help me, I did want to see him again. All the way over, on the highway from West Hollywood, I'd gone back and forth. Turn around and head home, or see it through? Obviously, *see it through* had won the internal debate.

I was a little excited, much as I hated to admit it to myself. Bill Wawrzniak: my life would be so different had I never met him. Sure, there had been some rough times, but overall I was pretty damned happy with my life and where I was at. So what would it hurt to see him one last time? To do this one last time, and then say good-bye for good?

I shifted my gym bag on my shoulder. *Yeah, right,* I sneered at myself, *good-bye for good. You'll never say no whenever he asks, no matter how mad you get or how disgusted you get with the whole mess. You jump whenever he snaps his fucking fingers. You've been doing it for years, even though you know damned well all you are to him is a body to use for a few hours in a hotel room. And you're never going to stop, are you? He snapped his fingers again and here you are. No matter how you justify being here to yourself, you* are *here, aren't you?*

I gritted my teeth and knocked.

The door opened, and there he was, wearing a T-shirt and a pair of jeans. He was still sexy, his blond hair now trimmed in a military style, his eyes still that startling icy blue, his skin tanned a reddish gold. He was a big man—just over six feet four and weighing a solid 240 pounds. He wasn't quite as well developed or defined as he'd been when we'd first met, but there was still that indefinable something about him that got under my skin. There was a big grin on his face, and the big biceps on his right arm flexed as he grabbed me and pulled me into a hug. He lifted me up a bit off the floor and said, "It's so great to see you, man!" My back cracked as he squeezed me. His delight was genuine, which was part of the problem.

It was hard to stay pissed off at someone who loved you.

Just not the way you want him to. That's always been the problem.

I let myself smile. "It's good to see you, too." And it was, which annoyed me even more. *Dysfunctional, party of one, your table is ready.* I hugged him back lightly, wrapping my arms around his broad back and barely exerting any pressure.

"Come on in!" He set me down and clapped me on the back. I shut the door and followed him past the closed bathroom door into the living room area of the suite. The love seat and table had been shoved against one wall, and a pair of queen-size mattresses, stripped of their sheets, had been placed side by side in the center of the room. Next to the love seat was the obligatory camera bag—he never went anywhere without his video and digital cameras. "You're gonna *love* this kid." He grinned at me. "Lots of natural ability and"—he whistled—"his body is pretty phenomenal."

"I'm sure," I said, putting my bag down and shrugging off my black leather jacket. I was wearing a black muscle tank top, and I made sure my biceps flexed as I deftly folded the coat and tossed it over a chair.

"Damn, you look hot," he said, shaking his head. "But then, you always do."

"Thanks." I sat down in the chair and leaned back, stretching my legs out in front of me. "So where's the kid?"

Bill's eyes glinted. "He's already dressed and in the bathroom, waiting." He rubbed his hands together. "So get dressed and I'll take some pictures."

I stood up and stretched. Pictures were a part of his ritual. He must have taken thousands of pictures of me during the years we'd known each other. He'd taught me how to pose, what gear looked best on me, and as my fame had spread in the underground gay wrestling circuit, those pictures had come in very handy. I kicked off my shoes and stripped down to my underwear—black Calvin Klein briefs with a red waistband. Bill always liked me in black and red. I unzipped my bag and removed a pair of black wrestling trunks with red stripes on the left hip. I slid off my underwear and placed it on top of my clothes. I pulled on the wrestling trunks and felt my dick start to stiffen a bit. Putting on gear was always a bit of a turn-on for me. I sat down and pulled on a pair of knee-high red socks, then my black kneepads, and slid on my black patent-leather wrestling boots. I started lacing them up. I focused on the laces while listening to him mess with the camera. I took my time, thinking, *Let the kid sit there in the bathroom until I'm good and ready—might as well get him used to Bill's self-absorption.*

Finished, I tied the laces and tucked them inside the boots.

I stood up. "Well?"

Bill looked up at me and whistled again. "Your body just gets better and better with age. How do you do it?"

"Diet and exercise," I replied.

He shook his head. "Still a smart-ass." He pointed the camera at me. "Give me a double biceps pose."

I raised both arms and flexed them, remembering to keep my index fingers slightly extended and my wrists bent so the biceps would peak. I stood there, going through pose after pose at his direction, remembering the first time I'd done this. It seemed like a million years ago, and in some ways, I suppose it was.

I'd always been a little ashamed of my interest in wrestling, thinking it weird and strange. For years, I'd only let very close friends know about it.

Then I met Bill, and everything changed.

"I saw your last video," he said, taking another shot of me from behind as I flexed my back muscles. "Great match—you really beat the fuck out of that muscle boy. But I really wish you wouldn't do that erotic stuff. That's for private."

"The fans like my cock," I said with a slight shrug.

"It's a gorgeous cock"—he snapped another picture—"but you shouldn't let everyone see it—the videos where you can see how big and thick it is in your trunks are a lot hotter than the ones where you blow loads on your victims."

Part of the reason I started doing the erotic matches on DVD was because I knew you wouldn't approve, I thought. That's me, putting the fun in dysfunction.

"Well, the kid thought it was a hot match." He put the camera down and lit a cigarette. "He's been hot for this match ever since he saw that one."

"Well, bring him out, then." I shrugged. "Don't you want some pre-match shots of the two of us?" I knew he did—he loved documenting the whole pre-match stare down and pose offs. He'd also tape the match, and when it was over, he'd have us pose for action shots. *They always look better when you're drenched in sweat* was his mantra.

It was like doing a BGEast shoot on a smaller scale.

Well, it was like doing a BGEast video shoot for fucking *free.*

There hadn't been a sound out of the bathroom since I'd arrived. I remembered the first time Bill had me hide in the bathroom so I could make an entrance. I'd been nervous. The only person I'd done a pro match with at that point had been Bill, and while he'd been a great mentor, teaching me moves, holds, and techniques, I was still nervous. The guy I was wrestling was an old friend of Bill's from the indie pro-wrestling circuit, and Bill had raved about him to me for so long I was absolutely terrified I wouldn't measure up, either as a wrestler or with my body. *Matt has his own private ring in Pensacola,* he'd told me, *and invites guys up to use it and work with him all the time. You're going to love him, and he's going to love you.* He'd shown me a picture of Matt—his body drenched in sweat, his red and white trunks clinging to his body, his arms outstretched in victory over his head, a championship belt around his waist.

He was *hot.*

The bathroom door opened and the kid stepped out.

I inhaled sharply.

Bill had been right, damn him—he knew me all too well.

The kid was a few inches shorter than me, and kid was an appropriate description. He didn't look a day over eighteen. He had close-cropped brown hair, pale skin with reddish cheeks, and his body was extraordinary. His shoulders were broad and his waist so narrow I could probably close my hands around it and have the fingers meet. His chest was strong, his pecs firm with quarter-sized erect purple nipples. His legs were muscular and defined, as well. He was wearing a white bikini that was barely a half inch wide on the sides, white kneepads, white boots, and a white Zorro-style mask over his green eyes.

My cock became instantly and achingly erect.

"Cage, meet Billy the Kid Weston." Bill glanced down at my crotch and smirked, damn him.

The Kid gave me a big, nervous smile, sticking out his right hand. "It's an honor to meet you, Cage."

I took his hand after a moment and squeezed it until he involuntarily gasped. "It's going to be a pleasure to kick your ass."

He pulled his hand away and got right up in my face, our chests barely brushing against each other. "The only ass that's getting kicked is yours." His voice was young and squeaked a bit.

"Okay then," I replied evenly. "Loser gets fucked. Deal?"

"You're going to love the way my cock feels in your ass, old man."

Nothing gets my cock harder than a cocky young muscle stud—and we kept mouthing off to each other as Bill took the pictures he wanted. I was ready for the match to start. As we kept posing, I admired his body and imagined how it would look writhing in pain as I twisted it into submission hold after submission hold.

"Okay, that's good." Bill put the camera down and picked up the video camera. "You guys ready?"

"I'm always ready," the Kid growled, getting up in my face again.

I drove my right fist into his abs. He doubled over, and I linked my hands together and brought them down on his exposed back, driving him down into the mattresses, gasping. "Too fucking easy," I said, straddling his back and reaching under his chin with both hands. As I pulled his head back, I slid my knees under his armpits, anchoring them and slipping his arms over my quads. I sat down on the small of his back, stretched my arms straight out, and leaned back. I flexed every muscle in my upper body and let out a howl of triumph. He was breathing hard, moaning every time he exhaled, as I cranked harder and pulled his head even farther back. I'd ease up for a little bit, listening to him trying to catch his breath, before pulling him back again. "I'll break your pussy back," I whispered in his ear. "You ready to give?"

I had to give him credit—most guys gave in and submitted to the camel clutch almost immediately. He held out for longer than most guys—but he finally surrendered to the inevitable, slapping my leg and half shouting, "I submit! I submit! *I submit!*"

I released the pressure and let him hang there, his arms still draped over my quads. It was tempting—oh, so tempting—to put him through it all over again, but I hadn't even broken a sweat yet, so I shoved his arms off and stood up. I flexed both biceps over him for the video camera and looked over at Bill. "This is it? I expected a bit of a challenge—at least to break a sweat."

"Fuck you," the Kid gasped out below me. He was rubbing his lower back with his right arm.

"I don't like your attitude," I replied, dropping onto his lower back with my right elbow.

He howled and rolled away from me almost to the edge of the mattress, clutching his lower back. I slowly walked over to where he lay. His cock was hard inside his tiny white trunks. I knelt down beside him, grabbing his cock through his trunks. "Looks like you like getting your ass kicked," I said, squeezing it ever so slightly.

"Fuck you," he gasped out.

I sat down on his chest with my knees on either side of his head. I reached down with my left hand, grabbed a handful of hair, and pulled his face up into my crotch. I rubbed his face against my hard cock. "You want to suck that, don't you?" I whispered as he tried to pull his head back. I let go of his hair, and his head dropped back against the mattress. I reached down and slapped him lightly before getting up and walking to the opposite side of the makeshift ring. "Whenever you're ready for more, boy—I'll be right here." I looked over at Bill. He'd stripped down to a pair of navy blue wrestling trunks with a yellow lightning bolt across the crotch, which was his trademark. His ring name had been Bill Lightning. His cock was hard, and there was a wet spot on the front of his trunks where the tip of his dick was. I was never really aware of him and his camera while I wrestled; when I'd started out, that had been good training for the video work. Some guys could never forget there was a camera trained on them, and it showed in the video later.

But Bill had trained me well, constantly screaming at me not to look at the camera. It hadn't taken me long to learn how to forget about it, to focus instead on the body of my opponent and what I was doing to it.

There'd been plenty of times when Bill had straddled my head and shoved my face into his crotch, growling at me to kiss his lightning bolt.

I watched as the Kid slowly got to his feet, trying to catch his breath. He glared over at me. Despite how easy that first fall had been, he was still cocky.

I love stomping the cocky out of boys.

"Fucker." He spat the word at me.

I smiled and pulled my trunks down a bit, so he could see the head of my cock. "You're going to have to work harder if you want me to fuck you, boy. I don't fuck pushovers."

"The only person getting fucked is you!"

I laughed. "It takes a man to fuck me—and you're just a little boy."

He launched himself at me, which I hadn't been expecting. He crashed into me and we went backward into the wall with a thud. He started punching me in the stomach, knocking the wind out of me before I was ready for it. I doubled over a bit, and he grabbed my head into a side headlock and dragged me back out onto the mattresses while I tried to catch my breath. He was squeezing pretty hard, and then he hip-tossed me over onto my back, managing to hang on to the headlock. I twisted, grabbing his wrists and trying to power his arms apart, to no avail. He just tightened his grip, and I could feel my teeth grinding together.

He was a strong little fuck.

I managed to get to my knees as he gripped tighter.

I drove my elbow into his abs and felt his grip loosen.

I did it again, much harder, and his grip broke as he fell onto his back.

I jumped to my feet. He was lying there, trying to catch his breath. I walked over and brought my right boot down on his stomach. His knees came up, and I stomped him again. I reached down and grabbed a handful of hair, dragging him up to his feet again. His legs were a little wobbly, and I slugged him hard in the abs.

He dropped down to his knees, both arms crossed over his stomach.

I stepped right in front of him and shoved his face back into my crotch.

I rubbed my groin against his face.

And he head-butted me right in the balls.

Hot iron spikes shot up into my intestines as I fell back, my body curled up as I groaned. Vaguely I was aware of him standing over me, saying things in a taunting, angry voice. He kicked me in the lower back, and I rolled away from him. I was breathing hard and I was furious. The little shit! You want to fight dirty, motherfucker? I'll show you dirty…

He rolled me onto my back and straddled my head. He grabbed the back of my head and shoved my head into his crotch. "You like that, old man? How do you like it?"

Actually, I liked it just fine. His cock was hard, and his balls felt heavy and full of young-man cum. He smelled musky and sweaty—a smell that drives me wild with desire. I let him rub his cock against my face, and then he was rolling over onto his side, taking me with him, and he gripped my head with his quads.

His legs were strong.

I forgot the dull ache in my balls as my head exploded with

crushing pain. He was trained well in applying a head scissors, too—Bill had undoubtedly let him know that head scissors were a huge turn-on for me. He knew exactly what to do—apply some blinding pressure and then ease up just as I was about to submit to it…and then once I was able to get some air into my lungs, tighten it up again. He twisted my head from side to side with his legs, pressed himself up onto his arms to get a better angle for pressure. But I wasn't going to give in to this punk, this little boy who thought he was tough enough to beat Cage at his own game…

Fuck.

The pressure built. Surely he couldn't keep that up…if I just resisted a little longer…

"I submit! I submit!"

He let go and I fell back onto the mat, holding my aching head. Through the roar in my ears, I could hear him taunting me, and I looked up to see him flexing and posing in triumph.

The little fucker.

He was going to pay.

I got to my knees.

"Anytime you're ready." He folded his arms and smiled at me.

I got to my feet. I slowly walked toward him. He unfolded his arms and watched my approach. As soon as I was in reach, we locked up, collar and elbow. I shoved him down and brought my knee up into his chest. He fell back onto the mattress, and I leaped into the air and came down with my elbow on his abs. His breath left him in an explosion, and I grabbed his abdominal muscles in a claw with my left hand and squeezed. Both his hands flew to my wrist, trying to get my hand off. With my right hand I grabbed his balls and squeezed. He half screamed.

"You like ball work, boy?" I panted as I gave his balls a brutal squeeze. I let go and he rolled up into a ball—until I grabbed his hair and picked him up, dropping his back across my right knee in a back-breaker. His oh-so-perfect abs were there, ripe for abuse, almost begging for it. I drove an elbow into them and ground it into the groove between his top two washboards. With my other hand I reached over and yanked his trunks down to his knees. His cock, oozing a little precum, arched up toward me.

I grabbed his neck and crotch and hoisted him back up in the air, then dropped him down across my knee again. He flipped off, landing on his stomach, and he arched his hard little round white ass up in the air. I reached down and smacked it. It was hard, with little black hairs in the crevice between the cheeks. I grabbed his trunks and yanked them all the way off. I stood over him before dropping down to my knees and wrapping his trunks around his neck, pulling him back. His hands went to his sweaty trunks, trying to get some air as I choked him.

My own cock was aching as I felt his hard little ass bucking up against me.

Once you submit, boy, I thought, *I am going to fuck you senseless.*

I let go, tossing the trunks to the side. I stood up and yanked my own trunks down. I flexed every muscle in my body as I let out a growl of lust, and with my right foot I nudged the boy over onto his back. I grabbed his ankles and hoisted him, turning him over into a Boston crab. He started screaming almost immediately, and the view of his twisted body, his hard cock hanging there, was sublime. I hoped that Bill's camera had a good view of it—I was going to want to see it in slow motion when I watched it later.

"I submit! I submit! I submit!"

"Say please."

"Please! Please!"

"You done, boy, or do you want me to beat on you some more?"

"I'm done! I'm done!" His voice quivered.

I let go, gently dropping him down to the mattress. I flexed over him a few times as he lay there moaning. I got up and went over to my bag. I slipped on a condom and lubed it up before heading back over to where he was lying.

I got between his legs and lifted his hips up over mine.

"You ready?"

He opened his eyes and smiled at me. "Fuck me, please, sir."

I eased my cock into his tight little hole, and as I did, I glanced over and saw Bill still taping. His own trunks were down, and he was pulling at his own cock.

Erotic is only for private, I heard him say again as I forced my cock into my groaning boy.

How many times had Bill taped me fucking someone I'd just beaten?

How many times had Bill taped me being fucked after getting beaten?

I leaned down and nibbled on one of the boy's hard nipples. He moaned, his eyes closing as I slowly worked my cock all the way inside.

Oh, he was so tight on my cock.

It felt so good.

I started to pull out slowly, gently. He began to writhe underneath me.

"Oh yeah," he breathed, "fuck me, oh please, fuck me, sir."

I slammed all the way back inside him. His eyes rolled back in his head as a deep moan reverberated in his throat. Once inside, I ground against him, and his entire body began to tremble.

I traced a finger from his throat down the valley between his pecs and along his abs.

I moved my hips back until all that was inside him was the head of my cock.

He opened his eyes. "Yes, sir, that's the way, that's so nice." He gasped, his eyes half-closing as I moved deep inside him slowly, resisting as he arched up against me, trying to get me inside all at once.

He shuddered as I reached full penetration, rotating my hips in a circular motion to loosen him up some, and he let out a shout as he starting spewing cum out of his cock.

I pulled back out, stroking myself as he finished shooting.

The first time Bill had fucked me, I'd come almost immediately.

I was you once, I thought as the boy smiled back at me.

I peeled off the condom, going up on my knees and stroking. He sat up and started playing with my nipples, and in three strokes I was coating him with my own load.

"Wow," he whispered, smiling at me.

Bill turned the camera off and set it down. "That was even hotter than I thought it would be."

I unlaced my boots and slipped them off. I stood up. "I'm going to take a quick shower." Without another word, I walked into the bathroom and turned on the shower.

As I washed the sweat and smell of the boy off me, memories flooded through my mind.

I'd fallen in love with Bill and had always wanted to please him. Even now, I was still trying to please him, even though he'd moved on to other wrestlers. It had hurt to realize that I wasn't special, that I wasn't the first and I wasn't going to be the last.

I thought about the Kid. I had, indeed, been him once, young and innocent, excited that an older guy wanted to make me a wrestler.

How many times had I shown up in a hotel room to wrestle Bill's latest find, for his videotaping pleasure? How many times had I been the first guy to wrestle the new boy, other than Bill?

This is the last time.

I toweled off and walked back into the other room. The boy was sucking Bill's dick. I closed my eyes and saw myself doing the same thing after getting beaten up and fucked by one of Bill's friends.

I got dressed without saying anything. I put my gear back into my bag and hoisted it up onto my shoulder.

"You want to get dinner?" Bill asked. The boy smiled at me.

I shook my head and walked out of the room.

Once out in the hallway, I leaned against the wall and closed my eyes.

This, I told myself, *was the last time.*

Three years of this was enough…

CHAPTER ONE

The Corinth County Fair was always the week after the Fourth of July, when the heat of the Alabama summer hung over the town like a wraith. The sun was relentless in a cornflower blue sky. An occasional wisp of white cloud drifted across the vast overhead expanse of blue. The levels of the rivers, lakes, and streams dropped. Farmers were praying for rain as the crops wilted in the windless heat. Scorching waves radiated off the softening blacktop on the roads. Parked cars baked in the sun, and steering wheels became too hot to hold. No breeze stirred the branches of the trees, and the stench of death from the meatpacking plant on the south side of town hung in the still air. The display on the Corinth County Bank sign showed it was 102 degrees as I parked my car in the dirt lot across the street from the fairgrounds. I sat in the car for a few moments, enjoying the cold air blowing out of the vents, getting up my nerve to face the heat again.

I was meeting some of my friends from high school at the fair. I was home for the summer from college and bored out of my skull. Every day was the same: get up, eat, watch television, read some books, and pray someone would call with something to do. The monotony stretched endlessly ahead of me, and the day I could return to college seemed a million years in the future. I'd always hated going to the fair when I was in high school, but then as now, there was never anything else to do. The fair was a way of killing time, wasting some money, and getting out of the house.

Next summer I'm finding a summer job and staying at school, I swore to myself for maybe the thousandth time that day as I got out of the car and locked it. I looked across the street at the fair. It was the same old fair it had been every summer of high school. Animal pens that smelled like shit, kids screaming, rigged games of chance on either side of the midway, and rickety-looking rides assembled by the long-haired stoner-looking dudes that operated them.

I wished I could say it was fun being around my friends from high school, but it wasn't. Time had passed and we'd changed. I was the only one of my old gang who'd gone to college. My lifelong best friend Tony was getting married in September to his girlfriend, Angela, whom I'd always hated. Tony was working at the meatpacking plant and trying to save enough money for a down payment on a house. To be fair, the reason I'd always hated Angela was because she diverted too much of his attention from me. I'd had a crush on Tony almost from the first time I'd seen him, and truth be told, I still hoped the day would come when he'd wake up and realize I was what he'd always wanted. He was so sexy, with his dark skin, blue-black hair, and blue eyes. He had the body of death, too—broad, strong shoulders, massive chest, flat stomach, and muscled legs topped by a gorgeous round bubble-butt I just wanted to bury my face in.

I didn't have anything in common with them anymore—not with Tony with his job on the kill floor, or Robbie who worked at the rubber-glove factory on the other side of town, or Kevin with his job on his father's dairy farm. They looked older than me, more weathered, and it seemed like all they ever wanted to talk about was their jobs, drinking beer, or getting laid. Robbie and Kevin were already physically going to seed, rolls of fat gathering around their waists and dark circles under their eyes. When I tried to tell them about my life at Gulf State, they just looked at me blankly, and one time I caught Kevin scowling at me. Their lives were already set, for better or worse. They knew they were never getting out of Corinth County, and whatever dreams they'd once had for getting out and seeing the world had died.

But not mine. I was getting my degree and getting as far away from Alabama as I possibly could.

And I think they resented me a little for escaping.

We were supposed to meet at the entrance in about five minutes. I broke into a sweat as I hurried across the street to the front gates. Sure enough, they were all standing there waiting for me, lounging casually. Despite the heat, they were all wearing jeans and sleeveless T-shirts. They waved absently as I walked up to them. "Hey, guys," I said, digging out my wallet to pay the entry fee. We paid, got our hands stamped, and walked into the midway. Despite the heat, it was crowded. There were lines at the rides, parents holding on to their children. The smell of hot grease mixed with the odor of the animal pens.

"What do you guys want to do?" Kevin asked after we'd gotten Cokes from a vendor. I took a drink and almost gagged. It was too syrupy and sweet.

"We should go check out the wrestling matches," Tony said, chewing on some ice.

That got my attention. "Wrestling matches?" I asked, resisting the urge to throw my nasty Coke into the nearest garbage can. "Seriously?"

"Yeah." Tony grinned at me. His straight teeth were starting to stain from chain-smoking. "They've got some guys up from Florida, the Gulf Coast Wrestling Alliance. They set up a ring and everything. There's some matches this afternoon and some others tonight." His left eyelid slid down in a wink. "Thought I'd surprise you."

I grinned back at him, and for just a moment it was like being back in high school again, the old connection between the two of us flaring up and blazing. *He remembers how much I love wrestling,* I thought and stifled a laugh. *Of course, he doesn't know why.*

It hadn't been easy growing up in a small town in Alabama and being attracted to boys instead of girls. There had been so many nights I'd wished I were dead, thinking I was the only one in the world. I still wasn't ready to tell anyone the truth yet, but someday, maybe when I had gotten out of college, I'd be ready. Now I knew there were others out there like me. I knew there were gay bars down in Tampa and the bigger cities in Florida. I knew there had to be other gay students at Gulf State—hell, there might even be a gay bar in Bay City itself—but I hadn't found one yet.

I knew my parents were never going to like it—they'd probably disown me.

That's just the way things were in Corinth, Alabama.

I was about eleven when I first discovered professional wrestling. I had been vaguely aware of it before—I'd seen the fan magazines in stores—but had never really given it a whole lot of thought. One night, I saw in the *TV Guide* that an old Katharine Hepburn movie was playing on the late-night movie and stayed up to watch it. After the news went off, the movie didn't start for another hour, so I curled up on the couch with one of my Hardy Boys books to read while I waited for the movie to start.

In the hour between the news and the movie, a pro-wrestling program came on. I was reading and not paying much attention to it, when I looked up and saw a beautiful young man climb through the ropes. He had shoulder-length curly brown hair, broad shoulders, and muscular legs. He was wearing a shiny blue jacket, and as he bounced around in his corner, I caught glimpses of tight white trunks beneath the longish jacket. When he took the jacket off, I gulped and felt my dick get hard. His chest was thickly muscled with huge nipples, his stomach flat, and his skin was perfectly smooth. His arms rippled with muscles, and those white trunks! They left little to the imagination, from the curve of his hard, muscular ass around to the front where a huge bulge was on display.

His opponent wasn't as hot or sexy—his chest and back

were matted with fur, he had a big belly, and he was wearing black tights that completely encased his legs—but when the bell rang, it was soon apparent the pretty young man was going to get his ass kicked. And the heavier, hairier bully threw him all over the ring, punching and kicking him and twisting his body in ways that didn't seem humanly possible. As I watched him suffering, his back arching and that oh-so-perfect white-covered ass going up in the air, I slid my hands inside my underwear and played with my dick until my entire body convulsed and liquid shot out of it.

Every Saturday night after that, I stayed up and watched.

Tony, of course, didn't know I masturbated when I watched wrestling on television.

He didn't know that sometimes I fantasized about the two of us in the ring.

We went inside the tent and gave our tickets to the bored-looking long-haired guy at the entrance. We took seats in the front and watched two matches before the main event. The matches were okay—none of the guys caught my attention. They were all heavy, with big guts hanging over their trunks, the meat of their arms jiggling as they maneuvered each other around the ring. I'd never seen pro wrestling in person before, and as these matches were boring, I found my attention wandering a bit as I looked around the tent at the other people inside. There were a lot of empty seats, which made me feel kind of bad for the big men sweating inside the ring. They tried to get the crowd into it, but the applause was sparse. No one booed or cheered the way they did when I watched on television. When the second match ended and the two wrestlers had left, the emcee climbed back through the ropes with his microphone and grinned at the thin crowd.

"And now for our main event! Making his way to the ring, put your hands together for Davey Reed!"

Davey Reed came in through the entryway on the opposite side of the tent where we were sitting. He had long stringy dark hair, and his face was dotted with angry red pimples. He was skinny, with long skinny arms, and his chest was underdeveloped. His legs were strong and thickly muscled, though, and his skin was pale aside from what we called a farmer's tan—his arms were dark. He was wearing shiny gold trunks that hugged his round ass like another layer of skin, and his kneepads and boots were a matching shade of gold. He held up his arms and flexed, trying to get the crowd to cheer or something, but other than some sparse applause, he got no reaction.

"And his opponent, weighing in at two hundred and forty pounds, Big Bill Lightning!"

My jaw dropped as Big Bill walked through the entrance. I bit my lower lip and felt my dick stirring inside my pants. He was gorgeous. He was at least six foot four, and his smooth, tanned skin glistened in the lights. He was wearing tight black trunks with a silver lightning bolt across the front, black boots, and black kneepads. His body bulged with muscle, and as he leaped over the ropes into the ring, I couldn't help but notice his cock was hard inside his trunks. He pointed at Davey and threw his head back, booming out laughter. Now the crowd was paying attention. He had charisma to spare, and everyone was watching his every move as the referee patted him down. When the bell rang, he didn't move—he just stood in his corner and waited for Davey to move in after him. As soon as Davey got close, Big Bill threw a huge forearm across his chest that sent the smaller man flying back across the ring. Big Bill laughed again and strutted his way across the ring as the crowd erupted in boos. He turned and flipped off the crowd, then went to work on the kid.

It was a mismatch, to be sure. The kid didn't have a chance, and Big Bill just treated him like he was a practice dummy. I couldn't take my eyes off the big man as he lifted, twisted, and tossed little Davey around like he was nothing. The crowd's boos got louder as he tossed Davey from side to side by the hair—and once, when the referee tried to reprimand him, he simply tossed the referee aside like he was nothing before moving back in for another assault on the skinny wrestler.

My cock was so hard it was aching.

Finally he put the kid in a sleeper, and after struggling for a few moments, the kid went limp. Big Bill lowered him to the mat and put his boot on his chest, flexed his muscles in triumph, and let out a primal yell that only resulted in louder booing. He pointed at a man in the audience, stalked over to the ropes, and started screaming about how he was going to kick the guy's ass. The ref pulled him back to the center of the ring and raised his thickly muscled arm in triumph. Everyone else erupted into another chorus of boos. Some people started throwing their crumpled-up Coke cups at the ring. Big Bill just smirked as he flexed his massive arms again, as though he was enjoying the jeers of the audience. He turned to face each side of the ring, striking muscle poses, and then he turned to our side. Tony, Robbie, and Kevin were booing just as loudly as everyone else—and Big Bill looked right at me and winked.

Our eyes locked for just a moment that seemed to last for an hour. My cock stirred inside my shorts. He looked away, leaped over the ropes, and headed out the way he had come in. I watched him go, the way those black trunks hugged his big muscular ass, and licked my lips. "Come on, let's go," Tony said, standing up. The referee was helping poor hapless Davey to his feet. Davey looked dazed, shaking his head from side to side like he was trying to figure out where the hell he was and what the hell had happened.

As we filed out, Kevin and Robbie started arguing over whether the wrestling was real or not. I fell out of step with them, and finally Tony whispered to me, "You should go talk to that guy. Big Bill."

"Why?" I looked at Tony, who gave me a big grin.

"He picked you out of the crowd for some reason." So Tony had seen him wink at me. My blood froze, but Tony just gestured to a group of trailers parked just behind the tent. They were the small kind, hooked up to big pickup trucks. "That's where the wrestlers hang out between matches. That silver one is Big

Bill's. Go talk to him. Get his autograph. Ask him about how you become a pro wrestler. Don't you want to be one?" He winked at me and stuck his elbow in my ribs. "Go talk to him, don't be a pussy your whole life."

"I…" I hesitated. I'd never really thought about becoming a pro wrestler. It was just something I enjoyed watching. It aroused me—but then it had aroused Big Bill, too. I couldn't have been wrong about him being hard in his trunks. I could hear my heart pounding in my ears. Big Bill was sexy as hell.

"Do it." Tony shrugged. "The worst thing that he can do is tell you to buzz off."

It was true. What the hell? "All right. I'll catch up to you guys later."

I swallowed again for courage and walked over to the silver trailer. I knocked, and the door swung open. "Yeah?" Big Bill said. He folded his arms across his chest, and the muscles bulged.

I stood there, in the blazing sun, and swallowed while I tried to get up my nerve to say something.

"You want an autograph, kid?" he asked, squinting in the bright light. He wasn't wearing a shirt, but had pulled a pair of sweatpants over his trunks.

"Good match," I blurted out. As soon as the words came out of my mouth, I wished a hole would open in the ground and suck me down.

"Thanks, kid." He put his right hand up to shield his eyes, and he smiled. "You're the kid who was in the front row." His teeth were even and white. He stepped aside, "Come in and get out of the goddamned sun."

I walked inside. It was cool inside the trailer, and as my eyes grew adjusted to the darkness, I glanced around. A pair of yellow trunks was draped over the little sofa against the far wall. There really wasn't much furniture inside the little trailer: just the sofa, a small table, and a chair off to one side. There were some mats set up on the little floor space, and there was a small door in the back.

The door shut behind me. "It's not much," the big guy said, "but it works for these jobs." He stuck his big hand out at me. "My name's really Bill."

"Bill?" I asked as his hand closed over mine, and I tensed, waiting for the massive pressure when he shook it. But his grip was gentle, and he pumped my hand up and down a few times.

"Bill Lightning's not my real name, it's my ring name." He smiled at me again. "My real name is Bill Wawrzniak." He walked over to a little refrigerator. "You want a beer?"

"Sure." He tossed me a can of Coors, and I pulled the tab and took a long swig.

He opened one for himself and plopped down on the couch. "So, what brings you here, kid?"

Maybe it was the beer, maybe it was his friendliness, but I heard myself saying, "I want to be a professional wrestler. How do I do that?"

He didn't say anything for a moment and gave me a long glance. "Take off your shirt," he said, finally.

"Huh?" I goggled at him.

"Take off your shirt."

I took another swallow and put the beer down. I pulled my shirt off and stood there, not knowing what to do next.

He got up from the couch and walked over to me. He grabbed my biceps with both of his hands and squeezed. He smiled. "Nice. You're a little on the small side, though. How tall?"

"Five-ten."

He whistled and walked around me. "How much do you weigh?"

"One sixty-five."

"You lift weights?"

"Not since I got out of high school."

He tossed the yellow trunks at me. "Put those on."

I thought, for just a moment, about going into the little bathroom to change. Instead, I kicked off my shoes and slid my shorts and underwear off. He was watching me with a smile on his face as I pulled up the yellow trunks. They were a little big for me—they couldn't possibly have been his—but I loved the way they felt.

"Flex your arms," he commanded.

Feeling a little silly, I did—and became aware that my dick was getting hard.

He walked up to me until our bodies were inches apart. I looked up into his eyes without flinching. He reached down with his right hand and grabbed my hard cock. I gasped before I could stop myself, and he smiled at me. "Wrestling turn you on, boy?"

I bit my lower lip and nodded.

With his free hand, he took my right hand and brought it his crotch. Through the fleece of his sweatpants I could feel his cock was hard, too. He bent his neck until his mouth was right in my ear. "Me, too," he whispered.

The feel of his breath on my ear brought out goose bumps.

This can't be happening, I thought to myself.

"You ever been with a man, boy?" he whispered. His mouth was right against my ear.

I shook my head.

Before I knew it, he let go of my cock and put both hands into my armpits. He bent his knees and lifted me up in the air, over his head, so I was looking down at him. He was still smiling, although my heart was in my throat. He was so damned big and strong…I was getting a little afraid. "Wrap your legs around me," he instructed, and I did as he asked, locking them together at the ankles behind him. He let me slide down until we were face-to-face and locked his arms around me. He pressed forward with his head until his lips were against mine. His big hands slid down and gripped my ass.

"You're very sexy," he breathed. "We might be able to make a wrestler out of you." And then he kissed me.

It was my first male-on-male kiss. I'd kissed my girlfriends before, had even gotten one of them to let me fuck her. And while the close body contact with girls had aroused me, gotten me hard, it had never been like this. This was how it was meant to be, this was what my body was wired for. If I'd ever had any doubts, they were erased as his tongue forced its way into my mouth and my body began to tremble within his big strong arms. He carried me over to the small couch and gently laid me down on it. He kissed my neck, and I began to moan.

No, it had never been like this with girls.

He smiled down at me as he slid his sweatpants down and off. Underneath, he was still wearing the sweat-soaked black trunks I'd watched him wrestle in. His body smelled of sweat, and he lowered himself on top of me until our crotches were touching. I could feel his big cock pressing against mine. I tilted my pelvis up so I was pushing against him. He cocked his head to one side. "Eager?" he whispered with a smile.

I swallowed and nodded my head.

He flicked his tongue over my right nipple, and in spite of myself, I emitted a low moan. "Like that, do you, boy?" he whispered and did it again and again until I could barely stand it anymore. He grabbed both of my wrists and pushed them over my head, holding me down while his mouth worked first one nipple, then the other. He licked my armpits, and I clamped my mouth shut to keep from screaming, it felt so good, so incredibly fucking good, I never had known anything could feel so great, and I wanted to put my hand on my cock, pull on it because my balls were aching, aching so hard for release, but he had me pinned down and I could do nothing as his mouth moved down my torso, his tongue flickering in and out of my navel. He tugged my trunks down with his teeth, freeing my cock, and his mouth was on it.

I writhed and bucked as his mouth slid up and down my cock, but I couldn't move, he was too big and strong. I finally stopped struggling, it felt so incredible, and I could feel my load starting to work its way up to my cock, and I knew it was going to gush out of me. He opened his eyes and winked at me, and my breathing was coming so fast and sharp—

—and then it was pumping out of me and into his mouth, the release so incredible and powerful, pleasure like I'd never known before, had never thought could be possible, it had never ever felt this incredible when I'd fucked my girlfriend, and I knew it would never feel this good with a woman. This was what I was meant for. I was meant to love men.

And when my body stopped shaking and trembling, he released my arms.

He wiped his mouth and stood up. He pulled the black trunks down, releasing his own huge cock, and I wanted it in my mouth—but when I reached for it, he pushed me away. "Not this time, boy," he whispered and straddled me, the cock just out of my reach, and he spat in his hand and started pulling on it.

His muscles gleamed with sweat as I watched, and I could feel my cock getting hard again.

I reached for his cock and he slapped my hands away.

Instead, I reached up for his powerful chest and started flicking his nipples with my fingers. He moaned and threw his head back, and before long his body stiffened, his defined muscles flexing, and his load rained down on my face and chest as he bellowed his pleasure.

When it was finished, he smiled down at me and reached for a towel. He wiped his cum off me and reached down to kiss me again.

"You live here?" he asked, as he lay down next to me.

"Uh-huh. But I go to Gulf State, down in Bay City. Just up the coast from Tampa a ways."

"You don't say." He lit a cigarette and blew smoke up at the roof of the little trailer. "I live in Bay City, own a gym there. Starr's Gym?"

I shook my head. I didn't know it.

"I got a ring there. I can train you." He kissed my cheek. "You've got a good body, but you're going to need to put on some more muscle before you'll be ready to work in a show. You willing to do that?"

I nodded.

"And I'll teach you some other things, boy." He nuzzled up against me. "You liked what we just did, didn't you?"

"Oh, hell yeah."

He laughed and kissed my neck. "Let's just lay here awhile, and then I'll show you a few moves."

I touched his sweaty chest. "I'll do whatever you want me to, Bill."

"I'll make a star out of you, boy." He laughed. "In more ways than one. Have you thought about a ring name for yourself?"

"A ring name?"

"It's as good a place to start as any."

"No, I haven't," I admitted. Out of the corner of my eye I could see his black trunks lying on the mat. The lightning bolt was turned up. "How about Johnny Lightning?"

"I suppose…" His voice trailed off for a moment, and then he shook his head. "Nah, we don't look anything alike—we can't pull off the brother act." He laughed.

"Oh." I thought for a moment and smiled when it came to me. "How about *Thunder*?"

"Cage Thunder." He smiled at me. "That's it, it's perfect." He reached over and pinched my nipple, and my cock got hard again. He looked down at it and smiled. "Oh yeah, Cage boy, we're going to have a lot of fun together." He pulled me over to him and wrapped those big arms around me again.

I didn't want him to ever let go of me, but he finally gave me a little shove.

He stood up and pulled his trunks on. "Put your trunks back on, Cage. I'll show you some moves." He winked at me. "And when we're done, maybe I'll let you suck my cock this time." He stretched to his full height. "There's nothing like a little wrestling to get you worked up for some sucking and fucking, Cage, my boy."

And we got to work.

CHAPTER TWO

Here we are," Bill said, turning the truck into a short little driveway on the right. He shifted into park and turned off the engine. He ran his right hand up my left leg, letting it rest just inches from my crotch, and squeezed. "Looks like we got here first—let me get the gate." He opened his door and got out.

I squinted against the bright afternoon sun. Directly in front of the truck was a big gate in a chain-link fence that looked to be about ten feet high, give or take. Three strands of barbed wire ran along the top of the fence. There was concrete on the other side of the fence, with weeds poking through cracks. About fifty yards away was an abandoned-looking cinder block warehouse with a rusted tin roof. I looked around. The whole neighborhood looked abandoned and not exactly the safest place to be, but it was the middle of the afternoon, so maybe that wasn't an issue.

I swallowed another drink of the Coke I'd gotten at McDonald's on our way into Pensacola. I had butterflies in my stomach and took another drink of the Coke, hoping it would somehow help calm me down a bit. Today was the payoff—the day Bill had spent the last few months preparing me for.

When the summer ended and I returned to Bay City for college, I'd started working with Bill several days a week in the ring. He trained me in the weight room and even rented me a room in his house. It was great being out of the dorms, and he gave me a part-time job working the front desk at the gym for some income besides what my parents sent me every month. He had a nice house, only a few blocks from the gym and from the bayshore.

It was weird living there, though. We spent a lot of time together, but every night we went to bed in our separate rooms. Every night before I fell asleep, I stared at the ceiling and wondered what it would be like to fall asleep in his big strong arms. We still fucked around some, but it was always involved with wrestling. We'd work in the ring with the door locked, and we'd play around sexually. But never outside the ring, which was strange to me. And every once in a while, one of his buddies would blow into town and I'd get to wrestle around with both of them. It always got sexual, but once everyone had shot their loads—once we were cleaned up—it was like none of that had ever happened. It didn't make sense to me. I knew Bill cared about me, I *knew* it.

He just doesn't know how to show affection, I told myself I don't know how many times.

But I pushed all of that out of mind. Today was the day I'd been preparing for all this time. Today I had a private audition for the Gulf Coast Wrestling Alliance, with a contract on the line.

Bill had told me not to be nervous—it would show, and that was never good. "You need to be cocky and confident," he'd told me over and over again since we'd gotten into the truck that morning. "Act like you're doing *him* a favor by coming to work for him. It'll show."

Easier said than done, I thought for maybe the hundredth time that morning, closing my eyes and taking a couple of deep breaths. *He wouldn't have set this up if he didn't think you were ready, if he didn't think you'd impress Matt. This is your big chance to make your dreams come true. Stop freaking out or you're going to blow it. And when are you going to get a chance like this again?*

Never, that's when.

I opened my eyes. Bill was unlocking the padlock on the gate. I smiled. The sun glistened on his long curly blond hair. I often wondered what his professors in the psychology program at Gulf State University thought about his hair, but I suppose when you're on a PhD track they don't question much. He was wearing a tank top that stretched across the big muscles of his back as he fought with the padlock. His broad back tapered down to a narrow waist, and his tight jeans gripped his big round ass. I felt my dick start to stir inside my own jean shorts. Finally, the padlock opened and he pulled the chain through and free before pushing the gate open. He turned and winked at me as he walked back to the truck. He climbed in, turned the key, and started the engine. Bill patted my leg. "Nervous, meat?"

The touch of his big hand on my bare leg made me shiver, and my dick got hard. I always loved it when he called me *meat*. "No," I lied, shrugging as I put my hand down on top of his, "I'm ready to get this show on the fucking road." He always liked it when I swore, when I spoke with a confidence I didn't really feel inside. But part of being a professional wrestler was acting, and so I figured I could fake it. I envied Bill the easy confidence he had in himself and in his body, a confidence so strong it almost crossed the line into arrogance.

I'd been to some of the shows, sitting in the audience and watching the big men in the ring. Every time Bill made his entrance, my dick got hard. He always wore black trunks, high in the waist and on the thigh, showing off his thickly muscled hairy legs over his boots, and a black leather vest open to expose the well-oiled muscles of his chest and abs. He would bellow the moment he stepped through the doors, so every eye would turn to him as he flexed his big biceps and pointed at the poor, hapless opponent who always climbed into the ring first. Sometimes, he'd wait for the bell to ring, go through the entire pre-match pat-down and rule explanation from the ref—other times, he'd attack his victim as soon as he stepped into the ring. And for the next twelve minutes or so, superstar Bill Lightning would kick the crap out of his opponent while the audience booed and jeered his every move.

While I sat there silently, shifting in my seat to ease the pressure on my hard-on, always wishing it was me in the ring with Bill.

"You brought the dance belt, right?" Bill asked as he put the truck back into gear.

He'd already asked me like three times. "Yes, I brought the belt," I replied. He wanted me to wear a dance belt under my trunks for the match because I always got hard, and that might not go over well with Matt. *Wrestling is family entertainment, so they don't want a sexualized product,* he'd told me over and over again, like there was something I could do to control my erections.

"Good," Bill said as he drove through the gate and put the truck back into park. He winked at me as he opened his door again. He hooked his thumb over his shoulder at a sky blue convertible Mustang parked on the other side of a Dumpster, which I hadn't noticed before. "Matt's already here—that's good. We'd better get a move on, though. He don't like to wait." He slid down out of the seat and left the door open as he went to close and padlock the gate.

I looked at the Mustang. The front plate read MATT MAN, which made me smile a little bit. I'd seen Matt wrestle—he was currently the champion of the GSWA, and he was also the talent scout/booking agent. His father owned GSWA, had even once been a star with one of the major promotions as Baron von Speer, and it was a family business. Matt's brothers were also wrestlers, his mother worked promotion—the whole family was involved in the business one way or another. Matt's oldest brother, Jake, was currently the number one contender to the champion of one of the majors—I saw his picture on the covers of the wrestling magazines in the grocery stores all the time—and he had an amazing body, as did Matt. They all used the von Speer name, but while their dad had been a heel, his sons all pretty much wrestled as *faces*, good guys the audience rooted for.

I'd seen one of Matt and Bill's title bouts—the big story in the GSWA right now was the feud between the two of them. The match had been one of the hottest ones I'd ever seen. Bill was thick and muscular, had maybe forty pounds or so on Matt. If seeing Jake von Speer on the cover of a magazine in his trademark canary-yellow trunks made my dick hard, Matt von Speer in his white ones *in person* was enough to fuel late-night jack-off sessions in my bedroom for months. Matt always beat Bill, or Bill was disqualified, but Bill hinted that relatively soon he'd win the belt away from Matt.

Being champion was a big deal for Bill—I knew it was something he desperately wanted, and that match was going to be televised. They were trying to find a big venue to rent for that night's matches, since it was going to be the peak of the story they were working. The fans were already getting revved up about it—the previous weekend, Bill almost had succeeded in pinning Matt, only to have Matt's brother Noah rescue him before the ref could slap the mat a third time.

Bill got back in the truck and drove closer to the warehouse. He parked near a short cement staircase leading to a door. He shut the engine off and grinned at me. "Okay, here we go."

I grabbed my duffel bag and got out of the truck. It was a Sunday morning, and we'd been on the road for about an hour or so. After I got off work at the gym the afternoon before, we'd spent the entire day wrestling and fucking around. My dick was actually a little sore, and so were my muscles—Bill had been rougher with me than he usually was, but that was his excitement about my audition today. But I was going to suck it up, because this private ring in a warehouse was where I was going to get my big chance.

I was going to impress Matt von Speer if it fucking killed me, and I would have to *really* impress him. It was rare for GSWA to sign someone who'd never been to a wrestling training school. Even Bill had spent a few months learning his trade at one in Missouri, right after he graduated from Louisville University and before starting his graduate work at Bay State.

Getting this contract with GSWA would be the fulfillment of a dream I'd had for almost as long as I could remember. Ever since I first saw a pro match on television, I'd fantasized about being a professional wrestler. I wasn't planning on making a living from it—that wasn't easy to do, and even the guys who got on with the big national promotions had to work at training schools or have some other source of income. But it wasn't about the money for me. GSWA taped some of its shows to be televised about a week later on independent TV stations throughout the South. Bill said the promotion's owner was even negotiating to get the shows on a cable channel, which would take the promotion national... which meant more money.

But I didn't care about the money, which I'd never said to Bill. He'd think me stupid to not care about the money.

It was hard to believe it had been almost four months since I'd met Bill at the fair. My body had changed dramatically in that time. My muscles were bigger and I'd lost some of the baby fat I'd still been carrying around. I had always hated weightlifting when I was in high school, but now, with specific goals in mind, I loved it. I loved the strain, the ache in my muscles from working hard. I loved pushing my limits in the weight room and in the ring.

I'd discovered that I could also enjoy pain—to a point.

I loved being in the ring with Bill. I loved it when he picked me up in a bear hug, our sweaty bodies clamped together, his big strong arms squeezing me until I couldn't breathe. I loved when he clamped his strong thighs around my head and squeezed, my face shoved into his sweaty crotch. And I loved when he stripped his trunks off and stood there, hands on his hips, in just his boots and kneepads, his big erection pointing right at me while I slid my own trunks down and off.

I loved fucking him, the feel of my big cock inside his tight ass, the way he moaned and groaned and writhed from the pleasure it gave him. He taught me how to suck a mean cock, too.

I loved sucking his dick.

And sometimes, he'd fuck me. I didn't like that as much as I liked fucking him, but I liked it. I liked having him inside of me, on top of me, holding me down and rolling me up to penetrate me.

I was more than a little in love with him.

And I wanted him to be proud of me.

He held the door open for me and I walked through it. The warehouse was dusty and empty. There was a single light on, a bulb hanging on a long cord from the ceiling just above a ring. There was a man in the ring, and I recognized Matt von Speer immediately. He was already geared up—red trunks, red knee and elbow pads, and red patent-leather boots with red laces. He was stretching, his right leg up on the top rope, his head touching his knee. All I could see was the curly black hair on his head until Bill shut the door behind us and he looked up.

"You're late," he called, bringing his booted foot back down. "I ain't got all day, you know."

"Fuck you," Bill said conversationally as we walked across the cement floor to the ring. "What have you got to do today, asshole?"

Matt grinned. He was very handsome, with big straight white teeth and thick red lips under a strong nose and green eyes. Freckles dusted his lightly tanned face. "So, you're Cage Thunder?" he said, turning his attention to me, looking me up and down. "Heard a lot about you. Get geared up so I can see what you got."

"Come on, kid." Bill steered me toward another door. He opened it and flicked a light switch. It was a changing area, with a sink, a shower, and a bench. Bill had already peeled off his shirt before the door had shut behind us and was undoing his pants, kicking off his shoes.

I swallowed and pulled my Bay State T-shirt up over my head. He tossed me a pair of shiny blue trunks with a crest in yellow brocade sewn onto the back. "Put those on," he instructed with a sly smile, adding a pair of matching knee pads and some white boots. "He'll come in his trunks when he sees you in those."

I got undressed, then pulled on the dance belt before the blue trunks, a little puzzled. Was he saying that Matt was gay?

I finished lacing up the boots and tied them. I stood up and looked at myself in the full-length mirror mounted on the wall. I did look good, I thought. My muscles were bigger than they had been, and there was more definition since I'd started following Bill's instructions. I turned and looked at my backside. The gold brocade design on my ass certainly drew attention to it—and it looked firm, big, and round.

Bill whistled. I turned and looked at him. He was wearing black trunks with a silver lightning bolt down the side, with black boots with matching silver trim and black kneepads with silver backing. He stood behind me, and we both flexed our biceps. "We make a hot tag team," Bill said, nuzzling the back of my neck and pressing his crotch against my ass. "Do good, little buddy, and get this contract and we could be tag team champions. Come on, let's get out there."

I followed him out of the little dressing room into the dark, and he whispered, "Don't come out of the dark until I tell you to, okay?" I nodded. He stepped into the circle of light and climbed over the ropes, going to an opposite corner from where Matt was standing in his red gear.

"Come on, boy!" Bill bellowed.

I hesitated for just a minute before stepping out into the light. I smiled to myself when I saw the look on Matt's face. His jaw dropped and his eyes widened. I climbed up onto the ring apron and over the top rope. I noticed there was a wet spot in the front of his red trunks, and I could see the outline of his cock. I wondered why it was okay for his cock to be so obvious in his trunks, when I had to wear a dance belt, but figured he wasn't the one trying to get a contract.

He strode out into the center of the ring and licked his lips. He gestured to me to come forward. Nervously, I walked out and met him in the center. He put the flat of both hands against my chest and pushed backward. I took a step back but then anchored my feet and my weight, so when he pushed again, I didn't move.

He smirked at me and stepped in until our chests were almost touching. He was about two inches taller than me, and he probably had about thirty pounds or so on me. I could smell his breath—peppermint chewing gum. He grabbed me by the hair and tilted my head back, slamming a forearm across my chest so quickly I didn't have time to react. I dropped to my knees and, still holding my hair, he shoved my face right into his crotch.

I froze. I didn't know what to do. He started grinding his crotch against my face, and I could feel his erection through the trunks. I tried to pull my head back but he tightened his grip on my hair, not letting go.

After what seemed like an eternity, he let go of my hair and stepped back. He was still smirking as he said, "Get up."

I got to my feet. He took another few steps back and leaped into the air. His boots caught me square in the chest and knocked me backward. I staggered back a few steps before losing my balance and going over, landing on my back with a loud thud that knocked all the air out of my lungs. Stars danced in front of my eyes as I looked up at the ceiling, trying to get my bearings and wits about me again. But before I could move or do anything, a boot kicked me right in the stomach. The ring bounced from the impact, and I went up into the air a few inches before landing again with an *oof*. I could see Matt looking down at me, the smirk still there, and I could see his cock was even harder inside his trunks. I turned my head to look for Bill as Matt started kicking me in the side, rolling me toward the ropes with each kick. Finally, as I rolled, I saw Bill. He was standing outside the ring in his corner, looking at me with a big smile on his face, and he was stroking his cock through his trunks.

When I reached the ropes, I pulled myself up to my feet and turned to face Matt again. He was standing in the center of the ring, smiling at me. I took a deep breath and launched myself toward him. He scooped me up as easy as if I weighed nothing and body slammed me down onto my back again. He grabbed my hair and pulled me back up. *Wham.* My ears were ringing and my back was starting to hurt, pain shooting out of my lower back up to my shoulders and down the backs of my legs. He grabbed another fistful of my hair and pulled me back up to my feet. It felt like my roots were being torn out of my scalp, and in that moment I hated him. I hated him and wanted to hurt him, to knock that smirk off his face, drive my boot into his nuts and grind them to powder.

He body slammed me a third time, but this time he brought me up to a sitting position and knelt down behind me, slipping an arm around my head and squeezing it backward. His knee went into the center of my back, and again all I could think was how much it hurt, how much pain I was in, how completely I was in his power.

And despite the pain, my cock was achingly hard.

He kept cranking the hold, never asking me for a submission. It was like he would let me get used to the pain, almost find a comfort level with it, and then would add a little more pressure just to let me know it was supposed to be painful.

Without warning, he released me.

I gulped in air and was about to get to my feet when he yanked me backward by the hair. His thighs clamped around my head and my face was right in his musky, sweaty crotch again. He was smirking at me as his muscles contracted and put more pressure on my head. I couldn't hear anything—his thighs were placed at my ears. All I could do was make noises and try to breathe as his legs squeezed. He rolled over onto his side, and I was able to twist somewhat so that I was on my side. He reached down and rubbed his cock on my face. I thought about biting his balls—that would take him by surprise, no doubt—but wasn't sure if it was the smart thing to do or not. I wanted the damned contract, after all.

He grabbed my hair again and yanked.

What was with the hair, anyway? I wondered. I'd never seen him pull hair in any of the matches I'd watched. His other hand went down and started pinching my nipple.

Oh. My. *God.*

I moaned.

He pulled and twisted my nipple.

The pain—Bill had worked it pretty hard the day before, so it was tender and sensitive, but the pain was so exquisite…I loved it. I wanted him to twist it harder, yank and pull on it. I shifted, my cock aching for release and pressing against the blue Lycra encasing it. I pushed my face deeper into his crotch and opened my mouth, tonguing his balls inside the red trunks. I looked up and his face registered surprise at first, and then the smirk turned into a pleased smile. He said something I couldn't hear but he tugged harder at my raw nipple.

And someone was pulling my trunks down, freeing my cock.

I tried to turn my head, but trapped as it was inside Matt's thighs, I couldn't. It had to be Bill—he was the only other person there. I felt the trunks and dance belt sliding down my legs, being maneuvered over my boots and off me. I struggled but his legs were too strong, and then someone—*Bill*—took my cock into his mouth.

I whimpered.

I was being overstimulated—the mouth working my cock, the hand playing with my nipple, the legs around my head—and all of it was pleasure.

My entire body began to tremble as Bill's mouth slid up and down my cock.

The pressure on my head relaxed, and I heard Matt say, "Poor little boy, are we making you crazy?" He let go of my nipple and gently slapped the side of my face.

I opened my mouth to answer him, but before I could say anything, he tightened his legs on my head again. I grabbed hold of both his thighs with my hands—they were solid, hard, with no give to them at all. I traced the definition in one of them with my forefinger while I allowed the other hand to just stroke the thigh. Matt's already damp trunks tightened against my face—his cock was getting harder, and I felt it moving through the Lycra. I slid my hand up and over his leg and found the tip of his cock. There was a wet spot there.

I heard him saying something I couldn't quite make out through the legs clamped on my head, but Bill stopped sucking my dick.

A few moments later, my head was set free.

My ears were ringing from the pressure, and as blood started flowing into my head again the way it was supposed to my vision clouded. I rolled over onto my stomach and got up on my hands and knees. I shook my head and looked up.

Matt had retreated to his corner and had his back to me. As I watched, he slid the red trunks down his legs and stepped out of them. His ass was white against the deep tan of his legs and torso, and it was solid muscle. There were some black hairs in the crack. I licked my lips and got to my feet. My legs were a little wobbly, and I could see Bill in his corner. He'd stepped outside the ring and taken his trunks off, too. His big cock was erect and standing at attention. He met my eyes and winked at me.

I wasn't sure if I was supposed to go back to my corner or not, so I just stood there in the middle of the ring, bare assed with my hard dick slick with Bill's saliva. Matt kept standing with his back to me, like he wanted me to get a good long look at his beautiful ass.

Out of the corner of my eye, I noticed Bill gesturing with his head. I looked and realized he was telling me to go after Matt.

I took a deep breath and took a step forward. My legs were still wobbly, and my knees almost buckled but I caught myself. Matt gave no indication that he was even aware of me, so I kept walking. When I was almost there he shook his head and spread his legs wide, bending forward, presenting that ass to me. I swallowed and looked over at Bill, who mouthed the words *fuck him* at me.

I pressed my dick into the crack of that strong white ass and heard Matt sigh as I pushed the head against his hole. It was slick—he'd lubed himself up at some point—and as I kept the pressure up, he relaxed his hole and the head slipped inside him. The muscles in his back flexed, the striations of the muscle fibers popping out under his tanned skin as I pushed deeper inside. Tentatively, I placed both of my hands on his narrow waist for balance and pushed again. He resisted, and I could hear his breath coming faster and faster as I eased my way inside him. Without warning, his resistance gave suddenly and I plunged all the way inside. His ass clenched, his triceps and shoulder muscles flexed, and his air exploded out of him in a cry that was part pleasure and part pain.

I slid my hands down from his waist to either side of that hard, beautiful ass and just stayed there, all the way inside. I could hear my heart pounding in my ears, could see his heartbeat pulsing in the big veins in the forearms grasping the top rope.

"Yeah, boy," he breathed, so softly I could barely hear his words, "fuck me with that big dick, boy. Ride me and make me your little bitch."

I didn't need to be told twice. I pulled back until all that was left inside was the head and then slammed back into him so hard he went up on his toes and cried out. I smacked his hard ass with one hand, and the sound echoed in the empty warehouse. He flinched a bit when I smacked him, so I kept spanking him as I fucked him, watching as the white cheek turned red and sensitive underneath my palm. Bill slid under the bottom rope and knelt in front of him and started worshipping Matt's cock while stroking his own. There was no sound other than the slapping of my hand on his ass and the sound of our bodies crashing together as I rode his ass as hard as I could, twisting and moving my hips up and down, side to side as I slid in and out of his ass. His head began moving back and forth as his moans got louder, and my balls began to ache for release.

He threw his head back and bellowed as he came, Bill taking his cock out at just the right moment so that his face and hair were sprayed with Matt's cum. He twitched and moaned, shivering as each load blew out of the slit and onto Bill.

I pulled my own cock out of his ass just as I started spraying a huge load all over his reddened ass cheeks and back.

A few moments later, Bill shot his out onto the ring.

We didn't move, just stayed there frozen, our heavy panting the only sound in the massive warehouse. I watched as my cum began running down Matt's thickly muscled back, dripping off that round hard ass.

And finally, he turned around. He smiled at me. "Yeah, kid, you'll do. You'll do just fine." He stroked the side of my face with one of his big, rough hands. He tweaked the nipple he'd made raw and I flinched a little bit. "You'll debut in our show next Saturday in Hutchinson. Can you make it down here on Friday night for practice?"

I nodded, too excited to say anything. I could see Bill beaming proudly at me.

Matt grabbed hold of my cock and leaned in. "I think you'll debut in a title shot," he went on, looking over at Bill. "Bill says you're pretty limber and can take a real beating. That true?"

I grinned and reached down and grabbed my right foot. I pulled it up and touched the toe to the back of my head. He whistled as I let go. "I was a gymnast in high school—I'm naturally flexible."

He climbed through the ropes. "Meet me here on Friday at seven p.m. on the dot, and we'll get the match worked out, get your contract signed." He hopped down to the floor. "Welcome to the GSWA, Cage. I'm going to get showered—I gotta meet my wife in a bit. You'll lock up, Bill?"

Bill nodded, and Matt strode over to the dressing room. Bill bounced across the ring and threw his arms around me, picking me up in a bear hug and kissing my neck. "You did it, kid." He grinned at me before setting me back down. I heard the shower start in the changing room. "Come on, boy, let's practice some more. You need to get used to being in the ring." He pushed me and I took a few steps back. My dick was already getting hard again, and so was his.

"Come and get me," I said, waving him forward.

And we tied up again, our hard cocks bouncing as we started wrestling.

CHAPTER THREE

*O*h *yeah man, fuck me!* Fuck me! *Yeah!"*

I opened my eyes with a groan and glanced at my alarm clock. It was just after two thirty in the morning on a Wednesday. I moaned, staring up at the ceiling. I closed my eyes and bit my lip. *I have to get up in a little over four hours,* I thought, covering my head with my pillow. It didn't help at all. I could still hear my rotten thoughtless asshole Bill moaning and talking in his bedroom. I counted to ten, making sure I took deep breaths to fight my irritation and rage, resisting the urge to pound on his door and scream at him to keep it down. Unfortunately, I knew damned well that would just piss him off, and we'd end up screaming at each other while his poor trick fumbled for his clothes and beat a hasty retreat into the night. *I've got to find another place to live,* I told myself for the thousandth time. But the need didn't change my financial situation. I couldn't afford my own place, not as long as I was in school and limited to working part-time. *But how long can I keep dealing with this?* I gritted my teeth and took another deep breath.

"Oh God, I love your cock, man, fuck me, yeah give it to me, man!"

I sighed and got out of bed, grabbing my cigarettes and a lighter. I went down the hallway to the living room and crossed over to the sliding glass doors that led to the backyard. I slid the glass door open and walked out onto the back deck. I slid the door shut behind me and, mercifully, could no longer hear anything. I lit the cigarette and sat down on a lounge chair, looking up at the stars. The deck ran the length of the house, sliding glass doors opening out to it from Bill's room and the living room. My bedroom was just down the hall from Bill's, in the front of the house. I took a deep breath and took another drag on the cigarette. Bill's curtains were open and light spilled out onto the swimming pool, which was just a few yards from his door. Bill liked to fuck with the lights on. "I like to be able to see the guy I'm with," he'd told me, "otherwise what's the point in bringing a hot guy home?" Then he quickly added, like he always did whenever he made a comment that sounded slutty, "It's just so romantic to look into his eyes…"

Like hearing *this* didn't make him sound like a whore: *"Oooooooh yeah, yeah, that's it, fucking pound my ass, man!"*

There were times when I positively hated him.

I crushed the cigarette out in the ashtray. I'd slowly come to the conclusion that moving in here had been an enormous mistake. Ever since I signed with GSWA, things had changed between me and Bill. And it hurt. It hurt a lot.

I don't know what happened, but once I'd signed the contract and started working shows throughout the Panhandle and Mobile, Bill seemed to lose interest in me. I now lifted weights at the gym by myself. The sessions in the ring became few and far between.

And Bill started showing interest in other guys. There were, it turned out, three gay bars in Bay City, and Bill would go out after the gym closed. More often than not, he brought someone home.

And they were always loud enough for me to hear.

Much as I hated to admit it, I was jealous. I wanted to be the one fucking him senseless. I wanted to kiss him, suck his cock, eat his ass, run my tongue over his nipples and down his washboard abs. I wanted to be the one driving him crazy with pleasure, making him scream out loud as I drove deep into his beautiful, round rock-hard ass. I wanted to be the one he spent the rest of his life with, the one he cuddled with on the couch while we watched old movies. I wanted to be the one with my arm around his waist when we walked into a dance club. I wanted to make him happy.

But he didn't want me—and he'd made that clear more than once.

About two weeks ago, on our way back from a show in Fort Walton—Bill had lost to Matt yet again, and I'd been the opening match, which hadn't really gone well; Matt had reamed me afterward—we'd stopped to eat at an all-night diner in a small town whose name I never knew. The waitress had just brought our main course, and I was taking a bite out of my bacon cheeseburger, when he said, "You know, Gary, I think you've got the wrong idea about the two of us."

I put my burger down. "Wrong idea?" I replied, my heart sinking. He'd stopped calling me Cage, too, which I hadn't taken as a good sign.

"I just think of you as a friend," he said in a rush, his tanned face flushing a little bit. "I mean, you're a great guy, and funny, and smart, and everything, but we're never going to be anything more, you know?" He bit his lower lip for a moment before continuing. "It's not like you don't have a great body—you do, you're sexy as hell—but that spark just isn't there between us, you know? I just don't think we'd ever make it as a couple, even if I felt that way about you. I don't." He brushed his hand over mine. "I just don't want you to have the wrong idea."

"Oh," I said, a smile plastered on my face as I died inside. He kept talking, but I couldn't hear anything he was saying. Somehow I managed to keep my composure while I prayed for a hole to open in the floor that I could dive into. There's nothing worse than when hope dies. But somehow I managed to make it through the rest of the dinner without letting him see how I felt, managing to smile and make jokes like nothing had changed.

I wanted to die.

Bill and I still hung out together, and he always introduced me to people he knew as his best friend. He got me a fake ID, and we started going dancing in the gay clubs. Out on the dance floor, he'd coerce me to take my shirt off. And guys started noticing me. It was amazing. It was everything I'd always wanted to have happen, and I started getting laid with some regularity.

But the one guy I wanted to notice me never did. Sure, he would give me compliments, but they didn't mean anything. He still didn't want me.

"Oh, my God, I'm coming! I'm coming! *Ooooohhhhhh! Oooooooohhhhhhhh…"*

Sometimes I wondered if Bill was deliberately loud when he was getting fucked, if he opened the curtains on purpose to tempt me to come down and watch him.

I walked back into my bedroom and turned on the light. I got that day's copy of *The Oracle,* the school paper, out of my backpack and stared at the ad I'd circled.

> *Wrestlers wanted for video company out of Fort Lauderdale. No experience necessary; will train you if you have the right look. All travel expenses paid, and excellent pay for the right guys. If interested, call Phil at 555-1781.*

I needed to move out of here. I needed to get my own place. The part-time job at the gym and the fifty bucks for doing shows every weekend wasn't going to cut it.

I decided to call Phil after my first class in the morning.

It couldn't hurt, right? The worst thing that could happen was they wouldn't want to use me.

"Oh my God, I'm going to come...oh oh oh oh oooooooohhhhh!"

And I reflected grimly, if it meant I'd never have to listen to *that* again, so much the better.

Chapter Four

I took a deep breath and rang the doorbell.

I was really nervous. Bill had no idea I was doing this, and to be honest, I really didn't care. I'd called Phil, and we'd chatted for a while on the phone. He seemed like a good guy and was really interested when I mentioned I was a wrestler for GSWA. "Experience is great," he replied. "When are you free to come out for a tryout?" We'd gone back and forth about it, finally finding a time we both had a few hours open. He'd also given me the link to the company's website and a password to the private members' section. I couldn't wait to get home to the privacy of my room and look up the site. Bill, of course, was out at a bar looking for Mr. Right Now. I scrolled through page after page. BGEast taped every kind of wrestling match, from mat scraps to pro stuff in the ring to erotic stuff. And the guys—my God. The wrestlers were all fucking gorgeous, with great faces and amazing bodies.

I knew I was in pretty good shape, but these guys all looked like underwear models.

The door opened. "Gary?" he asked. He was taller than me, about six-three. He was almost completely bald on top, with the rest of his hair clipped very short. He was wearing a gray sweater that stretched tightly across his chest and shoulders. His black jeans were tight. His voice was deep, almost rough sounding.

I held out my hand and he shook it. His grip was tight,

strong. The sleeves of the sweater were pushed up, revealing hard forearms with protruding veins. Physically, he looked even better in person than he did on the site, which was almost hard to believe.

"Nice legs," he said, smiling. I was wearing Lycra shorts and a white ribbed tank top.

"Thanks," I said, adding, "you look pretty good yourself."

He winked at me. "Come on in. You bring some gear with you?"

I nodded, holding up my gym bag. "Where's the bathroom?"

"Down the hall." He pointed, and I walked toward the open door. Just before I ducked inside, I glanced through another open door. It was a bedroom, but the carpet was covered by wall-to-wall wrestling mats. The curtains were open, and I could see a swimming pool in the backyard. One of the walls of the mat room was all mirrors. I felt my dick starting to stir a little as I shut the bathroom door behind me.

I pulled off my tank top and my shorts and slipped a red thong on, adding a red and blue striped bikini over it. My hands were clammy with nerves.

I opened the bathroom door, and Phil called from the mat room, "In here."

I stepped through and stood there, my arms self-consciously folded across my chest. Phil was wearing a black bikini, high cut on the thighs. His abs were sliced muscle. His pecs were thick and hard. A scattering of clipped hair covered them. The cleavage between his pecs was deep. His legs were solid and defined. My legs were bigger, but his looked strong. He walked up to me and tweaked a nipple. "Very nice," he said with a smile, "but I'm gonna kick your ass."

He dropped down to the mats and began stretching. I did the same, occasionally glancing over at him. His ass was round, tight, and hard. Muscles rippled in his back. I felt more than a little intimidated. *Stop that,* I chastised myself. *He's just another opponent, and Bill is just as sexy as he is—Matt, too.*

I took a deep breath and got up onto my knees.

He did the same, facing me, the handsome smile long gone. "Now is when you pay for all the shit you've been talking." He pushed me in the chest.

I felt my cock stirring. His body was beautiful. "Bring it on, you old fuck."

He pounced at me, and we tangled, arms trying to get some kind of leverage. I managed to get my right arm around his head and pushed with my legs. Off balance, he fell to the right. I moved my weight on top of him. He fell up against the wall on his upper back. I positioned myself so that he couldn't move. His face began to redden. He struggled and pushed, but I held firm. I looked down. His abs were exposed. Why not? I thought to myself, reaching down with my right hand. I curled the fingers. I grabbed hold of one of the washboards with my fingers in the cut and my thumb below and pinched the muscle hard.

"Fuck!" Phil half shouted, moaning at the same time.

Delighted, I lessened the pressure and then reapplied it. Again, he moaned in pain. "Give?" I asked quietly.

"Fuck you, you're not getting the first submission!"

I squeezed again. "Give?"

He moaned. "No way!"

I brought my left hand to another one of his washboards. I squeezed both, clenching my forearms. His back arched. "Okay, okay, okay!"

I moved back and sat on my haunches. He sat up, taking deep breaths. Beads of sweat were forming in the valley between his pecs. Damn, but he was hot.

"Good move." He rubbed his abs as he got back to his feet. "But now you're gonna suffer."

"Come on, then."

He rushed me, and his momentum carried me over onto

my back. I quickly twisted over onto my stomach, bringing my arms in tight to my sides, denying him the chance to get his arms through for leverage. Instead, he slipped his hands underneath my chin. Squatting on my back, he pulled my head upward. I strained my neck muscles, but he was too strong. My back started to arch as he pulled up and back. "Won't work." I grunted. "My back's limber."

Someone with a less flexible back would have been screaming by that point. Silently I thanked God for those gymnastics classes when I was a teenager. But then he started twisting my head. He sat up a little, and I turned to relieve the pressure on my neck. He was going to turn me over, I knew I was going to be vulnerable, but I had no choice. I turned but squirmed my legs out from under him. His long legs went around my waist and locked behind my back. Damn it. He fell backward, tightening his grip with his legs. I was now on top of him, but he was smiling as he started squeezing tighter.

I looked down at his face. I smiled. "Oh, ouch," I taunted him.

His face reddened. "You fuck!" He arched his back up and tightened his legs.

That hurt.

I started taking shallower breaths. He would lessen the pressure, I would draw in breath, and then he would squeeze again. The muscle cords in his legs rippled. Finally, the pain became too intense. "Okay, okay, okay." I groaned, tapping his right leg. "I give."

He relaxed and let go, sitting up with a smile. "How'd you like that, boy?"

"Nice." I shook my head, twisting my torso from side to side. He was smiling. My hair was slick with sweat. Damn, but he was hot.

We got up and looked at each other. This time, I got the advantage and managed to get my legs around his head. "How do you like that, tough guy?" I asked, squeezing. My ass contracted. "Give?"

"No way," he grunted. He swung his legs around and tried to get them around my head. I countered this by batting them away with my arms. He tried again, and this time I managed to grab hold of one of them. I twisted it slightly, tightening my legs around his head. His head was turning red. "Come on, big guy," I taunted, feeling my cock stiffening again. He tried to buck me off and tried to get his leg free. Smelling a submission, I tightened my grip on his leg and squeezed his head again, and with my free hand I punched his abs, three times in a row.

"Fuck, okay, okay." I let his leg go but squeezed his head one more time and got one last punch into his abs before letting go. He rolled over onto his stomach, breathing in air. I slapped his hard ass and sat back.

"That's two out of three," I said.

"You think this is over?" He was twisting his head from side to side. "Is that all you got in you?"

"I'm not even breathing hard." I shrugged. "I can go all day." I could see that his dick was hard, too.

"You ready?"

"Bring it on."

The next two submissions went to him. The first time, he managed to get me flat on my back, his legs around my head, squeezing until my ears rang and I was forced to give up. For added humiliation, he kept grabbing my head by the hair and pulling it into his crotch, rubbing my face on his hard cock, making me smell the musky smell of his mixed sweat and arousal. The next time, he worked me down with a combination headlock with a body scissors. With his free hand he was pinching my nipples. I fought it as long as I could, but there was no chance of getting out of it, and his damned legs were just too strong for me to keep holding out. I gave.

We took a break while he went to get us each a glass of

water. When he came back, he'd pulled his bikini off and was just there in a black thong. His bare ass, with just the Lycra triangle at the top in the crevice, was one of the most beautiful ones I had ever seen. I took a glass from him, put it down, and pulled off my bikini. My hard-on, which kept coming and going, came back. He drank his water and set the glass down. Both of our bodies were slick with sweat.

This time, I wasn't going to lose, and I didn't. After neither of us could get an advantage, I managed to get him on his back. I was on top and locked a full nelson on him. My hard-on was on top of his hard ass. He strained his arms, trying to break the nelson. I struggled to hold on. His ass just felt so good to my erection, I wanted to hold him there forever. I could feel that I was losing my grip. His strength and my own sweat were working to beat me. I held on and weighed my options. I pulled my own legs up underneath me and quickly let go of the nelson. In that split second when he was too surprised to move, I slipped my hands under his chin and pulled him up.

"No!"

I laughed. I held his chin up with one hand while I reached back and slapped his ass. "Give?"

"No way!"

"I'll break your fucking back!"

"No way!"

I stopped slapping his reddening ass and reached down and twisted a nipple. "I swear, I'll break it."

I slipped my legs around his waist and applied pressure there. That was it. He gave. I let go but didn't get off his back. I reached down and shoved his head into the mattress. "Not so tough now, are you, stud?" I taunted. I moved my legs up and around his head and contracted the muscles. He moaned again. "Give it up, stud, or I'll crack your head."

"Okay, okay, okay!"

This time I let him up, watching him warily. The tip of his cock was poking out of the top of the thong. I let him catch his breath for a moment and then attacked again. I forced him over backward, cradling his head between my legs again, squeezing and pulling his head up into my aching hard-on.

"You're gonna pay," he muttered between moans. "You are gonna pay. Okay, okay, let me up, you son of a bitch!"

Again, I released him and let him go. My balls ached from the pressure of the almost-constant arousal.

He got up, smiling. "You're pretty tough."

"Thanks." I was gulping in air myself. "You, too."

I shook my head, and that was it. While I wasn't looking he jumped me. My head was trapped between his legs. He was on his back, and I was on my knees. I grabbed his legs, trying to pry them apart. Through the ringing in my ears I could hear him laughing and taunting me. I opened my eyes and there was his cock, long, thick, red, and hard. He slapped my face with it. "Suck it, bitch."

"Fuck you."

He squeezed with his legs tighter. "I said suck it!"

I opened my lips and took it into my mouth. He leaned back and moaned. I started tonguing the head and swallowed it down into my throat. I tasted sweat and musk. I worked it with my tongue as I slid it in and out of my mouth. I thought that he might let go with his legs as the pleasure heightened, but no such luck. He held on to my head, just tightly enough to cause a little pain, but not enough to make me give in to it. I reached around his legs and started pinching his nipples. He started bucking a little bit, his tight ass contracting and loosening.

I pulled my head back from his cock just as it shot its load, spraying my face and hair. He shuddered and moaned until the last drops dribbled from the head. His legs relaxed, and I pulled my head out from in between them. He lay there panting. I pulled back a little bit, panting as well.

"Oh man," he said. "You give great head."

I moved around him. He was still lying on his back, eyes half-closed in the aftermath of his explosive orgasm. I straddled him and wrapped my legs around his head, rolling over onto my side, wrenching him over onto his back.

"You fucker!"

"Payback," I said and pulled his face up into my crotch. He began lapping my cock, sucking it down. I started smacking his ass with my free hand, grabbing those hard cheeks and squeezing, keeping my legs in position. It felt so damned good. He was a master. I felt the cum moving up my shaft and shoved his head back just in time to spray his face with my load. I moaned as my body convulsed and bucked with each shot.

Spent, I lay back, releasing his head. "Damn, that was hot," I mumbled, every muscle in my body aching and sore.

He laughed. "That was one of the hottest matches I've ever had."

High praise from a video star. "Thanks." I collapsed onto my back. Eyes closed, I sensed him lying next to me. He put an arm around me. I turned my head and we kissed, deep and wet and long.

When he pulled his head away from me, he smiled. "Yeah, you're going to do great at BGEast. They're going to fucking love you." He ran his fingertips gently down my back, making me shiver. "We're taping in a couple of weeks. You can ride down with me."

I smiled. "Sounds great."

I took a shower, whistling to myself as I lathered up—$250 a match, and a guarantee of at least three matches for the weekend.

I'd be able to move out of Bill's soon.

Chapter Five

The apartment was perfect.

It was a converted two-car garage, so it was one big room with wall-to-wall beige carpet, with a spot here and there. Directly opposite where the big garage doors used to be was a kitchen area, with plywood cabinets, a faux-granite counter, a double sink, an electric range, and the refrigerator. The ceiling was pretty high, and there was a metal spiral staircase leading up to a sleeping loft. The rent was affordable, it was in a nice neighborhood—a bit of a drive to campus, but I could deal with that—and best of all, my landlords would be a gay couple. Brett, who was showing the place to me, was a web designer and worked out of an office in the main house, and his partner, Jeffrey, was a doctor at Bayside General.

"I want it," I said, turning to smile at Brett, who was standing in the doorway. "Six hundred dollars a month and a security deposit?" I pulled my checkbook out of my back pocket. My parents were still giving me a rent stipend that would almost cover it, and my part-time work at the gym would hopefully cover everything else.

If not, I could always do more videos for BGEast.

I couldn't believe how much they'd paid me. I'd ridden down on Thursday night with Phil—I decided to skip my classes and got someone to cover my shifts at the gym. I wasn't on the card for the GSWA show that weekend in Jacksonville, so I didn't really have to tell Bill anything. Phil picked me up around three in the afternoon and we headed down. We got to the house where we'd be staying around eight o'clock. The BGEast guys were great, even though I was a little shy around them at first. Some more guys had already arrived, flying in earlier in the day, and it was, like Phil had said in his truck on the way down, a smorgasbord of hot guys. They were all gathered in the living room, the big TV on CNN, and tapping away at laptops. Phil introduced me to everyone—Steve, the owner, and Stuart, who was primary cameraman, and the other guys. Steve was an experienced wrestler himself, it turned out—he'd been a big star in Europe for years before coming back to the States and starting the company.

When I told him what promotion I was working with, he smiled a little. "Gulf States. Let me guess—Big Bill Lightning?" When I nodded, he made a slight face. "Hopefully he didn't teach you any bad habits we'll have to train out of you." He then patted me on the arm. "I'm sure you're going to do fine. You look great." He knit his eyebrows together and stroked his strong chin. "Do you object to wearing a mask?"

"A mask?" I wasn't sure how to answer that. *Do you think I'm ugly?*

"Great idea!" Stuart's face lit up. "He has the right size and frame to be a cocky heel. We can put him in a mask, make him a real badass, and then unmask him and turn him into a jobber for a while."

"Um, okay," I said finally.

"He'd make a good heel," Phil said from where he was sitting on the love seat, his long muscular legs stretched out in front of him and crossed at the ankles. "He's got the right attitude when he's wrestling." Phil winked at me. "I'll do a ring match with him, if you want me to."

Steve and Stuart exchanged a glance before Stuart said, "Wow—Phil never does ring matches."

"I'm not getting naked," Phil replied. "Down to a thong is fine, but no nudity and no sex."

"Sex?"

"Don't worry, kid." Steve patted my arm again. "It's not really sex." He shrugged his shoulders slightly. "Some matches get erotic. Nudity is a fifty-dollar bonus, erotic is another fifty. It's up to you."

"I—I don't have a problem with nudity," I said bravely. I bit my lower lip. I wasn't really sure if I did or I didn't. I knew BGEast did some erotic matches—I'd checked out their website pretty thoroughly—but I'd not really given it any thought.

❖

The whole process of taping a match was amazing, completely different from doing a show for GSWA. Before we even went over to the ring, we had to try on what we would wear, and Steve made the final decision. I tried on several different pairs of trunks before they settled on a skimpy pair of black trunks—Lycra in the back, leather in the front, with metal studs on the front. I gulped at myself in the mirror in the bedroom I was staying in. The trunks were really little more than a jock strap in the front, with thin straps leading around to the full back. I flexed, turned sideways, and examined myself every which way. When I walked back into the living room to show Steve and Stuart how I looked, Phil was modeling an aqua bikini for them.

He looked amazing. I could feel my dick starting to stir. He really did have a phenomenal body.

Stuart noticed me and whistled. "I think we have a winner here."

"Nice," Steve said, taking his attention away from Phil. "Turn around and let's see the back." I obliged, prompting another whistle from Stuart. "Definitely those," Steve went on. "Are you a heavy sweater?"

I nodded.

"Well, we'll have to put you into something else for your other matches today, then," Steve said, turning his attention back to his laptop. "Too bad because those could be your signature trunks."

Less than an hour later, I was standing in the ring with a black mask on, wearing the studded trunks, black knee and elbow pads, knee-high white socks, and black patent leather boots laced up almost all the way to my knees. My dick was already semi-hard as I posed for Stuart and his camera. It was cool in there—the air conditioner was running at top speed, and the ceiling fans way overhead were spinning. Out of the corner of my eye, I could see Phil using dumbbells to pump up his biceps while he waited his turn in front of the still cameras. His veins were bulging. He was wearing just the aqua bikini—no pads or boots for him, Steve had decided. He looked really, really sexy, and when he noticed me looking at him he winked at me. When it was his turn to pose, I loosened up, stretching and doing some push-ups to pump up my muscles while watching Phil.

It was a big room, with the ring smack-dab in the middle. There was a rack along one wall with dumbbells in differing sizes—Stuart had explained they had them for props and for the wrestlers to pump before tapings—and a couple of machines, a bench, and a squat rack. There were also mats set up, and a big punching bag hanging on a long chain from the ceiling just to the side of the mats. On the other side of the ring were two doors leading to locker rooms and showers. Some of the other guys were gathered around in chairs near the front door, waiting for their turns in the ring.

I was sweating. I could feel sweat trickling down from my armpits and running from my hair down my neck. It was nerves. I did, like I'd told them, sweat a lot—every show, I was soaked in sweat. Finally, they were finished with Phil, and they called me over to the ring.

Steve went over the story for the match, and the four of us discussed the choreography, went through a run-through of the first fall, and then it was time to roll tape. Because the air conditioner was so loud, it was shut off, and I started sweating even more. We started the match with me in one of the locker rooms and Phil in the ring, warming up. I felt a little relieved to see sweat glistening on his muscles—it wasn't just me. I would come out, walk slowly around the ring while Phil yelled insults at me for wearing a mask, and then would climb into the ring and stand, with my arms folded and every muscle in my upper body flexed, not saying a word.

I wish I could say it went without a hitch, but that would be a lie. We fucked up several times, having to stop tape, go over things again, and then start again. It took about forty minutes to tape the first fall, which ended with me forcing Phil to submit to a Boston crab after basically using him as a practice dummy.

Forty minutes to tape what would end up being only eleven minutes of actual footage.

The second fall was for Phil's revenge, and this went a lot smoother. It ended with Phil getting me in a vicious camel clutch, which left me moaning and clutching my lower back in the middle of the ring. The third fall started with Phil not letting me recover, going back after my lower back, until finally I reversed things with a low blow, stripped the aqua bikini off him to reveal a thong in the same color, and then just made him submit over and over to one submission hold after another until he was nothing more than a sweaty puddle of limp muscle for me to pose over.

"And that's a wrap. Nice job, guys," Steve called out from the ring apron, where he'd been taking stills of the match with a camera. "You boys get cleaned up, and let's get the next match going."

I wound up taping six matches over the weekend, and by the third match I was being filmed in the nude—and in the very next one (and all the ones after), jacked off on camera. Everyone was so nice, and easy to work with, and complimentary—there was a real camaraderie here.

Not like GSWA, where everyone was friendly but distant.

And when Phil and I left late Sunday evening for the drive back to Bay City, I had a check for fifteen hundred dollars tucked into my wallet.

Fifteen hundred fucking dollars—and an invitation to come back and tape again in a month. Eight matches next time. Two thousand bucks.

I was lucky to get fifty bucks a match from GSWA.

I'd made more in one weekend with BGEast than I had in all the matches I'd done for GSWA combined.

Monday morning I looked in the paper for an apartment, and here I was.

"Let's go back into the kitchen and sign the paperwork," Brett said with a smile. I followed him around the pool and through the sliding glass doors into the chef's kitchen. I sat down at the table and flipped open my checkbook. "Do you want some tea?" he asked, opening the refrigerator and retrieving a glass pitcher of iced tea.

I nodded. "Yeah, that would be great." He poured two glasses and sat down at the table across from me. "You don't want a credit check or references?"

"You're a student, aren't you?" Brett asked, running a hand through his wiry, curly auburn hair and smiling. He was a good-looking guy, with thick lips, a strong jaw, and dark freckles scattered over his pale face. His eyes were brown, and he was wearing a white tank top that showed strong muscles and some wiry chest hair poking out at the neck. "You're not going to have a whole lot of references, are you?" He opened a folder and pushed an application across the table to me. "Just fill that out—I can do a quick check online to see about your parents and so forth." He smiled. "Besides, it'll be nice to have a gay tenant."

I started filling out the form after I finished making out the check. Even after first and last months' rent and a security deposit, I still had a healthy balance in my account. *Thanks again, BGEast!* I thought to myself as I signed my name at the bottom of the form. I'd have to pay deposits for the power and cable, and

I didn't know what I was going to do about furniture, but I had my own place.

My own place.

No more waking up to Bill's loud fucking.

No more having to deal with Bill anywhere except at the gym and at the shows.

Honestly, though, I thought as I sipped my tea, did I even need to do the shows anymore? If I could pull off a two-grand weekend once a month filming for BGEast, wouldn't that take care of everything for me? Between the gym and the money Mom and Dad sent me?

Brett took the check with a smile. "When do you want to move in?"

I smiled back at him. "As soon as possible."

He stood up. "Let me get you keys."

He was a nice-looking guy, I thought, and it would be nice to finally have some gay friends. Bill wouldn't like me moving out—he wouldn't like me quitting GSWA, for that matter, but why should I spend my whole day Saturday driving to some bumfuck town and back, to make fifty bucks in front of a crowd of fifty if we were lucky? Matt kept saying I'd eventually get to work the shows in the bigger cities and make more money, maybe even tape for one of the televised shows.

No, working for BGEast made more sense.

Maybe I should look for another job, sever ties with Bill completely.

I wasn't ready to do that just yet.

I was still in love with him, much as I hated to admit it.

I pushed those thoughts out of my mind and smiled at Brett as he handed me a set of keys.

CHAPTER SIX

He'll pay us a thousand dollars each," Bill said, his voice low, like there was someone nearby he didn't want hearing what he was saying into the telephone. "I know you need the money—don't you?"

I closed my eyes and didn't answer at first. BGEast wasn't filming this month, and I'd been a little looser with my cash than I should have been. I had enough money to pay the rent and the bills, but that was about it.

I loved my apartment, and I loved the freedom of being on my own.

Bill hadn't said one thing about me moving out—he didn't act any differently at all. He didn't even say anything when I called Matt and quit GSWA. One of the trainers at the gym told me Bill had a new boyfriend. I somehow managed to keep my face expressionless, even though my heart had just been ripped out.

I missed him. I missed hearing his laugh. I missed him walking around the house in just his tighty-whities, or tanning out by the pool in a thong. I missed everything about him and couldn't figure out what I'd done wrong. I would find myself staring at myself in the full-length mirrors in the locker room at the gym, wondering what exactly was wrong with me. Why doesn't he love me? Why isn't he attracted to me?

So, lying in my bed studying for my medieval European history test, I'd been a little thrilled to see his name on the caller ID when my phone rang.

"Well, I can always use more money, that's not the point," I replied, my tone sharper than I'd intended. I didn't want him to know I was broke. I didn't want to admit my pride had made me move out of his house, and I couldn't afford to live out on my own, really. I also hadn't told him about filming for BGEast.

"It's a chance to wrestle," he replied with a sigh. "Since you're not with GSWA anymore…don't you want to wrestle anymore?"

"Of course I do," I replied carefully. *I miss wrestling you. I miss going to sleep in your arms after wrestling around and having sex. I miss getting in the ring with you and seeing you in your trunks coming after me, and knowing you're going to dominate me and take charge and make me your boy. I miss all kinds of things, Bill. But you don't miss me, do you?*

"You said a thousand bucks? Cash? To do what, exactly?" I bit my lower lip, waiting for the other shoe to drop. It was entirely too much money—and my dad always said things that seem too good to be true usually are. But in a part of my brain, I was already spending the money.

"Don't be so uptight, Cage," he replied. The only time he called me *Cage* instead of *Gary* when we weren't wrestling was when he was trying to talk me into doing something. It was like he thought I was two different people: Cage the adventurous one, Gary the conservative stick-in-the-mud. "It's a rich gay dude who's seriously into wrestling. He saw one of our matches one time in Pensacola, we exchanged numbers after the show, and he's here on a business trip. He was pretty damned excited when I told him you lived in Bay City, too." He paused. "He just wants to film us wrestling in a motel room—like we used to do sometimes, remember?"

"Just like we used to do?" I asked slowly.

"He just wants to film us, Gary."

"Wrestling and having sex."

"It's not like it's really porn, Gary," he said, making an exasperated noise. "All we have to do is act natural, like he's not even there, and do what we would ordinarily do. It's for his private collection—no one else is going to see it. And we can wear masks, if you're more comfortable with that."

What the hell, a thousand bucks is a thousand bucks, I thought, *and it's more than BGEast pays me.* Exhaling and hoping I wouldn't one day regret this, I agreed. He gave me the name and address of the motel. "I'll get there around three and check in—ask for me at the front desk and come on up."

"So, I guess I should bring my white gear?"

"Yeah." I could see the grin on his face. "Like I said, he saw you fight Matt for the title…so yeah, definitely the white. And no dance belt."

Of course not. I hung up the phone and walked over to the dresser. It wasn't noon yet—I didn't have classes on Thursdays, and I wasn't on the schedule at the gym. I put my book down. I knew the material pretty cold, but it never hurt to study some more. I'd thought about going to the gym and working out, or lying by the pool and getting some sun.

Making a grand was a much better option.

All of my trunks and kneepads were in the bottom drawer of my dresser. I actually had two pairs of white trunks—one a more traditional, professional-wrestler style cut Bill had given me, and a skimpier white bikini. I stood in front of the full-length mirror and stripped out of my clothes. I pulled on the traditional trunks first and checked myself out. I looked good, but I didn't like the way the waistband cinched my waist in the back and made me look like I had a bit of a roll there. They also made my ass look almost nonexistent. I slid them down and pulled on the bikini.

I smiled at my reflection. Oh, yes, these were much better. There was barely a half-inch of the Lycra material on the sides, which made my leg muscles look thicker, and the way the low-rise cut draped, my package looked huge. And they emphasized the round hardness of my ass and rode a bit low in the back as well, giving a slight hint of the crack.

My dick was starting to get a little hard.

Perfect.

A few hours later, I pulled into the parking lot of the Dew Drop Inn. It was in a part of Bay City I'd never been to before and probably would never come back to if I could help it. The motel itself was even seedier than I could have imagined. The parking lot was almost empty, and the few cars I could see had definitely seen better days. There were weeds growing through the pavement, and the big sign in front, which probably had been state-of-the-art around the time the Japanese surrendered, was cracked, dirty, and listing dangerously to one side. The entire neighborhood looked blighted, and maybe thirty years ago this place *might* have been appealing. But now it just looked like the kind of place you'd see on the news as the scene of a murder investigation—a body found in pieces in one of the rooms. *So, this rich guy wants to meet us here? Seriously?*

But I saw what looked like Bill's truck parked around the side, so I parked by the front doors and went in. The man at the front desk was smoking a cigarette and looked utterly revolting. He was wearing a wifebeater that might have been white when it was new, and suspenders were holding up his dirty-looking brown polyester pants. His gut was enormous, and he looked like he hadn't shaved in days. His graying hair was pulled back into a greasy ponytail. I asked for Bill Lightning and he grinned at me. He was missing a couple of his yellowed teeth. "Room two twenty-four," he said, "around the side and upstairs." His eyes moved up and down as he gave me the once-over.

I felt like I needed a shower, but I said thanks and got back into my car. I parked next to Bill's truck, grabbed my bag, and went up the stairs. I hesitated for just a minute before knocking on the door to 224.

The door opened, and before my mind could register anything I got pulled into a massive bear hug.

And I grinned. I couldn't help it as Bill's thick, muscular arms squeezed me, and he lifted me off my feet. He spun around like I was nothing, kicking the door shut behind him, and I wrapped my legs around his waist and kissed him. His tongue pushed into my mouth and I sucked on it, grinding my groin against his torso. He already smelled like sweat, and he squeezed an ass cheek in each of his big hands.

So much for the boyfriend, I thought, wishing I could push away, but his arms felt so good around me I couldn't bring myself to do it.

"Damn, I've missed wrestling you, boy," he growled in my ear once I'd let him have his tongue back.

He put some pressure on my lower back, flexing his big arms, and it felt good. "I've missed that, too," I replied in a low voice, putting my head down on his powerful shoulder. I had, that was the worst part of it all.

He set me down, and I became aware of the man sitting in the shadows in the corner. When I looked over at him, he got up and walked into the light.

He was taller than me—almost as tall as Bill, around six two or three would be my guess. He was wearing a sleeveless white T-shirt, and his arms were wiry, his forearms covered with bulging veins and black hair. His shoulders were far wider than his hips, and he was olive complected, with receding jet-black hair and wide, oval green eyes framed by long, dewy lashes. He looked to be in his mid to late forties, maybe, and his chest underneath the T-shirt looked strong, his stomach flat. He was wearing tight, faded jeans with strategic tears here and there. His legs were long and thin. He looked nervous as he stepped forward.

"Hi, I—I'm Jerry Brandon," he stammered, holding out a hand for me to shake.

I started to say my real name but then remembered why he was in the motel room with us and smiled. "Cage Thunder." I took his long, thin hand and squeezed it, and he shuddered a slight bit, his eyes closing.

Well, damn, I thought, *he really* is *a big fan, isn't he?*

Almost on cue, he said in a rush, "I'm a huge fan, a huge fan, you're such a wonderful wrestler, so sexy and innocent and young, and—" His face flushed as he cut himself off.

"Jerry's a big fan," Bill said, pulling his T-shirt up over his head and tossing it on the table. He made his big pecs bounce. He hadn't shaved, and the valley between the big pecs was thick with black hair.

It was hard, but I turned away from Bill and smiled at Jerry. "I appreciate that, Jerry." I pulled my own shirt over my head, and he was staring at me, his mouth open. I glanced at myself in the big mirror on the wall and didn't quite get it. I mean, why was he so into me when Bill was standing right over there? Bill was huge, his muscles thick and defined and beautiful. I wasn't repulsive, by any means, but my body didn't come close to Bill's.

To each his own.

Bill winked at me, and picking up his bag, he walked into the bathroom, shutting the door behind him. I knew what that meant—he went into the bathroom as Bill and would come out as Big Bill Lightning. It meant he'd be ready—and I had better be.

I smiled at Jerry and unzipped my duffel bag, kicking off my shoes. I undid my pants and pulled them off, folding them and putting them on the table next to my shirt. I could hear him breathing as I hooked my thumbs into the waistband of my underwear and slid it down my legs. I pulled on the skimpy pair of white trunks—barely more than a string on the sides—and adjusted my hard-on in the front. I sat down in the chair, pulled on my boots, and started lacing them up.

"Let—let me do that," Jerry said, kneeling in front of me.

I smiled and sat up, leaning back in the chair so my crotch was pushed up and forward. He gently laced up the white patent-leather boots, expertly tying first the right, then the left. I adjusted my white kneepads, and he stood up, stepping back as I stood up.

"You're so—so beautiful," he breathed out as the bathroom door opened.

I almost came in my trunks when Bill stepped out.

Bill wasn't wearing traditional trunks like he did in the ring. I'd never seen him wear anything other than that to wrestle—even when we were practicing at the gym. But now he was wearing a skimpy black leather bikini that was little more than a triangle in the front, and could barely contain him. All that connected the leather triangle in the front to the leather in the back were small brass chain links on each side. He had two black leather armbands around each biceps, which made them look bigger than they were. His black boots shone in the light, and he was wearing a black mask, with the holes for his eyes, nose, and mouth outlined in white. My knees almost buckled as he turned around and flexed the muscles in his back for my benefit. There was more material in the back than in the front, but still it was barely enough to cover each of his big, thick butt cheeks.

And around his waist was a championship belt.

He growled and tossed me a white pullover mask. I slipped it on and looked at myself in the mirror.

Yes, there was definitely something to wearing a mask.

Bill stalked over to me, and out of the corner of my eyes I could see Jerry had gotten a video camera out and was aiming it at us. At some point, Jerry had taken off his clothes except for a pair of red bikini underwear, and he had a long cock that was also fully erect as he watched us through the viewfinder of the camera.

Bill slammed his chest into mine, knocking me backward. He kept growling as he walked toward me again and slammed into me a second time. This time I was knocked backward into the wall. He growled and took the belt off, kissed it, and gently put it down on the table. He grabbed me by the throat and lifted me.

I struggled helplessly as he lifted me off the ground and then scooped me up and slammed me down on the bed. Before I could even think, he dropped an elbow to my chest and winded me… and the beat down was on.

For the next hour, Bill taught a clinic on submission holds, dirty tricks, and humiliation. After one particularly brutal torture rack, where he made me beg for mercy before he finally released me, he dropped me down on the bed and stripped my white trunks off and choked me with them. They were soaked through already with my sweat, and bare-assed naked as I was, I liked the taste of my own sweat. My cock was hard and dripping—it had been the entire time, but now it was exposed. I opened my eyes a bit and could see Jerry. He was still looking through the viewfinder on the video camera, but his free hand was massaging his own crotch.

I didn't even have time to smile before Bill flipped me over onto my stomach, and I felt a finger toying with my asshole—and gasped when it entered me. Bill massaged the sides of my hole with his finger, running it around the entrance until I started trembling. I felt the wetness of his tongue running along the patch of skin between my balls and my hole and couldn't control the involuntary trembling.

Bill had always worked wonders on my body with his tongue, and today was no exception.

As his tongue worked on my asshole, I arched my lower back and brought it up higher. I closed my eyes and forgot there was someone else in the room with us, and that he was recording everything. I didn't care as the pleasure from his tongue swept over me, and I certainly didn't give two shits about Jerry and his camera when Bill's big cock started slowly working its way inside of me.

"Like that, you little bitch?" Bill panted, slapping one of my ass cheeks with his open palm.

"Yeah, fuck me." I breathed out as he slid deeper inside me.

Nobody had ever fucked me besides Bill, and we knew each other's bodies intimately. For both of us, wrestling and fucking were so intertwined that it was hard—at least for me—to differentiate between the two. Yes, I always enjoyed getting my cock sucked, but nothing was more arousing to me than wrestling Bill and the fucking that came after. It was like Bill's cock had been somehow genetically designed to fit inside me perfectly. I couldn't imagine being fucked by anyone else—and he was so damned big...

When he was completely inside me, he somehow managed to hook his arms underneath me and lifted me, moving me so I was facing Jerry and the camera. Startled, I opened my eyes and saw Jerry's underwear was down around his ankles. He'd put the camera down—so my fucking wasn't being filmed, which was a good thing—and he was stroking himself. He saw me looking at him and he smiled at me, but my eyes closed as Bill slid out of me.

And like always, Bill's big cock pushed everything else out of my awareness. All I knew was I was being fucked by a stud with a big cock who'd earned the right to pound away at my ass, who'd dominated me and made me his bitch, claiming his prize. I loved the way Bill fucked me, the way he teased my ass with his massive dick, alternating between fast moves and slow ones, sliding out of me sometimes so slowly that I writhed, or slamming into me so hard it knocked the breath out of me.

And like always, he flipped me over and mounted me again, shoving my legs up as he started moving faster and faster...

My own load spilled out of me, the first blast shooting past my head, and my whole body convulsing as each load spattered over my chest and abs.

Bill was moving faster, sweat dripping off his face onto me, his eyes closed, and he howled, stiffening and gasping. He pulled out of me and coated me with his cum, and he kept shuddering each time he squirted more out.

I kept my eyes closed until I heard him chuckle.

"Let me get you a towel, boy," he growled, and I opened my eyes and sat up.

"That was amazing," Jerry said, smiling at me shyly. "If you give me your address, I'll send you a copy of the DVD."

"That would be great, thanks." I heard the shower start in the bathroom, and Bill stuck his head out, tossing me a towel.

"I'm going to shower," he said, "and then you can." Usually we showered together, but I figured he didn't want to leave Jerry alone in the room. I wiped myself down and then wrapped the towel around my waist. I picked up my sweaty gear and shoved it into my duffel bag. When I looked over at Jerry again, he'd pulled his pants back up and had his wallet out. He counted out ten one-hundred-dollar bills and held them out to me with a gentle smile.

"Thanks," I said, taking them and putting them in my wallet.

"Here's my business card." He held out his hand again. "Cage, you are such a hot man. If you ever—ever—need anything, please give me a call."

"Thanks." I carefully placed the card in my wallet.

"You're like my dream man," he went on. "I've always wanted a hot wrestler like you, you know…" His voice trailed off and he shook his head.

I stepped closer to him and took one of his hands and placed it on my chest. "Do you like that?" I whispered.

He swallowed and nodded.

I smiled at him and leaned down close to his ear. "You want me to do to you what he just did to me?"

His eyes wide as saucers, he just nodded.

I brushed my lips against the side of his cheek.

The shower turned off, and I stepped away from him. He was good looking—and he was rich.

Where does Bill find these guys? I wondered as Bill walked out of the bathroom stark naked, rubbing himself down with a towel. I went into the foggy bathroom and turned the shower back on and climbed under the hot water, letting it ease my stiffening muscles. I was a little bit sore—Bill always was a little rough, but I never minded. I kind of liked it, actually.

Once I was dried off and dressed again, Bill said, "We're going out for dinner, you want to join us?"

I shook my head. "Nah, I really do have to head back home and study. I'd best be getting back." Bill hugged me and kissed the top of my head.

"I'll call you soon," he whispered.

"Remember what I told you," Jerry whispered as I shook his hand, and I just smiled back at him.

"Thanks," I whispered back and winked at him.

I was grinning as I started my car.

Jerry preferred *me*.

That, I thought as I backed out of the spot and headed for the street, *might just come in handy someday.*

CHAPTER SEVEN

For the record, going to Blackbeard's for my birthday wasn't my idea.

I had actually turned twenty-one during Christmas vacation, a few days after New Year's, and I'd been in Alabama at the time. I'd gone out to the one bar in Corinth with my friends and drank a couple of beers, but I hadn't gotten drunk. But I'd gotten an e-mail from Phil wishing me a happy birthday, and promising to take me out on the town when I got back to Bay City. I'd just gotten in the afternoon before and called Phil, who insisted on taking me to dinner and then out to Blackbeard's.

I was excited a bit—this was my first time going to a gay bar—and could barely contain myself over dinner. Phil had just laughed at me. "Relax, champ." He shook his head. "It's just a gay bar, and it's not even the only gay bar in town. A few months from now, you'll be so over gay bars I'll have to drag you into one, kicking and screaming."

I just rolled my eyes at him.

And after he paid cover for both of us and we walked into Blackbeard's, he whispered to me loud enough to be heard over the loud music, "See what I mean?"

I nodded and smiled, but I didn't have the slightest idea what he meant. The bar was amazing. The Tavern in Corinth wasn't anything like this. There were plenty of guys inside, but it wasn't so crowded that we couldn't make our way over to the bar easily. Phil ordered us both something called a Cape Cod. It was red, and there was a strong alcohol taste beneath the sweetness of the cranberry juice. The bartender was good-looking, with dark hair, a good tan, and a muscular body. He winked at me as I picked up my drink and tasted it. I turned around and surveyed the bar. I didn't recognize the song the deejay was playing—it had a really fast tempo and the female singer was wailing. I took another sip of my drink and—

—that was when I saw Bill over by the pool table and video game machines.

He had his arm around a muscular guy who looked vaguely familiar.

"You know Bill?" I heard Phil saying next to me.

I nodded. "I work at his gym."

Phil laughed. "From the look on your face you do—or *did*— more than that."

I turned back to the bar. "I don't want to talk about it."

"Okay."

Before I could respond, the song that was playing ended, and the lights came up a bit. On the stage on the other side of the dance floor, an enormous drag queen came strolling out. I gaped at her as she started talking into the microphone, to hoots and hollers from the audience.

"I'm Floretta, and as you know, boys, tonight's *oil wrestling* night!" she said, throwing her head back and letting out a cackle. "And as always, we need some volunteers from the audience! Is anyone interested?"

"Do it," Phil hissed beside me. "Put up your hand."

"Come on, boys, don't be shy!"

"Bill will hate it if you do," Phil taunted me.

And that was all it took. I put up my hand, and Floretta cackled with delight again. "There's one! Come on up here to the stage, brave boy! I just need another volunteer. Just one."

The next few minutes went by in a blur. One moment, I was

standing up on the stage next to her and everyone was cheering—I tried to see if Bill was paying attention, but the lights on the stage were so bright I couldn't see anything. Another guy came up to the stage, and then Floretta was leading us back behind the stage to a dressing area, where she picked out a bright red thong and tossed it to me with a crooked smile.

I took a deep breath and changed. My hands were shaking a little bit.

And then I was back out on the stage next to Floretta again, and she was saying my name into the microphone, to cheers from the audience. "Let's get him oiled up!" And she pulled out a bottle of baby oil she'd hidden in her cleavage and squirted me in the chest.

"Are you nervous?" Floretta whispered to me, but not in her drag voice. Her real voice was even deeper than mine. "Don't be," she added, squirting oil onto my legs and rubbing it in. "This is just for fun, after all."

While I was backstage, someone had set up a tarp on the dance floor, with mats underneath it. So the dance floor was going to be the arena, and I was surprised that I didn't feel nervous at all. Of course, I'd wrestled in front of people before, but usually not in a thong exposing my ass.

And really, it was kind of *fun* standing up there in front of everyone.

"How does he look?" Floretta asked into the microphone. The crowd cheered. I just grinned at them all.

"Nice basket!" someone shouted.

Floretta looked down. "It is, isn't it?" She leered at me, prompting more cheers from the audience.

Okay, I have to admit, it was great listening to an audience of gay men cheering how I looked.

"Let's bring out his opponent!" Floretta said. "You boys ready to see Gary's foe?" They all cheered again. "Come on out, Lance!"

The door to the bar office opened. From where I was standing

I couldn't really see him, and I tried to play it cool, like I didn't really care. I was trying to get into my Cage Thunder character—the big bad heel from BGEast Productions, not Cage Thunder the jobber from GSWA. Lance came out from behind the stage curtain and I got a good look at him for the first time.

Mary Mother of God.

He was short, maybe five-six, and looked like he couldn't be more than twenty, but he was probably one of those guys who keep their baby face into their thirties. His body wasn't the body of a twenty-year-old, unless he started lifting weights when he was three. He had to weigh at least a hundred and eighty, and it was all muscle. Big, thick, hard muscle. His body gleamed in the lights from the oil. His pecs were as big as my head, I swear to God. His legs looked like tree trunks. He was wearing a yellow thong that was just a string running from the pouch, dropping into the deep crevice between his boulder-sized butt cheeks. His body was completely hairless. He lifted both arms and flexed his biceps, kissing each one. The crowd roared. He turned his back to the audience and made his ass bounce, flexing and relaxing it.

He was so gorgeous I couldn't take my eyes off him.

I looked out at Phil, who was grinning so big it looked like the top of his head might fall off. He gave me a big thumbs-up.

"All right, boys," Floretta drawled. "I want a clean fight, no biting, no punching, no ball grabbing, no choking, no kicking, no hair pulling."

Lance scowled at me. I scowled right back.

Floretta stepped down into the crowd. "Ring the bell!" Someone did, and Lance charged me, grabbed my legs, and dropped me neatly down to the tarp. He landed on top of me, and our heads were close together.

"Let's give 'em a good show," Lance whispered. I looked at his face, and he winked at me. "Just act like I'm hurting you, okay?"

"Okay," I whispered back. His body felt good on top of me, solid, hard muscle. He rolled me over onto my stomach and wrapped his fingers in my hair and pulled my head back, not hard, just enough pressure so I understood what he was doing.

I howled.

The crowd erupted into boos and catcalls.

Lance stood up, not letting go of my hair, and I got to my feet as well. He wound up and punched me in the stomach. It was nothing more than a light tap, his hand barely touching me, but I doubled over, selling it as the crowd jeered even louder. He smacked me on the back with his forearm, again, nothing more than a light tap, and I sprawled down onto the tarp. He started kicking me lightly in the side. I reacted to each tap of his foot by moving a bit. I moaned with each kick, each movement. He did it again and I flipped over onto my back.

I was having a blast.

He wound up to drop an elbow to my gut, and at the last second I rolled out of the way. Lance let out a bloodcurdling howl as his arm supposedly connected with the tarp. He rolled over and over, coming to rest on his stomach, clutching his arm. I stood and staggered over to him and kicked him in the side. Lance shrieked again, and the crowd cheered. He rolled over onto his back. I straddled him and started lightly punching his pecs. He kept howling, jerking with each hit, trying to buck me off.

His pecs felt incredible.

My dick was getting hard.

He grinned up at me and winked.

His hands came up under my chin, pushing my head back. He swung his legs up and around my head and pulled me back. I fell backward. He was lightly squeezing my head. It felt great in there, looking right at that beautiful ass.

Oh man, oh man—this is so fucking incredibly hot—I'm going to fucking shoot a load if this keeps up—but I don't want him to stop.

My dick was completely hard.

I felt something on my feet.

What the fuck?

Oh God, he's sucking my toes. Oh man, that feels so fucking good, oh man, oh man.

I stopped struggling against him. All I could think about was how good his mouth felt on my big toe, and then he moved to another toe, and my entire body was trembling.

Oh man, oh man, oh man—

He grabbed my dick.

I slapped his ass. It tightened. I smacked it again.

The slight pressure from his legs let up—he let me go. I slid my head out, even though I didn't want to, I could have stayed there forever, but he still had an ironclad grip on my leg, and he was now licking my instep.

Turnabout, I decided, was fair play. I grabbed his leg and bent it. I took his big toe into my mouth and started sucking, sucking like it was a Tootsie Pop, licking and sucking.

Why didn't I notice what pretty feet he had?

I licked his instep and his entire body went rigid. I pulled my leg away from him. I stood up and dropped an elbow onto his back. He screamed, and for just a minute I worried if I'd hit him too hard, and then he rolled over onto his back and winked to let me know he was okay, and then I started punching his abs, his razor-cut perfect washboard abs.

Hey, he's got a hard-on, too!

Cooooooooooool.

I straddled his abs again and shoved both my feet up into his face. He grinned at me and started tonguing my feet. *Oh man, that feels so great.* I reached back and grabbed his dick.

It was big, thick, and meaty.

Christ.

He winked at me again.

He bucked me forward, and I fell onto him, my crotch in his face. He rolled me over, and we slid in the oil on the tarp, rolling over and over again.

"You've got great feet," he whispered as we rolled.

"You, too."

"Do you care if I take off your thong?" He was on top of me, our crotches together, his legs wrapped around mine.

"What?"

"You can take mine off—but we have to make it look real." He kissed the side of my face. No one could see because we were so close together. "You're fucking making me so hot."

I'm making you hot?

"Okay," I breathed.

He sat up and pretended to choke me. His face looked intense, but he winked at me out of the eye the crowd couldn't see—hell, I'd forgotten we were in a bar. I tried to pull his hands off my throat. Finally, he let go and slapped my face, a nice stage slap that sounded really loud.

The crowd jeered.

He stood up and I lay there like I was too stunned, too disoriented to move. He grabbed my thong and yanked it off. My dick slapped against my lower abs. He waved it over his head and turned his back to me. He was flexing his muscles for the booing crowd. I got to my feet and slapped a full nelson on him and threw him down to the tarp again. He lay there like he was stunned. I looked at the crowd.

"Strip him! Feed it to him!"

I looked at Floretta. Her eyes were gleaming. She nodded slightly.

I walked over to him and stomped on his stomach. He moaned but nodded. I reached down and yanked on his thong.

The string broke in my hand.

The crowd cheered.

His dick was fucking huge.

I straddled his chest with it in my hand.

He grinned at me.

I shoved the thong into his face.

He screamed.

I threw it aside and stage-slapped him.

"Finish me off," he whispered.

I lay across his chest, holding him down.

Floretta jumped down onto the tarp and slapped the mat three times. "We have a winner!" she screamed, pulling me off Lance.

The crowd cheered as she held my arm up.

Phil was grinning like there was no tomorrow.

As I looked around the bar, I realized I was stark naked with a hard-on in front of a room full of strangers.

I kind of liked it.

And then I saw Bill, back in his corner, scowling at me.

"And what a nice cock our winner has!" Floretta reached down and grabbed it. The crowd cheered again.

I looked back at Lance. He was getting to his feet with a scowl on his face. His arms snaked around me, and he lifted me off my feet and threw me down.

Floretta screamed, the crowd was jeering again, and my foot was in his mouth again. What the hell?

He was working my foot with his mouth, bathing it with his tongue, and then went back to the toes. *Oh sweet Lord, it feels so fucking good.*

He was tugging on his own dick.

He shot a load all over me.

He winked at me, then grabbed Floretta's microphone. "There's your fucking winner!" he shouted into the microphone. "How does he look with my cum all over him?"

Okay, then.

I got up and grabbed him by the hair. He dropped the microphone as I pulled him back down to the mat. I punched him a couple of times in the abs and then stood up. I looked down at his beautiful body and shoved my foot in his face.

He started licking.

I started pulling on my dick.

I was so fucking turned-on, it didn't take long.

My load was bigger than his. As it shot out of me, I aimed

for his face, his chest, his abs, his legs, covering him with my cum.

For good measure, I stomped on his stomach one last time.

The crowd cheered as I raised my own hands in the air.

One of the bouncers handed me a towel and pulled me back off the stage, pushing me through the crowd. Everyone, it seemed, wanted to touch me, pat me on the back, grab my ass, pinch a nipple. He pushed me into the office, the door shutting behind me.

Oh man. I fucking just jacked off in public.

The door opened, and Floretta and Lance came in. Lance grinned at me.

"Helluva show." Floretta lit a cigarette.

"He's a natural." Lance winked at me.

"Okay," Floretta said, flicking ash onto the floor. "Gary, you got a nice look—sexy body. You ever danced before?"

Not sure what she meant, I nodded my head. "Yeah, I like dancing."

She rolled her eyes dramatically. "I mean for money." She jerked a thumb at Lance. "He's a dancer. A dick dancer."

"You mean like up on the bar?"

She gave me a sardonic look. "Ah, you're a college boy, aren't you? Yes, on the bar. We pay you a guarantee of fifty bucks a night, and you can make at least two hundred bucks a night—Fridays and Saturdays, sometimes Sundays. You up for it?"

"Two hundred bucks is a bad night," Lance chimed in.

Two hundred bucks on a bad night? In my mind's eye, I saw Bill making out with that guy in the back of the bar. Hell, even if I only made four hundred bucks per weekend, it was way more than I was making at the gym. "Okay."

"Great." She waved a hand at me. "You can start tomorrow night. Bring about six pairs of trunks to dance in. Boots are better than rubber-soled shoes—the bar can be slick and we don't want you falling off." She examined her nails. "We do the wrestling one Friday a month, and that pays two hundred, and you can dance afterward. But no more nudity, no more jacking off." She glared at Lance, then back at me. "Can you come by tomorrow for a photo shoot?"

"Photo shoot?"

"Promo shots. And we'll need to do employee paperwork for you." Her eyes gleamed. "We'll bill next month as a grudge rematch between you two. That should pack the house. Be here at three."

The door shut behind her.

This had worked out even better than I could have hoped.

CHAPTER EIGHT

I pulled up my red trunks and looked at myself in the mirror. I'd shaved my torso that morning, so all the muscles in my abs stood out in stark relief. I flexed my biceps. Looking good, I thought to myself. I took a deep breath.

I hadn't taped for BGEast in a while, and I'd missed it. While I'd met some wrestlers online and had a match here and there whenever I traveled to dance, it just wasn't the same. I'd had quite a few matches in the last eight months or so, but they were almost always disappointing. The oil matches at Blackbeard's— well, I got a lot of tips before and after those matches, but I didn't count those as actual matches. It wasn't remotely even close to actual wrestling, frankly, it was just sliding around like two greased pigs. And meeting guys online was always a mixed bag, at best. Some guys were just looking for sex, with wrestling as brief foreplay. Other guys just didn't know what they were doing or just liked to talk online about it, and when it came down to it, didn't show up or canceled at the last minute or the pictures they used online were twenty years old or whatever. But finals were now over, school was out for the summer, and I wasn't going back to Alabama. I was going to be doing a lot of dancing this summer—Lance had hooked me up with a booking agent, and I was doing a lot of gay pride events and a couple of circuit parties and some gigs in bars.

I walked out of the locker room, ready for the photo shoot that always preceded the matches.

Stuart was changing the batteries in his camera. He looked up and whistled. "Looking good, Cage."

"Thanks. What do you know about this kid?" I asked. I'd driven down to Fort Lauderdale and gone straight to the ring. I'd danced at a club in Orlando last night and had headed south right after the bar closed, at three in the morning. When I was too tired to drive anymore, I checked into a dump of a motel and wound up oversleeping.

Stuart shrugged. "Nice guy. He's a looker and got a great body. We worked with him some yesterday, so he's not a total novice."

"Cool." I sat down on the floor and started stretching my hamstrings. My stomach started churning a bit. I always got a little nervous before taping a match. You never knew how serious the other guy was going to be about it. You never knew if he was skilled enough to not hurt you. It also sucked when you didn't have the slightest idea what he looked like. What if he wasn't your type?

Not being able to get hard can be embarrassing.

The door to the other changing room opened, and I got my first look at my new opponent. He walked into the light. I whistled under my breath. Damn, but he was a beauty. He was about six feet tall and all muscle. Every muscle rippled and stood out with every step he took. He couldn't have been more than twenty-two or twenty-three. His shoulders were broad and corded with muscles. His waist was narrow. He was wearing a purple squarecut that emphasized the shape of his thick, hard legs. He had short curly dark hair. His face was beautiful. He smiled at Stuart. His teeth were even, white. He climbed through the ropes and started stretching. I watched him as he started posing for Steve.

His ass was round, hard as a rock. My dick started to get a little bit hard.

I stood up. I looked at the big mirror on the wall. My body fat was lower than it had ever been before, and veins bulged in all my muscles. The low-cut red metallic trunks caught the light and flashed a bit. I really liked them and made a mental note to ask Steve where he'd gotten them. I definitely needed to get a pair.

As I posed for Stuart, I could feel sweat starting to bead up under my arms and inside the mask. I was wearing a black latex mask that exposed my mouth and chin. It fit like skin, and I knew I was going to be drenched in sweat once we started wrestling.

"That's good," Stuart said with a big smile. "Let's get started."

I climbed through the ropes. I stood there with my arms folded, staring him down. He looked up and grinned at me. I smiled back. He got up and walked over to me, his right hand out.

"I'm Gino Matarese," he said.

"Cage." I shook his hand. He had a good hard grip. "Let's have some fun, okay?"

He nodded.

"Okay, guys," Stuart said. "I'm ready to start taping."

The bell rang.

Gino smiled at me and struck a pose. "You want some of this?" His muscles looked carved out of granite. Veins bulged.

Cocky little shit. I posed back, a double biceps, flexing my abs. "Come on, then, boy."

We started circling each other. I watched his hands. He feinted forward a couple of times, and I stepped back. We kept circling. We finally locked up and started pushing at each other.

Damn he's strong, I thought. He was muscling me back into a corner. *Okay, keep your head, watch for an opening,* I reminded myself. I felt the corner pads against my back. I spread my legs farther apart for balance. I started to brace myself when he dropped hold of my arms. He grabbed my head and neatly flipped me over his shoulder. I landed with a bang on my back in the center of the ring. He grabbed my right arm into an arm bar and cranked. I rose up onto my side with a yell. He shoved his right knee into my neck. Fuck, fuck, fuck, fuck…

"Come on, masked man, give it up." He grunted. I slapped at him with my free arm. The pain was blinding. He eased up a little, and I sucked in some air just as he tightened his grip again. Tighter. I yelled out again. "Give it up."

"No fucking way," I choked out through gritted teeth. He pulled again, applying pressure. A blinding jolt of pain wracked my body. An involuntary shout escaped my mouth. Jesus. He lightened up the pressure, and I took in some deep breaths. I wasn't stupid enough to think he wasn't going to put pressure back on. I braced myself for it and thought quickly. How could I get out of this—*"Fuuuuuuck!"*

"Come on, tough guy," he taunted me as I gasped for breath. "Give up. I'll break it."

"No way," I panted out. I tried to get my knees under me. There. I pressed up with my free arm and my legs. I was aware of his two legs on either side of my head. I looped my free arm around that leg.

He laughed.

And then let go.

My right arm dropped down to the mat. The shoulder and upper muscles of the arm were throbbing. I gulped in air, tested the arm.

Damn, he was good.

Then I felt his legs tighten around my head. Shit. He dropped to the left, and my head, trapped between his legs, turned my entire body to that side. A jolt of pain shot through my neck, and he tightened his legs.

"No way," I said through clenched teeth. I grabbed hold of his thighs with my arms. It was futile, I knew. His legs were too strong for me to pry them apart. He loosened the grip and tightened again. The blood was pounding in my head. My neck was screaming in agony. He lightened up the pressure and then cranked it on again. Hard. My neck. Red dots appeared in my vision.

He kept it on.

"Okay, okay, okay!" I slapped at his leg. "I give, I give, I give!"

He released the hold and rolled up to his feet.

I rose up on all fours and twisted my head from side to side. My neck was definitely stiffening up. My arm was still aching. I gulped in air. *Keep away from his scissors,* I said to myself.

"Get up, bitch. You want some more of me?"

I looked up at him. He had stuck a double-biceps pose, his abs standing out like a Greek god's. He was smiling at me, taunting me, striking more poses, showing off his muscles. And then I noticed that his dick was hard, longish and thick inside the purple squarecut clinging to him like skin. He ran his hands down over his chest and stomach, stopping just above the top of his suit.

I stood up slowly. I shook my head some more to clear some of the cobwebs. "You're gonna pay for that, boy."

"Oh, I'm scared." He laughed again. "Shaking."

Okay, boy, I thought. We started circling each other again. We locked up, and this time I powered him back into the ring corner. I stepped back, letting go, raising my arms. A clean break, not like the shit he pulled. He just smiled at me as I backed off. He came forward, darting for my legs. Before I could slip back he grabbed hold and knocked me backward. I felt his fingers grabbing my Speedo and pulling. He yanked my Speedo off and then threw it in my face. He backed off.

I got to my feet. He was standing a few feet from me, a big shit-eating grin on his face. Okay, then. This was a loser-gets-fucked match, and there was no way I was going to let this kid fuck me. Not when he had that gorgeous hard, round ass begging for my cock.

I jumped up and drop-kicked him square in the chest. His grin faded as he saw it coming, but it was too late for him to do anything. He fell backward in the ropes, which were strung tight and propelled him forward. I spun him around and slipped my arms through his, locking my hands behind his neck, forcing his head down.

"Damn!" he said, too low for the camera microphone to pick up.

I put my mouth next to his ear. "You're gonna get fucked today, boy."

He struggled, straining as he tried to break the hold by forcing his arms down. I positioned my legs and lifted him off his feet. He moaned. I brought him down hard and let go. He dropped to the mat on his stomach. I reached down and grabbed ahold of his trunks and yanked them down. His ass was so beautiful that I paused for just a second to admire it. He tanned in a thong, so there was a slight line of white running along just above those perfectly hard, round tanned cheeks that dropped down into the crack, a smallish triangle of white forming just where the line met in the center. I straddled his back. I grabbed his chin with one head and yanked his head back. With the other, I shoved the trunks in his face.

"Ready to get that pretty ass fucked?" I taunted, rubbing his sweaty trunks all over his face. I sat farther back, dropped the trunks, and used both hands to yank his head back. I shoved my legs under his arms. I settled in for a while. The camel clutch is a surefire submission hold. All the pressure goes into the lower back. If a guy is flexible, he can hold out for a while, but most guys aren't.

Let's see how limber you are, Gino, I thought as I pulled back.

"Oh God!"

"Come on, boy," I said. "How does this feel?"

He was gasping for breath, which exploded out of him in moans.

"Not so tough now, are you?"

"Fuck you!"

"I can sit here all fucking day if I have to." The muscles of his back were straining, but his arms were useless. I let go of his chin with one hand and reached back and slapped his ass. It was hard.

I felt my own cock stiffening.

I cranked back some more.

"I give, I give, I give, I give!" Gino screamed.

I let him go and stood up. He rolled over onto his back. His dick was still rock hard. He grabbed his back with both hands and rolled back onto his stomach. He came up onto his knees, arching his back.

I nudged him with my foot. "Get up, boy."

He stayed there.

I grabbed a fistful of his hair and dragged him up to his feet. I let go of his hair and turned him around, slipping my arms through his and locking my hands together behind his head. I shoved down, pulling him back against me. My cock slipped into the crack of his ass.

Damn, it felt good in there.

I cranked down on his head. He was slightly bent forward, and his hard ass was pressing against me.

My cock got harder.

I pulled him back and, using the nelson, drove him down to the mat. I was now lying on top of him. I let go and rolled him over onto his back. I sat on his chest and started gently slapping his face, not hard, but a little humiliating nonetheless.

"Come on, tough guy."

I leaned forward and allowed my cock to brush against his lips. Sweat was rolling down his face. So fucking pretty.

I stood up, pulling him up by his hair. I yanked his left arm up, wrapping my right leg over his left, and yanked him over to the side. Abdominal stretch.

He screamed.

"Okay, okay, I give, I give!"

Good enough for me.

I let him free, and he crumpled down to the mat, breathing hard.

I looked at him, lying there prone on the mat. Beaten. Beautiful. Sweating.

I climbed through the ropes and grabbed a bottle of lube and a condom. I climbed back through and stood over him as I slipped the condom on my cock, which by now was aching. I poured some lube over it.

I got down on my knees and pushed his legs apart.

He looked up at me. "Hey, what are you—"

I slipped between his legs, stroking my dick. I shot some lube onto his thick dick and rubbed it. He closed his eyes and dropped his head back. With my other hand I found his asshole and slowly started massaging it. A low moan escaped from him. He brought his hands up to his nipples and started pinching them gently.

I smiled.

I put the head of my dick up against his asshole and started slowly moving my hips back and forth. Not enough pressure to force my way in, just enough for him to feel a little bit, to make him want it. I leaned over him and took one of his nipples in my mouth, tonguing it, swirling my tongue over it, nipping it slightly with my teeth. He began moaning and moving his thighs up.

I slipped the head of my cock inside, just the head, and stopped.

His eyes shot open and he inhaled sharply.

I didn't move, just sat there, very still, waiting to feel his muscles down there relax and allow the intrusion. I started gently moving my hips from side to side, feeling it loosen just a little, and began nibbling on his nipple again. He brought a hand down and gripped his own cock and started stroking it slowly.

I eased my cock in a little farther.

"Ooooooooohhhhhhh yeah," he said, barely above a whisper, using what would have been a moan to form the words.

I started making a circular movement with my hips, feeling the resistance inside starting to give a little bit.

In a little farther.

His entire body was relaxing now. The movement of his hand on his cock began to go a little faster.

A little farther.

He brought his legs up, putting them over my shoulders.

He wanted it.

Bad.

I drove in fast, not getting all the way in, as he wasn't ready for the surprise of the sudden onslaught of my cock. His eyes popped open again. A loud shout escaped his mouth. I stopped, not moving, letting his body adjust to the sudden intrusion.

"Oh godohgodohgodohgod." He locked his eyes on mine. His jaw was trembling. "Fuck me, fuck me hard."

I laughed, not moving.

"Please."

I slowly began pulling back from him, my cock withdrawing in a slow, steady motion. His eyes closed again. When the head was all that was left inside, I plunged in fast and hard again. This time, I got it all the way in. I flexed my ass, trying to force everything in that I could.

"Oh my God!" he screamed. I started moving my hips again in a circular motion. He was panting. Sweat was running down his face. His entire body was trembling. His hand was jerking in a blur on his own cock. I raised up a little with my feet, bringing his ass up off the mat, and then leaned forward a bit.

"Thought you could beat Cage Thunder, did you?" I growled at him. I rolled him up a bit more, lifting his lower back off the mat. I slowly started to slide my cock back out.

He moaned.

I stopped withdrawing when all that was left inside was the head of my cock.

His eyes opened.

I stared down at him.

"Fuck me," he whispered.

"You want it?"

"Yes, oh please, yes…"

I laughed. "Beg me for it."

He squirmed a little, pushing his ass up. I moved my hips back. "Please."

"Please what?"

"Please, *sir*."

I slammed back into him as fast as I could, clenching my own ass and driving down.

He came with a scream.

His body trembled and convulsed as his cock shot. One landed in his hair, a couple on his face. His cock kept shooting. Onto his chest, onto his abs. He was trembling, convulsing, gasps coming out of his mouth with each shot that came out of him. When he was finished, I slid my cock out of him.

I straddled his chest and slipped my condom off. I lubed up my bare cock and started stroking. His eyes were half-closed and kind of glazed looking, but he brought his hands up and started pinching my nipples. I looked down at his beautiful pecs, glistening with his sweat and his cum, and soon shot my own load, into his face, hair, and pecs.

I stood up.

He grabbed his trunks and wiped his face.

We looked at each other.

He walked over to me and put his arms around me.

Our lips met in a sweet, tender kiss.

My hands went around and cupped his beautiful ass.

Our chests came together, our mingled cum slightly lubricating them.

He pulled his head back. "I want a rematch."

"Anytime, kid." I smiled back at him. I grabbed Gino's hand. "Come on, kid, let's get cleaned up."

CHAPTER NINE

I knew who he was the minute he walked into the bar, but I couldn't believe my eyes.

I had maybe another hour to go before I was done for the night and couldn't wait to get the hell out of there. This crappy bar in Pensacola was crowded, and I was smiling and flirting and doing my best, but my guess was I didn't even have two hundred bucks in tips. I was sick of smoky bars and grabby gay men who thought they could stroke me for fucking free. There was only one more week until school started again, and I was ready—more than ready. I'd managed to make a lot of cash over the summer, and maybe it was time to hang up my G-string and try something else. Some of the other guys who wrestled for BGEast charged to do private matches...maybe it *was* worth looking into.

I picked up my bottle of water and took another swig, stealing another glance. It wasn't my imagination, or wishful thinking.

It *was* Mighty Mike Armstrong, current champion of the Gulf Coast Wrestling Alliance.

I'd seen him in action enough times to recognize him in his street clothes. Anytime he was on a card anywhere within an hour's drive of Bay City, I was there, early enough to sit in the front row. I'd seen him wrestle in the ring five or six times, and I couldn't begin to count the times I'd jerked off thinking about him. He was a stud, no question about it. He was about five-ten and weighed about two hundred twenty pounds or so.

He was thickly muscled—no ripped abs for Mighty Mike, but with a solid body like that, who cared? His legs were tree trunks, his thickly muscled chest massive, and his ass always looked unbelievable in his black trunks. He always wore black trunks that rode up a little in the back during his matches, exposing a tantalizing glimpse of hard ass cheek. He was a handsome man, too—square jawed, black hair, blue eyes, and always with a bit of blue-black razor stubble on his cheeks when he stalked down the aisle, oozing attitude. He seemed to revel in the jeers of the crowd, always pausing on the ring apron to acknowledge the booing crowd with a mocking bow and a flex of his meaty biceps. As the howls of the crowd rose to a crescendo, he'd climb through the ropes and flex his arms again. My cock would leap inside my jeans every time those big muscles flexed. He was the sexiest stud I'd ever seen in the ring—but walking into a gay bar wearing a wifebeater damp with sweat where it stretched across his massive pecs and a tight pair of faded and ripped jeans, he was a god.

And here he was, walking into the same bar I was dancing at. Just last week, I'd seen him tear some lean long-haired kid with tattoos all over his pasty white skin to shreds, to the boos and catcalls of the majority of the audience in the Bay City High gym. I gave the kid credit for lasting fifteen minutes—as soon as he took off his ring jacket, I figured it would be over in a minute or two. It could have been, but Mighty Mike just toyed with the kid, playing with him to the fury of the redneck white trash sitting in folding chairs on all four sides of the ring. He didn't even try to go for a pin until the kid was nothing more than a quivering puddle of flesh in the middle of the ring. Mighty Mike rolled the kid over onto his back with a nudge of his black boot and pinned him by placing his index finger in the center of the kid's chest. Once the count was finished, Mighty Mike leaped to his feet and flexed his huge biceps as the audience jeered.

My cock was hard the entire match, like it always was when

Mighty Mike was in the ring. After he put his championship belt back around his waist and headed for the locker room, he passed maybe two feet in front of where I was sitting. For a moment, our eyes met, and I could have sworn he gave me a bit of a smile before walking on. I sat there for a while as the lights in the gym came on, and the crowd began to leave. I got up and looked at the locker-room door Mighty Mike had disappeared through. On the other side, he was stripping off those sweaty black trunks, unlacing his boots, and getting ready to get in the shower. I could picture him, the sweat glistening on his skin, as he wrapped a big white towel around his waist and headed for the showers.

My cock had ached inside my jeans as I walked out to my car.

I watched as he sat down on a bar stool at the other end of the bar.

Mike looked over at me. The eyebrows came together over those blue eyes, like he was trying to remember where he knew me from. I gave him a big smile, and a broad wink. He moved down the bar after getting a bottle of Bud Light, and I could feel sweat starting to form on my forehead.

"I know you from somewhere," he said as I squatted down in front of him, barely audible over the ridiculously loud music. His voice was deep and masculine.

I shrugged. What the hell? "You might have seen me at your match last week. I was in the front row."

He smiled but still looked puzzled. "Yeah, but that's not it—when I saw you out there, you looked familiar to me then, too."

"I've been to a lot of your matches," I replied. "That's probably it." I stuck out my hand. "Cage."

"Mike." His big hand swallowed mine, and he squeezed it—not hard enough to hurt, but hard enough for me to know it could. The puzzlement faded away, and he laughed. His smile—which you never saw at any time when he was in the ring—was dazzling. "Cage. Of course." He leaned in and lowered his voice. "You wrestle for BGEast—only they make you wear a mask."

My jaw literally dropped. I couldn't speak—I couldn't think of anything to say. He *knew* who I was?

He laughed. "Yeah, I'm a big fan." He touched my knee. "If I had a buck for every time I've blown a load watching you beat the shit out of Gino Matarese, I'd never have to work another day in my life."

"Cool," I managed to say, enormously flattered.

"We've even chatted online a few times."

"We have?"

"Hell yeah." He slid his hand up my leg to my inner thigh, and an electrical current went through my entire body. "We used to have some hellacious cyberfights." He winked at me. "All my pics online—I wear a mask, too."

And just like that, I knew who he was. An image flashed through my mind of a big, strongly muscled man in full pro gear, wearing a black mask with red trim. "No fucking way. You're Steelheel? No fucking way."

"Yeah, boy, I'm Steelheel." He nodded and gave me a sly wink. "I always wanted to meet you, boy—see if you were as much fun in person as you were online." He took a swig from his beer and put the mouth of it in the center of my chest. "Your videos are pretty damned hot. But I think I like you in person best." His grin got wider, deepening dimples in his cheeks. "I have to say, boy, I love watching you work over muscle boys."

For the second time in less than two minutes, I didn't know what to say.

I'd met Steelheel in a wrestling chat room, and he was right. We'd had some insanely hot cybermatches. He'd never sent me a picture with his face in it—in every picture he sent me he was wearing a mask. He'd told me he couldn't show his face in a wrestling context online because of his job, which really didn't make any difference to me. Who knows who you're talking to online, anyway? But the pictures he sent me were all of the same man—I could tell by looking at the impressive body—and that was good enough for me. It was a cyberfight, after all—the whole thing was about fantasy.

I'd saved the text of every single cyberfight I had with Steelheel. I used to get so turned-on reading and writing with his picture up on the screen! As soon as the instant message window opened, I knew I was in for a good time. I'd undress and sit there naked in my desk chair, with the bottle of poppers and the lube in reach. I'd open the folder where I saved his pictures and would randomly open one for a visual aid while we typed out a battle in the ring.

He was dominant, and I would always call him *sir*—he called me *boy*. I'd always e-mail him another picture of me—he couldn't seem to get enough pictures of me—and it turned me on even more to know he was sitting at his computer looking at my picture, stroking himself and imagining new and inventive ways to beat me down, to humiliate me and make me his boy.

And no matter how brutal and nasty he was to me, no matter how vicious he was to my body in the ring, once I'd finally surrendered, he would be tender.

We'd talked several times about meeting and actually having a match for real, but it never worked out. He was always vague about his job—I wasn't even sure where he lived. I also knew we'd probably never meet—how many guys that I talked to online did I ever actually meet?

Yet now, when I least expected it, here he was.

"Steelheel," I finally said, shifting a bit—my cock was hard and it was making me uncomfortable. "I can't believe it." I shook my head. "Dude, do you know how many of your shows I've been to?"

"Ah, you must have known it was me deep down." He winked at me again, taking another slug from his bottle. "Man, it's good to meet you at last."

I swallowed. "How'd you end up down here?"

"Why'd you disappear, man?" He changed the subject, not even acknowledging my question. "I missed you. That was the highlight of my day, boy. Have a cybermatch with you online, get all turned-on, and go pump iron at my gym."

"I missed you, too." I shook my head. "There's a lot of nice guys out there, but there sure are a lot of fuckin' freaks and weirdos." I resisted the urge to put my hands on his chest.

"Ain't that the truth." His leg brushed against mine, and it took all of my self-control not to shiver.

"You actually watch my videos," I replied, hoping my voice didn't shake.

"I couldn't fucking believe it when they released that tag match." He laughed, signaling the bartender to bring us both another beer. "I had to order it…and watching it, I was so proud of my boy. Should've had me as your tag partner—we'd have mopped the ring with those muscle boys—but you did a pretty good job." His knee brushed against mine again. "It's so hot watching you stand over a muscle boy after you've kicked his ass. A real turn-on, boy."

Hearing him say *boy* turned me on so much I wanted to tear his shirt off right there and run my tongue in the deep valley between his pecs. I managed to maintain my self-control and said, "I can't believe I never realized Mighty Mike was you." I felt like I was living one of my wildest fantasy dreams.

"I bought all your videos." Mighty Mike grinned at me. "You're a fucking badass, boy. I was proud as hell watching you kick the shit out of those job boys. And when you pull your big dick out and spray your load on them—*mmmm,* that's some hot stuff."

"You don't think I'm demeaning myself"—I turned my head away so he couldn't see my face—"and pro wrestling, by turning it into porn?"

Bill had told me that just a few months ago. He'd called me, wanted me to come over—he had a friend in town he wanted me to meet and wrestle with. Like an idiot, I'd gone, and I had a great time wrestling his friend. Afterward, while the guy showered, Bill had given me an earful about the videos.

"Someone tell you that?" Mighty Mike scowled, the look he usually gave his opponent when he first laid eyes on him in the ring. When I nodded, he went on. "Fuck whoever said that. Whoever told you that has some serious fucking issues." Mike pulled his wallet out and gave the bartender a twenty, waving off change. "You still living in Bay City?"

I nodded. "Yeah, I'm still there. One more year of college, and then we'll see."

He put his wallet back into his pocket and watched my face. "You better not ever disappear on me again, boy."

"Try to get rid of me." I grinned.

"Tell you what, boy, what time do you get out of here? We can head back to my hotel." He winked at me and lowered his voice. "You want to have that match we always talked about? You up for it, boy?"

An hour later, with my bag over my shoulder, I followed him out into the parking lot.

He got into one of those huge four-wheel-drive pickup trucks with the big lights on the top, and I smiled as I got into my own car. I followed the taillights of the truck to a dive fleabag hotel and pulled up beside the truck in the parking lot. He grinned at me as he climbed down from the truck, rubbing his big hands together. "Damn, boy, you look good in those jeans," he said, smacking my ass hard with his right hand. His right eye closed in a wink. "You got one hell of an ass, boy."

I leered back at him. "I got a big dick, too, *sir.*"

"I know, I've seen your videos." He grinned at me, and I followed him to a room at the far end of the first floor. He slid the key into the lock and turned on the light switch just inside the door. The room stank of stale air and the smoke of thousands of lodgers in years gone by. But what really interested me was the mattresses spread across the floor. The box springs leaned against the far wall.

I shut the door behind me. "Nice setup," I commented as I kicked my shoes off. "You knew I was coming?"

He pulled his T-shirt over his head, exposing his meaty pecs and thickly muscled arms. There was black hair around his nipples and around his navel. He grinned at me and made his pecs bounce for me.

"Oh man," I moaned. My cock was aching inside my jeans, so I undid the fly.

He walked over to me, getting almost right in my face. "The kid I wrestled tonight came over this afternoon for some private action," he said. I could smell him—the musk of his armpits, his breath, and I could see a trickle of sweat running down between his pecs.

"He was a big ole bottom." Mike leered at me, getting closer until I could feel his breath on my face. "He loved getting his ass pounded after I worked him over. He sucked my cock tonight in the locker room after the match."

I raised my hands and placed one on each of his solid pecs. There was no give to his flesh under my hands. "Think you can get it up again so soon, sir?" I asked.

A smile spread over his face, and he leaned forward, his crotch pressing against mine. "Can you feel that big cock getting hard for you, boy?" he whispered in my ear as his hands reached around and cupped my ass. "That's a nice hard ass, boy." He ran his tongue along my neck, and I shivered in response. "Yeah, you want Mighty Mike to fuck you all night long, don't you, boy?" he whispered again as one of his hands came around to the front of my jeans. He kissed my neck and I moaned as he used both hands to slide my jeans down. He leaned his weight into me, pushing me back tighter against the wall as his mouth worked its way down to the base of my neck. I shivered involuntarily. "Yeah, you like that, don't you, boy?" He grabbed each of my wrists with his big hands and raised them up over my head. He dropped his mouth down to my right nipple and began teasing it with his lips and tongue.

I closed my eyes and moaned, giving in to the pleasure.

"Uh-huh, boy, you like that, don't you?" he growled.

"Yes," I breathed.

His forearm shoved my chin up. "You think it's going to be that easy?" he growled into my ear. He stepped back away from me, his face stern. "No, boy, you want Mighty Mike's cock, you have to fucking earn it."

He walked around the mattress and rifled through an open duffel bag, squatting down next to it. "Perfect." He whistled, looking up at me and grinning. He tossed me a pair of shiny white trunks. "Put those on. No boots or pads this time, but that's okay. But next time you show up without boots and pads and I'll whip your ass, boy." He undid his pants and slid them down. He was wearing a pair of black wrestling trunks underneath, with a silver lightning bolt across the crotch. They clung to his heavy balls and his big hard cock as he flexed his big biceps.

I caught the trunks before they hit me in the face and pulled my shirt up over my head. I dropped it on top of my shoes and hooked my thumbs into the waistband of my underwear. I slid both my jeans and underwear off in one move, stepping out of both. My cock sprang up and smacked against my stomach. I slid the white trunks up. They fit me perfectly, outlining my cock and balls. I shifted my dick down and looked at myself in the mirror on the back of the door. Yeah, the shiny white looked hot against my tan, and I turned so I could look over my shoulder at my ass.

Sweet.

"Like the way you look, boy?" he asked, coming up from behind me. He'd put on a black mask, the holes for eyes, nose, and mouth outlined in silver.

"These aren't your trunks, are they, sir?" I asked, turning sideways and admiring the curve of my ass. His hands ran over my ass.

"They're too small for me," he said as his other hand grabbed my cock. "But they're hot trunks, so I bring 'em with me." He whistled. "Now I'm glad I did. They show off my boy perfectly." He slid a mask over my head, and I reached up and adjusted it a little so it was sitting on my head right. It was the same shiny white material, with the holes outlined in gold. He spun me around so I was facing the mirror again and brought his arms around me, his big hands coming up to my nipples. I could feel his hard-on through his trunks as it pressed against my ass.

I could feel his hot breath on my neck as his big hands closed on my pecs and squeezed them. His mouth pressed against the bottom of my neck as he grasped my nipples with the thumb and forefinger of each hand, tugging and pinching. I moaned and arched my lower back, pushing my ass harder against his crotch.

"Yeah, thought I forgot about your nipples, didn't you, boy?" he whispered as he tugged them even harder.

I could barely breathe. All I knew was I could feel his cock pressing against my ass, feel his lips on my neck, and the feeling from my nipples—it was all I could do not to collapse, I was so turned-on. Instead I leaned my head back, resting it against his shoulder, and closed my eyes, letting the wave of arousal sweep through my entire body. I started tapping my right foot so my body wouldn't tremble.

"That's a hot ass you got there, boy." His mouth was right against my ear, and I swallowed hard, trying to keep my breathing even and easy. One of his hands cupped my right butt cheek, squeezing it softly. Involuntarily I flexed the muscle, and he let out a low chuckle. "Carved out of stone, isn't it?" he whispered again and smacked the cheek he'd just grasped, hard. My body jolted, and the hand came around to the front. "Yeah, quite a monster you got there, boy." He squeezed my dick, still tugging on my left nipple. I wanted to collapse back against him, but I knew it was too soon.

I remembered this game from our online chats.

He stopped playing with my nipple and my dick, and his forearm smashed across my upper back. I fell against the wall with a loud grunt, and he grabbed my arm, spun me around, and hoisted me up like I was a bag of laundry, draping me across his shoulders. I could hear him laughing as I opened my eyes and looked at the room, upside down. One hand was on my chin, the other between my legs as he walked me over to the big mirror over the sink, next to the bathroom door. I turned my head so I could see our reflection.

There is *nothing* hotter than seeing yourself in a torture rack, and as I watched, he did some deep squats, which increased the pressure on my lower back.

"Gonna give up, boy?" he demanded.

"Fuck you," I sneered. "It feels good! I can outlast you!"

And it did feel good, so I relaxed into it even more, closing my eyes as he did a few more squats. Each time his body dipped down, the stretch intensified. I knew I wouldn't be able to outlast him—it would eventually start to hurt, and if I didn't give up I'd be sore for a couple of days—but for the moment, I wanted to enjoy the stretch and the feeling of his power. He was a strong motherfucker for sure—those muscles weren't just for show.

He emitted a delighted chuckle. "I knew you wouldn't disappoint me, boy."

He turned, and for a moment I was disoriented as he walked over to where the mattresses were placed side by side in the center of the room. He leaned to one side until my feet were on the mattresses, and he released me. The rush of the blood leaving my head made me dizzy, and before my vision cleared, he had scooped me up and slammed me down onto my back on the mattresses. He rolled me over onto my stomach and squatted down on my ass, grabbing my arms and lifting me up. His weight made my back arch as my head went up, and he draped my arms over his big quads, linking his hands under my chin and pulling back.

"How's that back feeling now, boy?" He grunted, but I could

hear the delight in his tone. His ass was on mine, and I could feel heat radiating from him, and the dampness from the sweat on his hairy arms.

What I really wanted was for him to fuck me right there and then, but instead I managed to defiantly say, "Fuckin' great! Is that all you have? Stretch me some more, big man!"

He let go of my chin and shoved my head from behind. My sweaty arms slid off his legs, and my head hit the mattress. He got off my ass, and in a flash I felt his elbow drop into my lower back, and a flash of pain forced the word *fuck* out of my mouth before I could stop myself. I rolled over onto my back and looked up into his masked face. He leaned down and grabbed my mask, pulling me up to my feet. He scooped me up again with ease and dropped my lower back over his knee. Right after the elbow, it hurt.

It hurt like a bitch.

He pushed my chin down and my back arched over his knee until the top of my head was touching the mattress on one side and my feet were on the other side of his bent leg. He reached down, grabbed one of my feet, and bent my leg so that my weight was balanced between my head, his knee, and the other foot. I tried to move to one side to ease up the pressure on my back, but he held me securely, and as the pain pushed everything else out of my mind, I could hear his low, sadistic laughter.

"I give! I give! I give!"

"Yeah, that's what I thought," he said, letting go of my foot and chin, shoving me off his knee. I rolled so I landed on my stomach, gulping in air.

It only seemed like I lay there for a few seconds before I felt his bare foot digging into the exact same spot in my lower back, placing more weight on it as I struggled to get away. He grabbed my left wrist and my right ankle, yanking them both up while his foot kept me down on the mattresses. I screamed out another submission, and he let me go.

I rolled over onto my stomach, looking up at him as he flexed his muscles for me. My back was in agony, my mind foggy, but watching his massive arms flex and his pecs bounce was one of the hottest things I'd ever seen. He placed his foot on my stomach. I could see his dick was hard inside his trunks—my balls were aching and begging for release.

He straddled my chest, one knee on either side of my head, and reached down, hooking his thumbs under my mask. He yanked it off my sweaty head and shoved it into my mouth, rubbing it over my face as I twisted and turned, trying to get away. But I was helpless beneath his weight, and I could taste my own sweat in the musky mask in my mouth. He tossed it aside and leaned forward, rubbing the crotch of his sweaty trunks in my face.

"You wanna suck that dick, don't you, boy?" he growled.

"Oh, hell yes, sir." I breathed the words out.

He pulled the trunks down a bit so I could see the head, a drop of clear liquid glistening in the slit. He pushed his cock down, the trunks moving down a bit, until it was almost within reach of my mouth. I flicked the tip with my tongue, and he groaned a bit as I circled the head with the tip of my tongue. His salty sweat tasted slightly of musk as my tongue worked the slit, and he groaned again before pulling his dick away from my mouth.

"Damn, boy, you trying to make me come before I'm done beating on you?" He laughed and pulled off his own mask, grinning down at me. His face was wet with his sweat, his hair damp, and a drop of sweat dangled from his chin just below the chiseled dimple. It fell, landing on my lower lip, and I darted my tongue out to lick it. He slid back until he was lying on top of me, his crotch pressing against mine, and I wrapped my legs around his waist.

He kissed me. My eyes closed and my head tilted back as his tongue entered my mouth, and my entire body shuddered as he started grinding his crotch against mine, his hard cock rubbing mine, our balls smacking against each other. I let my hands slide down his massive, wet back and grasped his ass with both hands.

His ass was as hard as he claimed mine to be, and I slid my hands inside his trunks, slipping a finger inside the crack and sliding it down until—

He grabbed my wrist, yanking my hand away and forcing it up over my head, and he buried his mouth in my wet armpit, licking and sucking on the tender skin there. I arched up against his strong body as his tongue toyed with my pit hair. It tickled slightly, but the pleasure was far more intense than the tickling, and both were so intense I began writhing under him.

He smiled at me. "Did I say you could fucking move, boy?" He got up and backed away from me, pure delight written all over his face as he wiggled his fingers, waving me forward in the unmistakable come-and-get-me wrestler's gesture.

I got to my feet, my balls aching, my cock straining against the Lycra-blend trunks.

"Flex for me, boy," he said, nodding his head. "Let me see those muscles."

I grinned and raised my arms, bending at the elbows till a ninety-degree angle formed. I made fists with both hands, remembering to angle the bent index finger up slightly, and pumped my biceps up. His hand on his dick, Mighty Mike stepped closer to me, a big lusty grin on his face. With his free hand he fondled my right biceps. He whistled and grabbed the other one with his left hand as he stepped right up to me.

"Nice, boy," he breathed out before dropping his hands and wrapping his arms around my waist. He bent his legs and lifted me as his linked fists applied pressure to my lower back. I collapsed forward, my head and shoulders going over his right shoulder as he began applying the power of his beefy arms to my lower back. My crotch rubbed against his stomach as he started walking around with me in his arms, completely helpless.

It felt incredible.

I didn't ever want him to let go.

But my back was starting to hurt again, and I was having trouble breathing.

Yet pressed against his sweaty, heaving chest, I didn't want to surrender. I didn't want the moment to end. I wanted him to keep squeezing me, asserting his dominance. He carried me over to the wall and slammed me back against it. All my breath was forced out in an explosive gasp as he stepped back and slammed me into the wall again.

And I couldn't stop myself even if I had wanted to.

My balls clenched and I came in my trunks, gasping for air and convulsing and shaking as he just stood there, holding me, my helpless limp body completely at his mercy.

He set me down, and I fell back against the wall again, my head ringing. I could feel him stripping the trunks off me, and then his hands were on my shoulders, forcing me down to my knees. I opened my eyes and his cock, his oh-so-beautiful cock was right there in front of me, his trunks down to his knees.

I started licking him, worshiping his mighty cock, licking and sucking, moving my head back and forth as he moaned, and I worked faster and faster, and his entire body went rigid.

I pulled my head back, rocking onto my haunches as he shot his load into my face and on my chest, convulsing and moaning with each hot blast, until he was finished coating me.

I didn't want to ever clean it off me.

"Come on, boy," he said, pulling me up to my feet. "Let's get cleaned up." He pulled me after him, his cum running down my torso. When we reached the bathroom, he turned back to me and asked, "You don't have to get back to Bay City tonight, do you?"

I shook my head.

He smiled. "Good." He winked at me. "We can play all night long." He looked me up and down, shaking his head again. "I gotta get you in the ring sometime, boy."

"Anytime, sir, anytime," I replied as he turned on the shower. "Anytime."

CHAPTER TEN

I can't believe I am doing this, I thought to myself for maybe the thousandth time, drumming my hands on the steering wheel.

School had started a few weeks earlier, and I was still dancing at Blackbeard's. The booking agent Lance set me up with kept trying to get me to do out-of-town gigs, but if I couldn't drive there and back I wasn't interested. The last time he'd called and I'd said no, he'd threatened to drop me as a client. "Go ahead," I'd replied, but he was all bluster. Every once in a while I thought maybe I should go ahead and take one of the gigs—I wasn't making as much at Blackbeard's as I used to. Lance told me it was pretty normal, which was why I had to take gigs in other towns.

"The regulars get used to you and they're not as willing to give you money," he'd said as he pulled his jeans on over his strong, thick legs, "as they were when you were fresh meat. That's why you gotta go out of town, man. When you're fresh meat, they can't give you money fast enough."

Yeah, whatever, I'd thought at the time.

But last weekend, I'd only brought home about three hundred bucks, total. I had a shoot scheduled with BGEast later in the month, so I wasn't too worried about the drop in income—I still had quite a bit saved up from all the dancing over the summer— but shit, that just fucking wasn't worth my time.

So when Phil called me about this dude coming to town being willing to pay me five hundred bucks for a match—why the hell not?

But sitting in the parking lot of the hotel, I felt like a *whore*.

I knew Phil did it, and some of the other guys from BGEast did, too. It didn't have to be anything more than wrestling—that's what the guys paid for, a chance to wrestle a video star.

And this guy—this Chase guy—had made it clear all he was expecting was a wrestling match.

I opened the picture he'd sent me on my phone again, remembering getting the e-mail with the picture and his phone number.

Why does he have to pay for it? I asked myself again, as I had every time I'd looked at his picture. *People would pay* him *to wrestle.*

It was a picture of a bare torso, and it made my mouth water. His body was smooth and tanned, the muscles huge and defined. With my hand shaking a little bit, I'd picked up my phone and dialed the number. He'd answered on the second ring. "This is Chase." His voice was deep, masculine. My cock started to move inside my underwear.

"Um, hi, Chase, this is Cage. Thanks for the e-mail. You'll be in town on Wednesday?"

"Well, yeah, I'll be free about four. Does that work for you? Phil said five hundred for two hours?"

"Yeah," I'd replied, trying to keep my voice steady. "Cash only, and I get paid up front before we do anything. That a problem?"

"No, that's not a problem." He lowered his voice. "And what do I get for five hundred bucks?"

"I need to tell you up front, I don't do anything anal. We can do oral, that's fine, but nothing more than that."

He laughed. "No anal. You like to wrestle, Cage?"

"Yeah, I do."

"Then that's all I care about. I'll text you the room number."

And now it was five minutes to four, and I was nervous as hell. I took another swig of water. I was wearing a black T-shirt and sweatpants. I had a thong on under the sweats.

I hadn't told Mike about this gig. He didn't seem to care about the matches for BGEast—he took great pride, as he told me any number of times, in me being such a stud for the cameras. "I love seeing you pull that big dick out on camera and spraying your victims, and knowing how many guys are getting off on it, and knowing you're fucking mine."

But this—how would he feel about this?

We'd been seeing each other as much as we could since that night in Pensacola. It wasn't easy, since he lived in Tampa and I was two hours north in Bay City. He was usually wrestling somewhere on the weekends, and I of course was dancing. But I didn't have classes on Tuesdays and Thursdays, so whenever possible I drove down and spent the night, driving back for school.

He was an architect, an associate in a really successful firm in Tampa. When I asked him what they thought about him being a professional wrestler, he just laughed. "They don't care what I do as long as I bring money into the firm," he replied, nuzzling my neck.

I took a deep breath. I went inside and took the elevator up to the fourth floor. I knocked on the door of room 414, and the door swung open.

Standing there with a big grin on his face was a tank of a man. He was five-nine, for sure, a few inches shorter than me, but that was the only way he was smaller. He was wearing a white string tank top that showed off the heavy veined muscles in his shoulders and arms perfectly. The deep cleavage between his massive pecs disappeared beneath the white cloth, but a tanned, half-dollar-sized nipple peeked out on the left side. He was also wearing baggy black nylon sweatpants, but they didn't hide the size and power of his mighty legs. His black hair was buzzed short, marine style, and his green eyes stood out brightly against the dark tan of his skin. "Cage? I'm Chase." He stuck out his hand and I shook it. "Um, come in." He stepped aside and let me in.

I sat on the bed. "Your body is gorgeous," I blurted out, feeling like a complete dork.

"Thanks!" He smiled at me, a genuine smile that lit up his eyes. "You've got a pretty nice one, too. I have to say, your videos are fucking amazing."

"Thanks." I shrugged.

"I mean it." He smiled at me. "I was pretty pleased when Phil said you'd wrestle me." He gestured over at the dresser. "Your money's over there."

Not sure what the protocol was, I hesitated for a moment. Then I figured *fuck it* and walked over to the dresser. Five crisp one-hundred-dollar bills. I put them into my bag.

"Take your shirt off."

I obliged, pulling my tank top up and over my head. He whistled. "That's nice, man."

"Thanks," I replied, folding the tank top and placing it next to my bag.

He placed one of his big hands on my leg. I jumped a bit, and he laughed. "Relax, man, I'm not going to bite you. We're gonna have some fun, right?"

I nodded.

He stood up and pulled the miniscule tank top over his head and tossed it into a corner. I just stared. The cuts in his stomach were deep enough for me to stick an entire finger inside. His torso was shaved completely smooth, and there was no hair under his arms. His armpits were really white. He gestured to me. "Come here."

I walked to where he was standing. "Jump up on me and wrap your legs around my waist," he instructed.

"Okay." I did, and he put his arms around my back and pulled me in close to him. His skin was warm and smooth against mine, and I felt my dick growing. His skin was also surprising soft over the steel-like muscles underneath. He carried me over to the bed and laid me down gently on top of it, stood there beside the bed, and popped his arms up and flexed them. Huge veins popped out in his forearms, on his biceps, and in his shoulders. "Damn," I breathed out.

He grinned at me and slid his hands inside his sweatpants, then inched them down. All he had on underneath was a black thong. His pubic hair had been waxed so none showed around the Lycra hugging the big hanging package. He had a bikini tan line that showed stark white, like his armpits, against the deep tan. He slid my sweatpants down, folding them and putting them on top of the dresser. When he turned, I got a great look at his beautiful muscled ass. The thong was just a couple of strings running above the top of each perfectly molded cheek, then a tiny triangle just above the deep canyon between them. He bent over and touched his toes, making his ass flex and curve.

I almost came right then.

He turned back around and grinned down at me. He ran his fingertips down both of my thighs. "Nice legs." He whistled. "You have to promise to head scissor me at some point. I fucking *love* that."

"Okay."

He jumped up on the bed, which bounced, and lay down beside me on his side, resting his head in his hand, the biceps bulging. "What do you feel like today, Cage? Sub? Pro? Jobber/heel? Give/take? Just trading holds?" He put his top leg over mine. It was heavy, but I liked the way it felt on me. His free hand began tracing around my left nipple.

"I like it all," I said, hearing my heart beating in my ears. "Dude—you're paying, you decide."

He rolled over on top of me, our crotches against each other. His dick was hard, too. He grabbed my arms and held them down over my head, making my back arch up, just a little bit. He bent his head down and started flicking his tongue over my neck. My body started to tremble. He grinned up at me. "Why don't we just roll around a bit and then see what we feel like?"

I swallowed. "Sure." I actually liked what he was doing but didn't say anything. I wanted to see what he would do next.

He let go of my arms and rolled off me, getting up on his knees. I didn't move for a minute, just sat there and admired the beauty of his body. He sat back on his haunches and grinned at me until I finally got up on my knees. "Flex your arms," he ordered.

I did. He whistled and grabbed each biceps with one of his hands and squeezed. "Nice, man." He let go and traced an index finger from the base of my throat down between my pecs and down to my navel.

"Do you"—I swallowed—"do you want me to put you in a full nelson?"

"Thought you'd never ask." He turned around so his back was to me, the hard cheeks staring at me. I put my arms underneath his armpits and locked my fingers behind his neck and pressed down, moving in closer so my crotch was right up against the boulder butt, my hard cock between the cheeks. He groaned a little bit, put up a bit of a struggle against the hold, so I had to apply more pressure to hold him in it. He began alternately flexing his butt cheeks, so that my dick was kind of getting a massage back there.

It felt incredible.

"Oh man," he breathed, "that's nice. A little tighter, do you mind?"

I squeezed and he let out a long moan.

"Yeaaaaaaaaaaaaahhhhhh…"

I leaned and fell backward, pulling him with me so he landed on top of me, and I put my legs around his waist and locked the ankles, squeezing.

"Oh yeah, man, that's hot…fuck, yeah…torture me, man…I can take it!"

I squeezed my legs together with every bit of strength I could muster, and he groaned, his breath coming faster and shorter as I pushed his head down farther, squeezing with my arms, until finally I couldn't squeeze anymore and relaxed.

"Fuck!" he said, rubbing his back against me. "You're good, man."

I squeezed again and he cried out a bit, fighting against it, until after a few seconds more he said, "Okay, man, okay! I give, stud!"

I let go of him and he rolled off me onto his stomach. He grinned at me, shaking his head. "You know what you're doing, man. Fucking hot! So many guys don't, you know? That's why I figure it's easier to hire a pro."

"Actually, I'd wondered about that," I replied. "I mean, your body is amazing. BGEast would snap you up in a minute to tape, you know."

He shrugged. "Yeah, well. I don't need to do that." He smiled at me. "Wrestling is a private thing for me. Although it must be hot to know that guys are so turned-on by watching you."

"Yeah, it kind of is," I replied, putting my hands underneath my head. "And I know what you mean. I've gotten to the point where I don't meet any of the guys on the contact sites anymore. It's just disappointing."

He shrugged. "Most of 'em don't really wrestle—it's just a fantasy for them, and sadly, many of them aren't in very good shape—they don't know how to put on holds or anything." He rolled onto his back. "Sit on my chest and work my abs over."

"Okay." I climbed up on his massive chest, enjoying the feel of his hard pecs under my ass, and punched him lightly in the stomach.

"Yeah, nice. You can go harder."

I started punching, the punches becoming harder and

faster. With each punch, his body reared, reacting, and he was moaning. The head of his cock was sticking out of his thong. I kept punching, harder and faster until he finally tapped me on the back. "Break, man, break!" I sat back and looked over my shoulder down at him. "That's hot, guy, I fucking love this! Your back looks so fucking hot up there." He traced a finger down my spine, and I trembled a little bit. "Now, my turn."

"What do you want me to do?"

He pushed me off and smiled. "I'm going to scissor you, man, so you can see what my legs can do." He slid his legs around me. He squeezed a bit, not hard, just enough for me to feel the power in his legs.

"Yeah." I grinned back at him. "Really give it to me, man."

He rose up on his hands and flexed his ass, his legs squeezing together. All the breath was crushed out of me, and I could feel the blood rushing to my head, but still I didn't give in, even thought spots were appearing before my eyes. It just felt so fucking incredible, those big powerful legs around me, his balls up against my side, looking at the rippled stomach and those big strong pecs…I felt like I could die right then and there.

He let up and whistled. "Damn, you can take it."

I gulped in breath, my vision clearing a little bit. "Feels good, stud."

He squeezed again, but this time I couldn't hold out, couldn't resist. I smacked his legs, and he immediately let go, and I rolled out from between them, gasping for air. I reached for the bottled water on the nightstand.

"You okay?" he asked, concern in his voice. "I don't want to hurt you."

The water felt good and I gulped down another swallow. "Fuck no, man, that was fucking hot!"

He smiled. "I'd love to get in a ring with you sometime. There's nothing hotter than wrestling in a ring, is there?"

"Yeah." I reached over and tweaked his right nipple. "I'd be glad to meet you down in Lauderdale sometime. I can use the ring whenever I want, you know. One of the benefits of being part of the BGEast family."

"Cool." He reached over and rubbed my dick. "You wanna lose these thongs?"

I leaned down and grabbed the strap of his with my teeth and started pulling it down. I heard him laughing as his cock sprang out and slapped up against his lower abdomen. I kept it tight between my teeth until it was down around his ankles, then used my hands to get it off the rest of the way.

"My turn." And he did the same thing, his hot breath blowing on my legs as he worked the thong down. He grabbed my ankles and pulled me down onto my back and stood, holding my legs apart. Before I could wonder what he was going to do, he started running his tongue up the inside of my left calf, and my entire body went rigid. His tongue kept sliding farther and farther up, until he was licking my inner thigh. I closed my eyes and moaned. My God, no one had ever done that to me before and it felt fucking amazing. I was going to have to remember that the next time I was with someone, and trying to get them worked into a frenzy. It felt so fucking good, I could barely stand it, and then his tongue was up, licking my balls and then going up the underside of my cock. Then he was lapping at the head.

I put my hands down on his shoulders, kneading the hard muscles, digging my fingers in and working them. They were tight and hard, full of knots, and I started working one of the knots out.

He moaned, letting my cock go. "Oh man, that feels great! Don't stop!"

I swung out from under him and straddled his back. His head went down, and I started sliding my thumbs down the muscles along his spine, digging in deep with them, and he kept moaning, his ass flexing and unflexing, his legs swinging at the knees and slapping against the bed. When my thumbs reached where the curve of his ass started, I hesitated. *Nothing anal,* we'd said.

Instead, I sat down on the small of his back and grabbed

both of his arms, bringing them up and backward. The muscles of his back jumped out in relief. *"Ooooohhhhh!"* he grunted, the skin turning red as he fought to bring his arms back down. I kept applying pressure to them, struggling against his incredible strength. A bead of sweat rolled off my nose and dropped onto his back. Beads of sweat popped out along his back, as he strained and struggled. "Fuck you, man!" he half shouted. "I'll never give!"

I drove my knee into one of his sides.

"No way!"

I did it again, and his body convulsed.

"Okay, man, fuck you, I give, man!"

I let his arms drop and sat down on his back again. He was breathing hard, and his back was shimmering with sweat in the late-afternoon sunlight. I wiped sweat off my own forehead and leaned down to kiss the back of his neck.

He rolled me over onto my back and came on top of me, his cock against my stomach. He grabbed my arms and forced them over my head again, putting his weight against them. He smiled down into my face. His own was wet with sweat. "Nice sneak attack, stud." He then put his face down in my right armpit and started licking it.

Oh, wow. My whole body tried to arch up, but he was too strong, holding me down and helpless as he started kissing the sensitive skin there, then nibbling. It was incredible, my cock was straining, my whole body straining, and I could feel the sweat trickling down all over my body, I had to get up, I had to get his mouth away from me, it was too much, it was too much, if he didn't stop I was going to come, I couldn't believe how fucking amazing it was, how it felt—

—and then, he stopped.

I lay there, panting. "Jesus."

"Pretty intense, huh?" He didn't let go of my arms. I didn't mind. I liked lying there with his hard, heavy body on top of mine, completely in his power. Then he got up off the bed and stood there for a minute, just looking down at me, and then he had one hand under my neck and the other under my lower back and he was picking me up. *My God, how fucking strong is he,* I wondered as he got his legs underneath me and then pressed me up and over his head until I was lying stretched out over his left shoulder, one hand around my neck and the other under my balls, balancing me up there.

The stretch on my back felt good.

"Doesn't that hurt?" he asked, his voice amazed.

"I was a gymnast," I gasped out.

"Damn, I need to get you in a ring," he said, bending his knees then straightening them out so I kind of bounced on his shoulder, my back arching farther with each movement, and he kept going until I felt the pain start, and I shouted, "Okay! Okay! I give!"

He neatly flipped me onto the bed, where I bounced a bit before settling in.

"How was that?" he asked.

"Fucking hot," I said, trying to catch my breath. "No one's ever done that to me before."

He kept standing there, looking down at me, until I sat up and got off the bed. I grabbed his head into a side headlock and dragged it down to my hip, turning him until I could flip him over onto his back on the bed, which groaned.

I drove down on him, squeezing and flexing my arm as much as I could. His face started to redden, and he struggled, trying to break the hold with his own arms, but somehow I found the strength to hold him off until he was tapping my arm. "Okay!" he squealed. "Okay! Okay! Okay!"

I let go and moved away from him, but not fast enough. He grabbed my shoulders and dragged me toward him until our faces were inches apart, and then he pressed his lips against mine. I opened my mouth to take his tongue into it and then sucked on it. He began moaning, and I rolled over on top of him, my cock rubbing against his. His pelvis started thrusting, and I matched it, so our cocks were stroking each other. I moved my mouth down his throat, tracing his Adam's apple with my tongue, and then sucked a little at the base of his throat then moved down to the pecs. I started flicking my tongue over his right nipple while pinching the left with my left hand. I moved my right hand down and grabbed his cock with it, squeezing it tightly.

"Oh, you fucking stud, yeah, that's the way, man, that feels good." He kept up a steady stream of talk while I worked his nipples over with my tongue, before bringing it down and starting to work on his navel. His back arched up, and I pinched both nipples hard.

His legs came up around my head, resting on my shoulders as I took his cock in my mouth, and as I worked it, his legs came together, squeezing gently against my head. Just enough pressure for me to know they were there, not hard enough to hurt. They felt awesome there, and then I brought my hands to his quads and ran them up and down them while I sucked his cock.

He put both hands on my head. "Dude, you've gotta stop or I'm gonna come, and I don't wanna come yet."

I pulled back from his cock and looked up at the gleaming torso, the beautiful face smiling down at me.

"I want you to fuck me," he said. "I want you to come inside me."

"I thought we agreed no anal."

He pulled me up alongside of him and put his arms around me. "That's a rule I have to start with, until I meet the guy and know what he's like. I don't let just anyone fuck me—but you've gotten me so fucking hot, I have to have it."

"What about your boyfriend?"

He shrugged. "I don't have a boyfriend. That's just my excuse."

"I can't believe you don't have a boyfriend!" I ran my hand down his torso, and he shivered.

"Just unlucky that way. Never met anyone I wanted to be involved with—and besides, he'd have to wrestle." He grinned at me. "That makes it a little harder, you know? What about you? You single?"

"No." I shook my head. "I'm seeing a guy—no commitment or anything yet, we're just seeing where it goes."

"Does he wrestle?"

I grinned. "Yes—he's a working pro."

"Does he know you do this?"

"We haven't gotten to the point where we need to talk about that kind of thing." I shrugged. "Maybe someday. We'll see."

"Most guys aren't that cool, so I might as well take advantage of you while you're still on the market," he said, placing his hand on my inner thigh. "I got to say, you're the kind of guy I could see myself getting involved with. Like I said, you're hot and you wrestle. My dream guy."

It was flattering, and for a brief moment I heard Bill's voice in my head again. *You're just not my type, Gary, sorry.*

It still fucking hurt.

He reached over and licked my neck for a moment. "You must be beating guys off with a stick. So fucking sexy." He grinned. "Your body"—he grabbed my dick—"and this cock! Hell, man, I've gotta have that inside me. You sure you want to?"

"Hell yeah."

He got up and walked over to the dresser, pulling out a condom and a bottle of lube. He tore the package open with his teeth, then gently slid it down over my aching cock, then squirted lube on it until it was nice and wet. He squirted some more into his hand, reaching back and lubing his ass.

He then lay down on the bed, his legs apart, and beckoned to me. "Come fuck me, stud."

I knelt between his legs, and he spread his legs farther, his eyes open and staring up at me. I grabbed my dick and guided it in between those massive cheeks till I found the tight little opening and pushed gently. He moaned, then relaxed, and I slid my cock in about halfway before meeting resistance. He was growling, a low sound that only let up when he needed to breathe in some more air, as I started sliding my cock slowly in and out, not trying to force it all the way in. *Let him get warmed up and turned-on some more, and then I'll try*, I figured. Besides, it felt good.

His eyes closed, and I started lightly punching his stomach as I slid in and out, and he started stroking his own cock.

"Yeah, that's nice, you can punch harder."

I started slamming my fists into his abs when I moved my cock out, letting him breathe as I went back in, and then, just as I thought, just as his legs got slick with sweat, the resistance gave and I plunged all the way in. His entire body bucked, his back arching, and his eyes flew open.

"Oh, you fucking stud, fuck me, fuck me, *fuck me!*"

I started moving faster, slamming my fists into his gut with greater power as I slammed my cock deeper inside him, and he kept groaning, and moaning, and then suddenly he was shooting a load, cum spitting out of the slit of his cock, his entire body jerking and a cry coming out of his lips with each shot. I stayed deep inside as he came, until he was finished and his body relaxed, and then I slid out. I peeled the condom off and started stroking my cock.

"You didn't come?" he asked, his eyes half-shut. I shook my head. "What do you want me to do to help you?"

"Scissor my head," I said, lying down. He swung his big legs around my head, so that I was staring at his beautiful ass, and started squeezing. It didn't take long—the feel of his legs and the sight of his ass had me shooting in maybe six strokes.

He let go of my head and got up and walked into the bathroom to grab a towel. He wiped me down. "Damn, look at the time!" He shook his head. "I hate to run you off, but I've got to meet some people for dinner shortly."

I looked at the clock and was shocked to see it had been well over two hours. He wiped himself down and then gave me a big hug and a kiss. "Thanks, man, that was fucking awesome."

I slid my sweatpants on and pulled my tank top back over

my head. He was counting out more money. He held out another couple of hundreds. "Here you go, Cage."

I looked at him, then at the money. "You don't have to give me more money. You already paid me my rate, and I had such a good time I don't feel right keeping it."

"Take it." He tucked it into my sweatpants. "I'm leaving tomorrow morning, but I'll be back in a couple of weeks. Maybe I'll come down early, and we can head down to Lauderdale, use the ring." His eyes twinkled. "We can get a room down there, spend the night. What's your overnight rate?"

"I—"

"Let's say two grand. Does that work for you?"

I nodded.

He kissed me again at the door, long and hard and slow. "Count on it, stud."

I started whistling as I headed back to my car.

CHAPTER ELEVEN

M ike was snoring beside me in the bed, his back to me.
It was a Monday night, and he had to work in the morning.
I'd driven down to Tampa as soon as I got out of my last class—
The Modern Essay—and he'd made an amazing dinner for me
before we wrestled around, had sex, and he'd fallen asleep. But
me, I couldn't sleep.

And I knew exactly why.

In the dark, with my hand on the remote control, I hit play
and watch the match again.

Mike surprised me with the DVD, a new release from
BGEast, right after dinner. They'd already sent it to me, but I
hadn't watched it until Mike put it in the DVD player in the
bedroom. He'd meant well—he thought it would turn us both on,
which would make our own wrestling even hotter—and I'd gone
along with it, not letting him know how mortifying I thought the
match was to watch. Mikc was proud of me, like he always was.
"You're so fucking hot when you wrestle," he'd said, kissing me
on the neck—and I'd had to play it off.

Almost every match I've ever taped had a sequence where
my opponent got the upper hand and beat on me for a while.

So, why did this particular one get under my skin so much?

It didn't make any sense.

I couldn't let it go. There had been so many matches since

that one, in front of the camera and in private, that I couldn't recall some of them. Some of my private-match clients fantasized about beating on me, and since they were paying, that was perfectly fine with me. Mike loved to dominate me in our matches, and I fucking loved it when he made me call him *sir,* when he draped me over his shoulders in a torture rack and made me beg him to stop.

Yet somehow I couldn't put this match out of my mind. I didn't understand why, why this match ate at me, gnawing away at my ego until I could think about nothing else. Sometimes I found myself sitting in traffic running an errand, listening to the radio, when out of nowhere, suddenly I felt his smooth, thick legs around my waist, my right arm twisted behind my back, and that moment of submission coming closer and closer as my mind clouded with the pain raging from my shoulder and the squeezing of my abs constricting my already labored breathing. I remembered hearing his voice through the fog, demanding my submission, threatening to tear my arm from its socket, the exquisite agony as I tried to resist the urge to just say the words and make the hurting stop. But I could not, I had to resist, somehow find the strength of will to resist the pain, and somehow, some way, fight my way out of this trap. The pressure relaxed for a just a moment before it returned, expelling my air out in a gasp as the arm twisted so far back that my shoulder rose off the mat, and I knew I could not go on much longer. The match was lost, lost, lost…and then without warning or expectation my arm went free and the legs around me went slack. I gasped for breath and watched my partner stomping on him as I crawled away to gather myself…

Then I came back into myself and shake my head.

No other wrestler had ever gotten inside my brain the way he had.

I hit the pause button before clicking back a chapter on the DVD.

We were circling in the center of the ring, him barefoot, his big body wearing only a skimpy pair of aqua trunks that clung to his magnificent muscular ass. Confident I was about to finish him off—Maxx and I had beaten both him and his partner mercilessly since the bell rang—I moved in and drove a knee into his midsection and he dropped down, and I landed a forearm to his exposed back, sending his big, beautiful Russian body sprawling. This was the moment before the direction of the match changed, and I hit the frame-advance button and leaned forward. I watched, in slow motion, as he gathered himself as I got closer, thinking he was cowed, beaten, ready to submit at last   when somehow he grabbed both of my legs, raised me up, and then slammed me down, flat on my back.

Again I hit the pause button. This was where I went wrong. There was no way I could have anticipated or blocked the sudden move that left me writhing and almost defenseless. I was at his, and his partner's, mercy for what seemed like an endless rhythm of punishment to my back. Body slams, over-the-knee back breakers, single-leg crabs, and then the final, ultimate humiliation...my submission to a swinging pendulum. Through it all he taunted me, tagging in his partner who slammed me again before tagging out, and back into the ring he came, mouthing insults as I desperately, through the intense pain in my lower back, tried to get to my corner to tag in my partner and get a respite from the vicious punishment. He enjoyed torturing me, punishing me, beating me. After I finally gave in and lay sprawled, unable to get to my feet, he leaned down and whispered to me, "You look good down there..."

Maxx had to come help me to the corner. I couldn't stand, my legs were wobbly, and without his support I would have just been lying there defenseless when the bell rang again.

And per the rules, the second fall started with the last two wrestlers back in the ring.

He was merciless when the bell rang, absolutely merciless, and he *enjoyed* torturing me. It was more than trying to win, I was convinced of it. He could have gotten me to submit in the first fall long before he did, but he was enjoying himself. He loved hearing me scream out in pain, bending me into shapes I didn't know were possible, taking his time so he could savor every delicious second of my disgrace in front of the camera.

How was it possible he'd gone down to defeat in almost every single one of his matches when he was able to toy with me like that?

It was *humiliating*.

Had his own partner been his equal, Maxx and I might have lost the match and never been able to hold our heads up at BGEast ever again.

Nicky *fucking* Romanov.

I hit the eject button on the remote and sat there, in the dark, brooding.

I got up and walked over to my laptop, signed in to my e-mail program. I sat there in my underwear scrolling through the e-mails from fans, boosting my ego as I read about how hot they thought I was, what a great wrestler, how sexy—but it still wasn't enough for me.

Because Romanov was still under my skin.

Finally, I signed into my chat program, and I smiled to myself. The boss was online, as I knew he would be. I sent him a message:

> Cagethunder: I want to wrestle Romanov again. I'll even do it for free.

I chuckled to myself as I hit send. The boss doesn't really like rematches. BGEast hasn't done many. But the boss is a businessman, and he likes to save money.

> Kidleopard: You know we don't do rematches.
> Cagethunder: It's not a rematch. We did a tag match. Besides, I wrestled Jody in a single match after we did the tag.
> Kidleopard: Jody begged.

Cagethunder: So you want me to beg?
Kidleopard: Couldn't hurt.

I stared at the screen. I bit my lower lip.

Did I want to get Romanov back in the ring badly enough to humiliate myself before the boss? I leaned back. I knew Steve well enough to know that I could crawl naked over broken glass and hot coals, only to have him say, "No, I don't think it's a good idea—but nice job."

I started typing *fuck you* when another message window opened on my screen.

Sexynicky: Pussy.
Cagethunder: Eat me, bitch.
Sexynicky: You lucky you had a partner, pussy, or I would mop the ring with you.

I could hear him sneer the words in my head, in that thick accent.

I heard his voice in my head as I lay broken on the mat. *You look good down there.*

I could feel his feet on the small of my back as he stood on me again.

I could feel his legs crushing my midsection.

Cagethunder: Anytime you want a rematch, be glad to make you my bitch. Again.
Sexynicky: Boss says you afraid to get in ring again with me. Pussy.
Cagethunder: Anytime, anywhere. I'll beat you and fuck your ass.
Sexynicky: You lucky if all I make you do is suck dick. You like suck dick.

In spite of myself, I was getting hard.

And a big *fuck you,* boss.

I cut and pasted the conversation into the chat window I had open with the boss and clicked send.

Stew on *that,* asshole.

Cagethunder: Your dick is so small it's not worth sucking.
Sexynicky: Big uncut Russian dick tear your ass apart.
Cagethunder: Tell me when and where, whore.
Sexynicky: Two weeks. Fort Lauderdale. Saturday. Man enough?
Cagethunder: Man enough.
Sexynicky: Start training.

And he signed off.

My computer dinged, and I clicked over to my e-mail. There was one from Romanov with a picture attached. I opened it. The e-mail said simply *Big enough?* The picture downloaded, and my jaw dropped.

It was Nicky, taken with his computer cam. He was stark naked, leaning back in a chair, and smirking at the camera. One arm was draped over the top of his head, his exposed armpit hair damp and dark. His other hand was cupping his hard cock.

He wasn't lying. His cock was fucking *huge.*

Kidleopard: Does he want to tape this?

I smiled to myself as I typed back, *Don't know, don't care.*

Kidleopard: He's never gone nude on camera before. Maybe taping a rematch is a good idea.
Cagethunder: Beg.

And I closed the chat program while laughing to myself. Licking my lips, I raised a bottle of poppers to my nose and inhaled deeply up each nostril. As my heart beat faster, my cock got harder. I squirted some lube onto it and started stroking myself as I stared at the picture of the naked Russian. I felt his legs around my waist again as he twisted my arm up behind my back. I felt his sweaty skin against mine and heard him whispering to me again, *You're close, why don't you stop the pain and say what you know you want to,* in that accent. I felt him on top of me, sneering into my ear as he worked my body, torturing and twisting me as I moaned and screamed.

It didn't take long before I shot a massive load all over my chest.

I took a few deep breaths.

As I wiped my torso down I looked at the picture still smirking at me from the computer screen.

Sexy Nicky, indeed.

❖

I trained hard over the next two weeks, talking Phil into working with me on the mats whenever he had some spare time, and driving down to Tampa to work out with Mike in the ring there. I lifted weights every day, did an hour of cardio, twenty minutes in the tanning bed, and watched what I was eating. Phil got pissed at me for being a little too rough the last time we worked out before I left for Lauderdale.

"Christ!" he swore at me, backing away. "Dude, I think we're done working until you get back." He shook his head. "I'm not Nicky, asshole."

"Sorry." I walked over to the side of the mats and picked up a towel, wiping the sweat off my head. I shook my head and walked over to where he'd sat down, on the edge of the mats. He was scowling at me. I plopped down beside him. "Really." I ran the towel over my head again and took a really deep breath. "I don't know why he gets under my skin so much."

"Because he worked you over," he replied, taking a swig of water from his bottle, "and made you look bad, and people think he'd kick your ass one-on-one." He laughed.

I couldn't stop thinking about Nicky. I watched his other matches before I went to bed every night, looking to see how other wrestlers had beaten him down—how they'd managed to put him away. I sniffed the poppers as I frame-advanced his beatings, rubbing lube on my hard cock and pulling at it until I came.

Mike kept telling me I was overthinking it. *Boy, you know you're a stud and you're going to punish him,* his e-mail the morning of the trip said, *so stop obsessing about it. He's just a pretty muscle boy, and you eat them for breakfast. Don't disappoint me now, or I'll give you a beating you'll never forget the next time I see you.*

That made me laugh as I typed out my response: *Yes, sir. I will make him my punching bag.*

And I headed for the airport.

❖

The day of the match I woke to sunshine coming through the sliding glass door leading out to the pool at Steve's place. The boss was a man of few words, and I knew better than to ask about Nicky or the match. When the boss was ready to talk wrestling, he would, and there was no sense in bringing it up before he was ready. It would be a waste of time.

I brushed my teeth, washed my face, and pulled on a pair of Andrew Christian bikini briefs before walking out into the living room. I started the coffee—the other wrestler there for the weekend wasn't up yet, but I knew from other taping weekends he liked the way I made coffee and would probably be up in a little while. I was standing in front of the coffee machine willing it to go faster when I heard the refrigerator door open and close behind me. I turned around and was startled to see the boss, who usually was never seen before eleven at the earliest.

He raised his eyebrows at me as he poured a glass of cranberry juice, looking me up and down. He seemed to approve, so I turned back to the coffeemaker.

"The ass is looking nice, Cage," he said and walked back out of the kitchen.

Faint praise was about the best anyone ever got from the boss.

The match was scheduled for one, so I drank coffee and stretched out on a towel next to the pool, trying to relax and not get worked up, psych myself out.

I hadn't known the last match was going to be a tag battle until the last minute. Maxx and I had done a couple of tag matches for the cameras, and our styles meshed together really well, but Jody and Nicky were new to each other. I'd thought I was going to take on Jody first, followed in the ring with Nicky fighting Maxx, and maybe it was the size similarity between them—no one ever knew with the boss—but Steve decided to put all four of us in the ring together in a tag bout. I'd been confident about the Jody match; I knew I could kick his ass pretty easily, which was borne out when we did our singles match the next day. Nicky I wasn't so sure about; I knew he almost always lost his matches, but the ones I'd seen showed him to be tough and skilled with a bit of a nasty attitude of his own.

I kept remembering that moment when I'd dropped him to his knees and was moving in to finish him off only to have him take me down.

You're psyching yourself out again, stop thinking about it, stop remembering it.

Bill had told me once, the hardest part about a rematch when you lost the first time was doing that—psyching yourself out. "Once you let a wrestler inside your head, you'll never beat him," he said. I never had before—until now.

Stupid fucking Russian.

At one fifteen, I walked out of the locker room in my black-and-red boots, with red kneepads and a red mask with black trim covering my face. I was wearing bright red trunks that matched the rest of my gear, red trunks that hugged and accentuated my package. My cock was already semi-hard, and it was pretty obvious when I stood in front of the big mirror outside the ring and flexed. I'd trimmed my body hair down the previous weekend, so it could be seen, but the definition of my muscles was also visible. Up in the ring, Nicky was posing for portraits. I folded my arms and stood there, watching.

He was wearing white posers that barely covered his round bubble butt in the back. They rose low in the front, and he was wearing white knee and elbow pads. He was barefoot, his big size 14 feet planted shoulder-width apart as he flexed. He was leaner than he'd been for the tag match—his muscles were more defined, his stomach flatter.

He saw me looking and pointed at me, the muscles in the arm and shoulder rippling. "I'm going to fucking kick your pussy ass!" he yelled at me in his thick accent.

I didn't say anything, just reached down and grabbed my dick with my right hand, flipping him off with the other one.

"Save it for the ring, boys," the boss commanded, walking up to me, the camera strap around his neck. "Let's get your portraits done, Cage, since you're both so ramped up."

I could see Nicky as I posed, always keeping him in focus in the corner of my eye as the boss took picture after picture. He was hard to please—posing for him always took a lot longer than it did with any of the others. He wouldn't snap the picture until everything was perfectly positioned, every muscle shaped the right way, the light gleaming off my skin perfectly.

It was always a pain in the ass, but no one else ever made me look as hot as he did.

And finally, we were done.

I was already sweating under my mask as I got into my

corner and started stretching, warming up my muscles. Stuart the camera guy was on the other side, filming Nicky as he twisted and turned, bouncing on the balls of his feet. I swallowed and watched, focusing.

He's a big pussy. You can take him. He's bigger than you are but who gives a fuck? It never mattered before. Take him down and humiliate him. Take those trunks off and shove them in his mouth, spank his big round ass, fuck him up like he's never been fucked up before.

The bell rang.

I stalked out into the center of the ring, but he just stood there, resting back against the ring ropes with a lazy smirk on his face.

"You want me?" he hissed in that heavy accent, beckoning me forward with a wave of both hands. One of his eyebrows went up and his lip curled in contempt. "Come get me then, pussy."

I didn't stop to think, I didn't pause. The sound of his voice, the way he sneered *pussy* at me, the memory of how Maxx had to come to my rescue—all of those things raced through my mind in a millisecond, and I stormed forward, drawing back my right arm to give him a forearm smash across his pecs—

—and his bare foot swung up and caught me right in the throat with considerable force, knocking me backward.

I choked and fell back.

My eyes watered as I rolled over onto my stomach and got up onto my knees. I kept gasping, trying to suck some air in. I was vaguely aware of camera flashes. I could hear Nicky saying something, but I couldn't make out what it was.

He kicked me in the side, his foot just missing the bottom of my rib cage and smashing into my obliques. The force of the kick knocked me over, and the momentum kept me rolling, over and over, still not able to breathe, until I came to a rest against the bottom rope. I lay there on my back, and finally my air passage opened again. I gulped in air, my eyes closed. I could feel his footsteps vibrating through the ring as he walked closer to me.

I knew I was vulnerable, exposed, completely at his mercy but didn't care. *Do your worst, motherfucker,* I thought, *you won't break me. And payback is going to be a major, major bitch.*

He grabbed me by the mask and started pulling me away from the ropes. I let my body go limp, and I could hear him grunting from the exertion of pulling me. But he was even stronger than he looked, and he was using the mask to drag me up to my feet. His arm went through my crotch, and he picked me up as easily as if I were a bag of garbage, and I kept my eyes closed as he launched me through the air.

My back hit and I bounced up into the air, pain radiating from my lower back as I came back down on my back again. All the air left me, and my right hand involuntarily went to my lower back, rubbing it as I rolled onto my head and my knees, arching it, stretching it, desperately trying to make the ache stop.

"You look good down there, your ass up in the air," I heard him say just above me. I felt sweat dripping onto my back from his chin. "Like you're ready to get fucked. That what you want, Cage? You want my big Russian dick in your pretty ass?"

"Fuck you." I somehow managed to choke the words out.

He kicked me in the side again, knocking me over onto my back again. I opened my eyes, and all I could see were the lights over the ring. Then his face blocked out the lights as he reached down and grabbed my mask again in his big hands. He pulled me to my feet and launched me into the corner. My lower back caught on the middle turnbuckle, and I fell to my knees, my arms draped over the top ropes. I could feel sweat running down my neck. It was so hot in the mask under the lights and so hard to breathe…

His big right hand grabbed me underneath my chin and pushed me back up to my feet. His forearm crashed into my upper chest—once, twice, three times. He stepped back, and my eyes focused on his smirking face. He was bouncing on the balls of his feet, and that smirk…that fucking smirk. His chest was glistening with sweat, his close-cropped dark hair was soaked through, and his white trunks were wet and becoming more and more see-through. I could see his pubic bush, dark against the wet white Lycra, and his thick cock nestled against his balls.

He planted his foot right into my abs, but I saw it coming and was able to tense them. He grabbed my arm and whipped me across the ring, and I crashed into the opposite ring corner. Unable to catch myself or stop the momentum, I fell facedown. I shook my head, trying to get my bearings, willing myself to get to my feet, to do something, anything, before the big motherfucker attacked again.

I got to my hands and knees and looked up. He was standing, that same nasty smirk on his handsome face, a few feet in front of me. He was taking his time—there was no need to rush in, press his advantage—because he thought I was beaten.

That was all it took. I got to my feet, a little wobbly, gulping in air and my back still aching, the pain from the kicks in my side starting to subside a little bit as rage burned through my veins. I made fists with both hands and realized I was trembling a little bit.

Oh, he was going to pay.

He took a step forward and launched himself into the air. I tried to move but my reflexes were still too slow. Both of his feet hit my chest, and he pushed off with them. I didn't see where he went as I was driven backward to the corner, but the entire ring shook when his big body landed. I had just enough time to hope he landed wrong before I crashed back into the corner so hard I was propelled forward again, and before I knew what was happening, he'd scooped me up in his arms and was dropping me.

My lower back crashed down over his upper leg, and I bounced and rolled off his leg. I hit the mat with my forehead first, the rest of me hitting a split second later. I was dazed again, unable to move, and I was vaguely aware of him grabbing my right leg and lifting it. My back arched as he slapped a single-leg crab on me, and before I could think or stop myself I screamed in agony as my lower back cracked. He yanked my leg up and backward again, and his free hand cupped my balls and squeezed.

Miniature daggers stabbed into my lower abdomen from the pressure in my balls. He was saying something, but I couldn't hear or understand a word. All I could think about was the dueling pain in my back and my balls. I couldn't help but remember that this was how the back torture had started last time—a single-leg crab.

The son of a bitch was going to put me through the exact torture he had the last time, I realized through the agony, and there wasn't a damned thing I could do to stop him.

Sure enough, just when I thought I couldn't take any more, he let go, slamming my knee down into the mat. He got off me and scooped me up, dropping my lower back over his knee and bouncing me off. He did this twice more, and more out of instinct than anything conscious, I reached for the ring ropes. Grasping the center rope with both hands, I managed to drag my aching body closer to them. I pulled myself up and, grasping the top ropes, it took every ounce of strength I had to get to my feet. My legs wobbly, I tried to catch my breath.

That was when his big size 14s slammed into my upper back, one right between the shoulder blades, the other slightly lower, and the momentum from the dropkick carried me right over the top rope.

Everything spun in a bizarre kaleidoscope as I seemed to flip over in slow motion. I managed to somehow land on my feet, but the momentum was too much and my legs were still too wobbly to hold me, and I kept going, smacking down on the concrete floor outside the ring with my shoulders first, followed by my head.

Pain exploded inside my skull and stars danced in front of my vision.

I tried to sit up but my body wouldn't respond.

My head was ringing.

I was vaguely aware of camera flashes as I tried to get up, tried to move, tried to do *something,* anything.

I couldn't resist as the son of a bitch picked me up and carried me. I could hear him saying shit, but it was just sounds I couldn't hear over the ringing in my ears and through the fog in my head. I could feel his sweaty torso pressed against mine as he effortlessly carried me—

—and slammed the small of my back into the ring post.

And did it again.

I was stunned, in agony, unable to move, completely helpless as he rammed me into the post a third time.

To add insult to injury, he then placed me down on the ring apron and rolled me back into the ring as gently as if I were a baby.

I felt him grab my leg and roll me up onto my shoulders. The ring vibrated as he slapped the mat three times and let me go. Somewhere in the distance, I heard the bell ring.

I closed my eyes. My legs started trembling. My back was on fire with pain. My eyes were stinging from sweat rolling into them. I was vaguely aware of someone kneeling down next to me.

"Cage, you okay?"

Somehow, I managed to turn my head and look at the boss. There was concern in his eyes. "Yeah," I croaked out. "I'm good."

"We can stop here, you know," he replied, helping me get to my feet. "We've got some good footage. And we can sell it as Nicky wins a big match—"

"No."

I shook off his hands and managed to walk to my corner unassisted. I leaned back against the ropes and looked across the ring where Nicky was talking to the cameraman. His body glistened with sweat in the lights. The white trunks were soaked through, and I could clearly see the crack of his ass through the fabric. On the right cheek the trunks had ridden up a bit. I grabbed the bottle of water the boss held out to me, and I took a gulp before looking him in the eye. "Two out of three, like always, boss." I wiped the sweat out of my eyes with a towel.

"You sure you can go on?"

I nodded. "Damned sure."

I took another gulp of water and watched as Nicky wiped some of the sweat off his head and his chest with a towel. I looked at his handsome face, free of expression and unconcerned about what he had just done to me, not worried about what was going to happen next. The boss walked across the ring and I couldn't hear what he was saying, but at some point after he started talking, Nicky looked over at me.

And smiled.

He fucking smiled at me.

And I felt the anger begin to burn inside me.

Pain to rage, buddy, pain to rage, was what Maxx had said to me in the tag match after Nicky and the big jerk Jody Riddle had worked me over until I was almost completely helpless, totally at their mercy. Jody had paid for it in the ring the next day.

And I wasn't going to let Nicky do this to me again and get away with it.

Fuck no.

I closed my eyes and focused my will.

I could do this.

I would do this.

I heard the bell ring and opened my eyes.

He was leaning back in his corner, a big smile on his face, as he beckoned me to come forward, taunting me.

I walked forward out of my corner, never taking my eyes off his. I knew exactly what I was going to do. He didn't move, just stood there, and when I was almost within reach he said clearly, "I'm giving you a free shot, okay?"

I nodded. "Okay," I said and kicked him in the balls.

His eyes almost bugged out of his head before his face became an exquisite portrait of agony. I stepped aside and let him fall to the mat, both hands clutching his violated testicles as he rolled up into a quivering, moaning ball.

"You stupid *fuck,*" I said conversationally as I grabbed both of his feet and hoisted them up in the air and apart. "You really think you could get away with that? I'm Cage *fucking* Thunder!"

I planted my big boot right in his balls again, and he screamed as I put my weight behind that leg.

The sound of his scream shot adrenaline through my aching body, and the pain, the suffering—everything—went away as I tossed his legs aside and planted my boot in the small of his back.

"You like back torture, big guy?" I asked, grabbing a leg and arm, pulling upward as he screamed. "How's this bow and arrow feel, huh?"

He managed to gasp out something I interpreted as *fuck you,* so I ground my boot into his back a little more.

I took a deep breath and pulled harder, was rewarded with another scream.

My dick was starting to get hard.

I slammed his arm and leg down and stomped on his back a few times. I was going to stomp another time when he managed to roll away from me. I followed him as he rolled, and he went under the ropes and outside the ring.

I followed, grabbed the back of his head, and slammed his forehead into the ring apron. He reeled back, so I scooped him and slammed him down on the concrete floor. I picked him up again and carried him over to the ring corner. I hoisted him up—he was hard to hold, since he was dripping with sweat—and slammed him into the corner. What was good for me, after all, surely was good for him?

After I softened his lower back up a few more times, I

swung him around so he was wrapped around the ring post, his abs facing the center of the ring. I grabbed his legs in one arm and hooked my other arm under his chin and yanked back, wrapping him like a pretzel around the ring post.

I could almost feel his vertebrae snapping as he screamed, "I give!" over and over again.

I released him and slapped his wet face before turning to the cameras and flexing for them.

And then I climbed back into the ring.

I went back to my corner and grabbed the towel, wiping down my neck and chest. I was soaked, but I wasn't sure if it was my sweat or his—I'd forgotten sweat came off him in buckets. He was still lying in the corner around the ring post where I'd left him, Steve and Stuart talking to him in low voices.

I hoped he wasn't done—because I wasn't.

I adjusted my hard-on in my trunks.

Oh, hell, no I wasn't done with Sexy Nicky.

Now it was humiliation time.

The boss and Stuart climbed through the ropes, and Stuart picked up the video camera.

Nicky and I looked at each other.

I blew him a kiss.

The bell rang again.

I didn't move as he walked out to the center, his hands up. Sweat was running down the sides of his face, dripping off his chin. I stepped out of the corner and spread my arms wide.

"Free shot, bitch," I sneered. "Better make it count, though."

He paused, gave me a mistrustful look, and I tilted my head back so I was looking at the ceiling. I was completely exposed, vulnerable. The ring shook as he lunged for me. I quickly moved and drove my knee up into his abs, driving the air out of him and doubling him over. I then brought my knee up again, slamming my upper leg into his ribs with brutal force. The momentum flipped him, landing him on his back in the center of the ring.

"Stupid bitch," I sneered as I leaped into the air, landing on his abs with all my weight on the knee connecting with him.

His eyes bulged and he convulsed as I straddled him, scooting up so my knees were on either side of his head. He kept struggling underneath me as I flexed my right biceps, and then the left, letting sweat drip from my elbow onto his face. I slapped him a few times before grabbing the back of his head and pulling his face up into my crotch, rubbing my sweaty balls and hard-on on his mouth and nose.

He tried to move his head, get away, but my hold on his head was too strong. I could hear him gagging against the smell of my musk and sweat, and it just made me prolong it. "You like the smell of my balls? The taste of my cock sweat?" I taunted as he kept trying to buck me off. His legs pounded the ring in frustration. I reached back with my left hand and grabbed his balls. I didn't apply any pressure to them, just held them in my hand. His cock stirred. "You like squeezing balls, don't you?" I reminded him as I moved my hands slightly from side to side. I let go of his head and smiled down at him.

He stopped moving. He was absolutely still, just breathing beneath me. His eyes were wide and round. A drop of sweat clung to the tip of his nose. There was no sound in the gym other than our breathing. It was almost like time had stood still, like we had somehow slipped into some other dimension where it was just the two of us, predator and prey. His eyes had a cornered, defeated look to them—the defiance and resistance gone. "No, man, don't," he whispered, barely audible.

Another drop of sweat dripped from my chin to his face. "Why wouldn't I?" I whispered back to him. "You're mine now, bitch."

And I squeezed.

His entire body went rigid, and he bellowed as my hand closed tightly around his heavy balls. He started trembling as I squeezed, his head thrashing back and forth between my knees and thighs.

When his eyes filled with tears, I let go.

I stood up, standing with his head between my boots. He was panting and rolled over onto his side, bringing his knees up into a fetal position.

He was done.

But I wasn't.

I flexed, posing for the cameras as the flashes went off, going through an entire litany of every muscle pose I knew while sweat dripped onto his beautiful, battered body. I stepped away from him and let them take some pictures of his suffering. He really did look like a work of art as he lay there in the center of the ring. My art, my creation, a sculpture made from flesh and blood and muscle.

My balls were aching as my cock strained against my trunks.

But his suffering was just beginning.

I climbed through the ring ropes and found my bag, where I'd stashed it next to the ring. I pulled a small bottle of lube from the side pocket and slid it inside my trunks, right alongside my angry hard-on. I walked around the ring until I was in front of the mirror. I looked at my reflection. My chest hair was drenched, clinging to my sweaty skin. The trunks were soaked through with sweat, turning a darker color from the bright scarlet they'd been when I'd put them on, outlining my long, thick cock. Behind me I could see him, still suffering in the ring. He was now up on his knees, his head still pressed down against the mat, his big meaty ass up in the air.

I climbed through the ropes and came up behind him. His ass was something to see, the little dimples in his wet lower back prominent as I raised my boot and kicked him square in the center of the ass.

He sprawled flat with an *oof*.

I sat down in the center of his lower back and hoisted him up, draping an arm over both of my knees so I had him in a camel clutch. He didn't even resist as I put him in the hold that would finish him once and for all.

I cupped his chin in both hands and leaned back, hoisting his head and chest even higher and forcing his back to arch even farther.

He started screaming almost immediately, slapping at my leg.

"I give! I give ! I give!"

I let go of his chin and let him hang there limply for a moment before I slid my arm under his chin and nestled his chin into the bend of my elbow, wrapping my other arm around it as I cranked him back in a combination camel clutch/sleeper. My right forearm cut off the carotid artery, so no blood could reach his brain. He struggled desperately at first, but with each passing second he got weaker, and he went limp in my arms.

I released him gently and set him facedown on the mat.

I stood and went through my litany of poses for the cameras.

When I was finished, I reached down and slid his wet white trunks down and off, exposing that delicious-looking ass.

Turning to the cameras, I first held his trunks to my nose and inhaled deeply of his scent.

Then I tilted my head back and twisted them in my hands, so that his sweat ran off into a steady stream into my mouth.

I tucked his trunks into the back of mine, and with my foot I rolled him over so he was face up.

I stood with one foot on either side of his hips and slid the front of my trunks down. I squirted lube onto my dick and started stroking it.

I was already so turned-on it didn't take long for me to blow a big load onto his sweaty torso.

I bent over and wrote CAGE on his chest in my cum.

I posed for the cameras one last time and pulled my trunks up.

I slipped through the ropes and headed for the locker room.

Once the door was closed behind me, I closed my eyes and took a deep breath.

He was out of my head for good.

I turned on the shower and undressed.

CHAPTER TWELVE

Y ou *are* turning into a bit of a whore, you know?"
I stopped chopping lettuce and turned to look at Phil.
He was leaning against my kitchen counter, holding a glass of
red wine in his left hand. He had an amused look on his face,
which kind of took the sting out of what he'd just said. His eyes
were open wide, and a slight smile twitched at each corner of his
mouth. His eyebrows were arched up toward his hairline.

"No, I'm not." I finished chopping the lettuce and wiped
it off the cutting board into a bowl. I started chopping up some
bell peppers. "Besides, you're the one who told me to charge for
private matches," I reminded him, tossing the bell pepper slices
on top of the lettuce and reaching for a red onion. "Remember?"

"Yes, but I don't have sex with them." This time, there was a
hint of subtle teasing, a faint note of mockery, in his tone. "How
exactly does Mike feel about all this, anyway?"

I cut the onion in half the way I'd seen a chef do it on the
Food Network and started slicing it. "Mike knows I wrestle for
money. He buys all my videos." I shrugged and tossed the onions
into the bowl. "It's not like I don't blow a load for the cameras in
every match." I picked up the cucumber and started peeling the
skin off. "He also knows I still dance sometimes." But I hadn't
really been doing much of that lately—I hadn't needed the money
in a while. I had a couple of regular wrestling clients, and even

though it sometimes meant driving to Orlando or Jacksonville, the money was too good to pass up.

I set the cucumber down. "My God, I am a slut." I rolled my eyes at him and started slicing it.

Phil laughed. "I'm not judging you, believe me. We've been friends too long for that." He winked at me and started tossing cherry tomatoes into the salad bowl. "I'm just wondering if, you know, maybe Mike's the right one for you. Have you considered that?"

I finished slicing the cucumber and started on the mushrooms. I didn't answer him right away.

The truth was, I hadn't really given it any thought. Sure, I liked Mike a lot. He was sexy as hell, and I'd miss spending the night with him, curled up in his arms, if we stopped seeing each other. But I wasn't in love with him, I didn't think. Not the way I'd been in love with Bill.

"You still think Bill's going to change his mind?" Phil went on. "Baby, that's just not going to happen, and you know it." Phil refilled his glass and took a sip. "I saw him the other night at Blackbeard's—he was with some new guy. Good looking. He introduced me to him, said he was a wrestler"—he made a face— "you know how that goes."

Yes, I knew all too well how that went.

Besides the wrestling connection, Phil and I had also bonded over the fact that he, too, had been one of Bill's protégés. The difference? Phil hadn't been stupid enough to fall in love with him. Then again, Phil hadn't been a naïve teenager when Bill had sucked him into his web.

It still stung, even after all this time. It still hurt that I wasn't good enough to be Bill's boyfriend. Guys paid me to wrestle them, guys bought DVDs of me wrestling, guys stuffed money into my G-string when I danced in bars. Photographers wanted me to pose for them—I had any number of business cards in my desk drawer, and some of them I'd even posed for.

But I couldn't get over Bill not wanting me.

"You really need to think about what you might be missing out on," Phil went on. "Seriously, I'm trying to be a friend—don't roll your eyes at me! I've been meaning to talk to you about all this for a while." He took my arm. I looked at him. His facial expression was as easy to read as a large-print newspaper. "You're still in love with him, too, aren't you?"

"Don't be ridiculous." I mixed raspberry vinegar and extra-virgin olive oil together for the salad. "I'm not in love with Bill anymore. It was just a stupid teenage crush, is all it was. I know that now. And I'm not going to blow things with Mike."

"All right. If you say so." Phil sat down at my small round kitchen table and started rolling a joint. "But talking about it might help, you know."

"There's nothing to talk about," I insisted. *And maybe if I keep saying that,* I thought to myself, *it will prove to be true.* I knew Phil wouldn't judge me, but saying it out loud—I just couldn't bring myself to do it. And he was right—Mike was great for me. He was perfect for me. He liked wrestling. He didn't mind that I wrestled other guys, never complained about anything, even if I had to miss one of his shows because I was *whoring* myself out as a wrestler for money. Easy money. It was better than flipping burgers or waiting tables or slinging cocktails. And if the guy was willing to slip me a few more hundreds for getting him off, well, who was it hurting?

The salad was finished and it was just a matter of the chicken breasts finishing broiling. Phil lit the joint and inhaled deeply, lovingly. He blew the huge cloud of smoke out and up and passed it to me. As I inhaled, he said, "So, they're taping down in Lauderdale weekend after next. You going down for it?"

I blew out the smoke and coughed until I thought a lung might possibly pop out. I took a swig of my wine to cool my burning throat and wiped water out of my eyes. A warm, tingly, fuzzy feeling began to creep in on my mind. "First I'm hearing of it. Are you going?"

He took another hit, offered it to me, and when I waved him

off, he pinched it out between his thumb and forefinger. "Nah." He laughed. "I've pretty much wrestled everyone in the stable, you know? I need to recruit some new guys if I want to work again."

"Yeah. I think I might be in the same boat. They haven't asked me down in a while." I closed my eyes. I did miss it. There were a couple of guys at the gym I might be able to recruit, I thought as I picked up my wineglass. They were both pretty hot, and one of them had even asked me about dancing at Blackbeard's. And if they didn't mind dancing in a jock or a thong in a gay bar, making some wrestling videos for a lot more money probably wasn't going to be much of a problem for them, either.

The timer on the stove started beeping, so I got up and walked over there. The chicken was finished, so I pulled the cooking sheet out of the oven. I put two breasts on each plate, and then a healthy helping of tender broccoli and cauliflower out of the steamer. I filled two bowls with salad. I placed a bowl and a plate in front of Phil and then settled in with my own across the table from him.

"So, you're not in love with Mike?" Phil asked. "This chicken is really good, by the way."

"Thanks. The recipe was in the paper last week." I smiled at him. "And no, I'm not. I like him a lot, though."

Phil sighed and pointed his fork, with a piece of lettuce and a cucumber slice speared on it, at me. "You need to talk to Mike, you know. Find out how he feels, figure out where this is going." He put the fork down and stared at his plate. "You don't want to do to him what Bill did to you, do you?"

"No." I picked up my fork. "No, I really don't."

Later, after Phil had left and I was in my bed staring at the ceiling, I wondered if I was being fair to Mike.

I closed my eyes. Maybe Phil was right. Maybe it was time I had a chat with him.

CHAPTER THIRTEEN

I climbed through the ropes, naked.

I couldn't help but smile. I had lost count of how many times I'd wrestled in this ring, but one thing I did know was I'd never climbed into it stark naked before. *Of course I've frequently* been *naked in here,* I reminded myself with a bemused smile, *but never, ever to start with.*

Usually when I got into the ring I was in full pro regalia: from my boots to the kneepads to the trunks to my gloves to the mask. But this time, I was barefoot and my cock and balls were out on display. I'd already stretched in the locker room, and stripped down. The air-conditioning wasn't on—one of the conditions for the match we'd agreed to beforehand—and all the lights were off save for a single one directly over the ring. The rest of the gym was in darkness, and the bulb in the working light had been switched out from a white to a red one. The entire ring was bathed in an almost eerie red light, which gave it a seedy, almost sleazy air, and I kind of liked it. It was easy to imagine a crowd sitting out there in the dark, waiting for the main event. My dick was starting to get a little hard as my armpits got sweaty, and beads of sweat broke out on my forehead as well. It was a hot, humid night in south Florida, and once the fight started we were both going to be drenched in sweat.

And nothing turns me on more than sweaty muscle.

When Joe e-mailed me with a challenge, I'd been caught off guard. We'd worked together my second weekend taping matches, and while the match was fun—they always are—I'd also been a little disappointed. The boss always put the wrestlers he's pairing together for a taping in touch with each other beforehand—sometimes it worked, sometimes it didn't. Once the boss sent me a picture of Joe and his fucking amazing body, I wanted him in the ring—but he didn't tape much anymore and pretty much considered himself retired from the wrestling video world. So when the boss told me Joe was up for a match with me and gave me his e-mail address, my dick had immediately gotten hard and I didn't waste a second in e-mailing the big stud while still exchanging messages with Steve.

My initial e-mail was brief and to the point. *So, I hear you want to work a match with me.*

The response came within ten minutes. *Fuck yeah, I want to tape with you, man. I've wanted to ever since I first saw you.*

That made me smile. I remembered the first time he saw me quite vividly.

Joe had stopped by the gym the afternoon we taped my match with Jody Riddle, and I was in my full bad-ass garb—the black mask, the leather studded bikini, the knee-high leather boots, and my gloves—and the boss had instructed me not to shave off any of my body hair. When I came out of the dressing room, I bit my lower lip. Joe was standing on the other side of the ring talking to Steve and looking fucking amazing in a tank top and a tight pair of jeans. There was another hugely muscled guy with him, and I kind of smiled to myself. *Ah, so that's the kind of guy he goes for,* I thought, *I'm probably not big enough for him. Ah, well.*

You can't take things like that personally in this business—it's a sure way to drive yourself crazy.

But he smiled at me as I walked past to the mats so I could finish stretching. Jody was up in the ring getting some pre-match portraits taken, and I sat down on the mats. I spread my legs and stretched to the left with my eyes closed, centering and trying to find my focus. *Don't worry about Big Joe, just think about what you're going to do to Jody when the bell rings.* I visualized myself kicking Jody's ass, working him over in the corner, just beating the holy hell out of him, and my dick started stirring in the bikini. When I leaned over to my right, I opened my eyes as Big Joe and his friend walked past me on their way out. Big Joe grinned at me and hooked his thumb back over his shoulder. "He's a big boy. What's he got, like forty pounds on you?"

"Five inches taller and forty-five pounds, to be exact," I replied, trying to bring my forehead down to my right knee. "Won't matter, though."

"Oh?"

"I'm going to kick his muscle ass, and then I am going to fuck him into next week." I smiled up at Joe. His friend looked a little disconcerted, but Joe laughed.

"That"—he winked—"is something I'd like to see."

I'd been tempted to say, *You can experience it yourself sometime,* but chickened out with the words on my lips. Instead, I'd closed my eyes and gone back to focusing on my stretching.

I wiped sweat out of my eyes. In the gloom outside of the pyramid of red light over the ring, I could hear Joe moving around, but he didn't say anything. I could feel adrenaline coursing through my veins. I took a deep breath and walked to the closest ring corner. I grabbed the ropes and extended my arms, leaning backward and feeling the stretch in my shoulders and back.

We'd taped a match a few months later, in full pro gear and in the ring. We'd exchanged a few e-mails, talked some shit to each other, and I got the impression he was up for a match that ended nude and with both of us shooting loads on camera. But when it came time for the taping, it didn't happen. Big Joe didn't seem all that into me, and it ended up just being a regular taping.

I was enormously disappointed, obviously, but didn't take it personally.

And then, about a month ago, he'd e-mailed me out of the blue. Not recognizing the return e-mail address, I almost deleted it, but the subject line *Wrestling match?* made me pause and click it open instead.

> *Hey, stud:*
>
> *Remember me? We met at the ring when you were taping with that big guy, and we taped a match a few months later. I was really into you, but I get shy in front of the cameras. Would love a chance to wrestle you in private, man. You and me, no one else around, on the mats working up a sweat in jocks. You up for it? I hope so.*
>
> *Joe*

I sat there staring at the e-mail for a moment, my cock stirring in my sweatpants. There was a photo attached, and my hand shook a little as I clicked it open, hardly daring to hope it was him. The picture downloaded, and when it opened, my breath caught.

It was him, all right.

Drenched in sweat, his head tilted back, wearing only a jock so soaked with his perspiration it was almost transparent.

I hit reply.

> *Joe:*
>
> *I'd love to wrestle you—any time, anywhere, any kind of match. Mat, ring, jocks, full gear, no gear, on camera or off—anything you want.*
>
> *Cage*

A few moments later I got an answer.

Cage:
Fuckin'A, bud. You up for a dog collar match? I just had two made with a strap to connect 'em together—in the ring, bare assed, dog collared, rough, turn off the a/c so we both sweat buckets. You up for stakes?
Joe

I was so turned-on my balls achcd. I slid my sweatpants down. A drop of precum oozed from the head of my cock.

Joe:
Sounds hot, man, you're talking my language now. You name the stakes.
Cage

I couldn't take my eyes away from the picture. My God, he was a *man*. The soaked jock outlined his long, thick cock and heavy balls. Dark hair covered his entire torso, and his strong muscled legs were also hairy. His face was classically handsome: square-jawed, strong nose, and gorgeous eyes. He had a mustache and goatee, thick and black. His hair was trimmed close on the sides and a little longer on the top, receding a bit on both sides. And the muscles—my God, the muscles! They were thick and powerful. His biceps looked as big as my head, and blue veins snaked down over them from his shoulders.

Staring at his picture, his sensual masculinity, the thought *I'd let him fuck me* raced through my head.

Another e-mail popped into my inbox.

Cage:
Loser is winner's sex pig slave for an hour. Can you handle that, boy?
Joe

Another drop oozed from my cock as I responded.

Joe:

> *Sure, that sounds great—but I'm not sure I'd be finished with you in just an hour.*
> Cage

I reached for the lube and squirted some on my cock.

Cage:

> *Grrrr. When can you be here?*
> Joe

And now, a month later, I was in the ring bare assed.

And he was out there somewhere in the dark.

The ring squeaked as he stepped onto the apron, and the ropes jiggled as he stepped through them. I didn't turn to face him. *Get a good look at my ass, big man,* I thought as I started twisting from side to side, stretching out my lower back. The ring bounced as he moved, and finally I turned to face him.

He was completely nude, standing in the center of the ring with a big smile on his face. In each hand he held a black leather dog collar. A strap was hooked to both of them and hung down between his hands.

His swollen cock bounced as he shifted his weight from one foot to the other.

"You ready to get rough?" he growled. His voice was deep and masculine.

I smiled lazily as I took a few steps toward him. "Collar me up, man. Let's do it."

He returned my smile as he put the collar around my neck. "You don't know what you're in for, *boy.*" He pulled it tight and fastened it behind me. The strap was attached to a loop in the front. He walked back in front of me and held out the other collar.

I took it and he turned his back to me. His back rippled with muscle. His big white ass had dark hairs in the crack. Sweat was already rolling down his tanned skin. I could smell him—one of the things we'd agreed on in advance was no deodorant. His armpits smelled ripe and manly. I wanted to put my mouth into one of them, lick the sweat off, and taste him. My hands shook a little as I slipped the collar around his neck. I resisted the urge to rub my cock in the crack of his ass.

Much as I wanted to, I hadn't earned the right yet.

Rules are rules.

I pulled the collar tight and fastened it.

His broad back was an inviting target.

I swung my right arm back and smashed my forearm into it.

A loud grunt exploded out of him as he dropped forward onto his knees. I kicked him in the center of his back with my right foot, and he fell onto his stomach, making the entire ring bounce as he hit. I leaped into the air and brought my foot down on the small of his back—once, twice, three times. "Fuck," he breathed as he reached around, placing his right hand on the reddening spot where my foot had connected. He arched his ass up, coming up a bit on his knees. I put my foot against his side and shoved hard, rolling him over onto his back. I dropped my right elbow into his hairy abs, driving out all his air, and as he started to curl up into a ball I straddled his stomach, sitting down hard. I leaned forward and dug the fingers of both hands into the tender spot where his pectoral muscles connected with his shoulders. I put my weight onto my hands, clawing into the hard muscle.

Instinctively both of his hands came up and grabbed my wrists, trying to pry them off.

He was breathing hard, loud inhalations and exhalations, and his eyes were wide, his face mottled with rage.

His massive hands closed around my wrists, and his huge biceps flexed as he squeezed, veins bulging.

Christ, he's strong.

I tried gripping harder, but his skin was too sweaty and his arms too strong. My fingers slipped off, and defensively I shifted more weight forward, but he was pushing me up. His face reddened with exertion. Sweat ran off my nose onto his face. I went farther up as his arms straightened. His big legs swung up and locked around my torso, and he snapped me backward. My back hit the ring, and he used the momentum to roll me back onto my shoulders, my legs up in the air. He was still gripping my wrists, and as I shook my head he flexed his legs, squeezing.

Instinctively I contracted my abdominal muscles.

He tightened his legs again.

I could barely breathe.

I opened my eyes.

He was smiling. I could see his face above my crotch.

I closed my eyes and, in one motion, arched my lower back and swung my legs up and back, bringing them together as hard as I could around his head.

He bellowed and relaxed his legs.

I brought my legs together again.

He fell back, his legs coming loose.

I tried to roll backward over my shoulders and head to my feet, but I'd forgotten about the strap. It caught and yanked me forward, headfirst to the mat. I barely had time to put my hands down to prevent a face-plant—which would have been fatal to my hopes of winning the match. I got up on my hands and knees. The strap was underneath him. He was holding his head and moaning. I grabbed the strap with my right hand and tried to free it but it wouldn't move.

I had to move him.

I took a deep breath and grabbed one of his legs, trying to roll him to the left and off the damned strap.

He grabbed the strap and yanked on it.

My neck and head wrenched forward.

He planted a big foot right in the center of my chest and yanked on the strap again.

For a moment I was suspended like that—his foot pushing my chest backward with his arms pulling my neck and head forward. It felt like my spine was going to snap in half. I took a deep breath. My chest was soaking in sweat, so I slid to the left and off his foot. He was still holding the strap and he was smiling.

Fuck this.

I reached over and grabbed his hairy balls, squeezing.

He let the strap go and clamped his hands on my wrist.

I squeezed tighter.

He bellowed in agony. His shoulders came up off the mat, his legs rising also, bent at the knees.

I let go, grabbed both of his legs, and rolled him back up onto his shoulders. I stepped over, trapping his knees behind mine, and put my weight down. His knees came to rest on other side of his reddening face. With my weight now anchored, I reached down and started slapping his face with my hard cock.

He squirmed, but leverage was on my side. "All that muscle and you're still fucking trapped." I couldn't resist taunting him as he struggled. I slapped his face with my cock again, running the head against his lips as he twisted his head from side to side to avoid it. "Come on, lick my cock. You know you want to."

"Fuck you." He grunted. He gave a lurch and I almost lost my balance.

"All those hours in the gym and you're still not strong enough," I replied, knowing he was trapped.

But I'd forgotten about the fucking strap.

"You think?" he growled, and before I could think or react he grasped the strap in his right hand and yanked. My head snapped to the side, and he shoved with his legs at the same time. I flew off him to my left and grabbed the bottom rope to keep from going through them. My head snapped back, and I started to choke a bit as the pressure from behind on the dog collar intensified. Instinctively my hands went to the collar to try to relieve the pressure and let some air in as he dragged me backward. I flipped over to my back. I opened my eyes in time to see him over me, his big right foot lifted and heading down toward my abs. I barely had time to tighten them as he connected. My head was spinning and I was doing my best to suck in air when his hands went under my armpits, and he lifted me into the air. My feet were off the ground as he pressed me up over his head. I could hear guttural laughter as he turned and threw me into the corner. My back slammed into the turnbuckle, and pain flamed through me. His forearm went under my chin and forced my head back. I went up onto my toes as my aching back arched backward and his other forearm smashed across my chest. My legs buckled, and I would have fallen to my knees had my arms not somehow draped over the ropes. My head spun. I was vaguely aware he'd grabbed me by the collar and spun me around before my head was driven into the turnbuckle. Colored lights exploded behind my eyes, and he did it again. I dropped to my knees and fell forward. I lay there, my arms grasping the ropes, as I tried to clear my head and breathe.

Pressure on the collar again brought me to my feet, wobbling, and he spun me around and pushed me back into the turnbuckle again. I grabbed the ropes again to keep my feet as he punched me in the right pec. My head snapped back and fell forward again. Through the haze I sensed his body right in front of mine. He grabbed my head, and as my eyes began to focus I saw his massive hairy chest right in front of my face as he pushed my mouth up against his huge left nipple. "Suck it, boy," he growled.

I opened my mouth and took his sweaty nipple into my mouth. He tasted of sweat and hair, and I darted my tongue around it. Through the ringing in my ears I could hear him moan from deep inside his diaphragm. *Distract him while you regroup,* flashed through my mind, so I closed my lips around the big nipple and sucked on it. I could feel his thick cock against my chest. I opened my eyes and glanced up as I worked him with my lips and tongue. His head was back, his eyes closed, but he still had the goddamned strap gripped in his other hand.

He was too strong for me to overpower. He'd obviously done strap matches before. *What the hell were you thinking agreeing to this? How fucking stupid are you, anyway?*

If I was going to win this, I had to outsmart him, out-think him. It was my only chance.

As I kept working the nipple, he started moving his hips, rubbing his meaty cock against my chest.

Grab his balls again.

Just as I started to untangle my right arm from the ropes, he pulled his nipple back from my mouth and grabbed the collar again, pulling me back up. Again, his forearm went under my chin and he shoved my head back. The blow was brutal, and my knees buckled from its force. He raised me back up and unleashed a fury of slaps and punches into my chest—one pec then the other. My pecs were throbbing as the force of his blows sent drops of sweat flying.

Panic surged through me. I was completely at his mercy.

Just say I quit *and be done with it. So what if you have to be his slave? There are worse things.*

But I couldn't—*wouldn't*—say it.

The onslaught ceased.

I sensed his body just fractions of an inch from mine.

"I could finish you off now," he whispered in my ear, "but where's the fun in that?"

"Fuck you," I managed to gasp out.

He laughed mockingly in my ear. "No, boy, the only person getting fucked around here is going to be you—when I'm done toying with you, of course."

I felt one of his arms snake through my legs, and he hoisted me sideways up into the air in a stunning raw display of masculine power and strength. *Fucking stud* flashed through my mind as he swung me around in the air and effortlessly tossed me into the center of the ring. I tucked my head just as my body hit the mat and bounced up. I rolled onto my stomach as pain flared in my lower back. The ring shook as he walked toward me, and I saw the strap just in front of me.

The strap—use the fucking strap!

I grabbed it with both hands and put all of my weight into a downward yank. The strap tightened and then went loose as he bellowed and catapulted forward and down. I managed to roll to the side as he landed headfirst right where my head had been. His head bounced and his entire body shuddered. He rolled away from me, both hands going to his head and covering his face. I got to my knees as he rocked back and forth, moaning. I sat there for a moment, looking at his magnificent body, the sweat shining in the dim red light from overhead.

Get on top of him!

I couldn't, though. My back was throbbing, there was a dull ache in my head, and I was gasping for air. *Rest, rest for a minute, you have some time.*

His thick pubic bush glistened with sweat. His cock was hard, swinging from side to side as he rocked.

And despite the agony, mine was, too.

I somehow got to my feet and twisted, trying to relieve the pain in my back. Standing over him, I dropped an elbow into his abs.

He bellowed loud enough to echo through the empty gym.

Rather than trying to get to my feet again, I placed my right elbow just above his navel and put my weight onto it and started grinding.

His eyes flew open and his shoulders came up. His breath was shallow, and I kept grinding the elbow into his hard, flat stomach.

You can do it, you can finish him off, and then he's yours— for the rest of the night he's your slave!

I took my elbow out of his abs and smiled at his writhing magnificence.

Humiliate him.

I got to my knees and swung my left leg over him so I was still on my knees, straddling him. I lowered my ass onto his face and drove my right hand into his abs at the same time. He writhed, and I kept hammering my fists into his abs. The sweaty skin began to redden under the blows. Yet I didn't stop until I needed to catch my breath.

Which was when his tongue snaked into my asshole.

I caught my breath in shock, and my entire body went rigid for a second before involuntarily relaxing as his tongue began lapping at my hole. He knew what he was doing, all right, and my right foot began to shake a bit as the pleasure swept through my body, the aches and pains going away as ecstasy began taking control of my consciousness. I closed my eyes, tilting my head back—

—and he tossed me aside as easily as he would swat a fly.

I landed on my side with a thud, my head spinning.

And again, pressure on the collar.

He dragged me up, first to my knees and then my feet. I was vaguely aware of him in front of me as I struggled to breathe. The pressure ceased, and I gulped in air as his arms went around my waist and he hoisted me up in the air, pressed close against his slick chest. I felt his lips pressing against mine, and I parted my lips. His tongue darted into my mouth. I tasted sweat, salty and tangy, and I could also taste myself. I closed my lips around his tongue and started sucking on it, my head pounding. My cock was pressed up against his furry wet abs, and I started grinding a little bit as he held me there.

My hands dropped to his huge wet biceps and caressed them.

They suddenly flexed, and I cried out as I felt his power squeezing against my lower back.

It hurt—God how it hurt. His biceps were like steel in my hands. I could feel the power coiled in them and felt my resolve and determination ebbing out of me.

He's not even squeezing hard.

Just say I quit.

I felt him growling low and deep in his throat as the bear hug got tighter.

And the intense, blinding pain crossed the line into pleasure.

I lowered my head to his neck and started licking the sweat.

"You like that, boy?" The deep timbre of his voice sent chills through my body.

"Oh God, yes," I gasped out in a bare whisper.

I could feel the head of his cock against my ass, and I wanted it inside me.

I wanted him to fuck me until I screamed.

I wanted to shoot my load all over myself while his cock pounded my ass.

I wanted to be his slave, his toy, for as long as he wanted me to be.

I wanted to lose myself in his body, to his lusts and desires and needs. I wanted to suck his cock until his balls were dry. I wanted to worship his godlike body, to please him. I wanted him to blow a load in my face. I wanted to feel his powerful arms around me as long as I could stand it, I wanted him to break me in half, destroy me, humiliate my manhood and break my spirit until all I could say was *Yes, sir*, I wanted our bodies to merge until we were one flesh, one spirit, one desire.

And my tongue brushed against the warm leather collar around his neck.

The collar.

I slid my hands up his wet skin until they rested on his powerful shoulders. I kept grinding my cock against his stomach. I kept licking his neck. He was breathing harder, but I was well aware of the difference between heavy breathing induced by exertion or pleasure, and this was pleasure based. He loved holding me helpless in his arms while my hands ran over his powerful muscles, the feeling of having me completely at his mercy.

And I liked it, too.

But I also liked the thought of having him at *mine.*

I slid my hands along his shoulders while I moved my head up to his ear. I started kissing his ear, lightly nibbling on his earlobe as he let up some of the pressure on my back.

I grabbed the strap with both hands and yanked.

His eyes opened wide, and he let go of me as I pulled as hard as I could. I dropped my feet down to the mat and jumped back, not letting go of the strap.

His hands went up to the collar reflexively as he dropped to his knees.

"How do you like being dragged by the throat?" I hissed as I yanked on it again. I ran around behind him, never letting go, and placed my foot in the small of his back and pulled back again.

He let out a choked gurgle as his head came back, his back arching while my foot kept him in place. His arms swung, grasping up behind him until his hands closed on the strap. He tried pulling, but he couldn't get all of his strength into it—the leverage I had and being behind him rendered him effectively powerless.

And completely, totally, at my mercy.

He looked magnificent, like a sculpture of helpless masculinity, the muscles in his ass contracted, the muscles rippling in his back, arms, and shoulders as they struggled helplessly against the pressure on the strap pulling against his neck.

"Say it," I said.

"Fuck you!" he bellowed and yanked on the strap, almost making me lose my balance.

He had to quit.

This was my last chance.

I pulled back again, leaning back to add my weight.

He screamed as his back arched backward.

"Say it."

"I…quit," he gasped out, and his entire body relaxed, all the tension gone from his muscles as he sagged. I dropped my foot and let go of the strap, and his head went forward as he sat back on his haunches.

I'd done it.

I'd beaten Big Joe.

I sat down hard, my body spent and exhausted.

We both sat there, motionless, no sound but our labored breathing for several moments.

Finally, I managed to get to my feet.

I walked around to where he sat and knelt down in front of him. His head was still bowed. "Wow," I said, allowing a smile. I wiped sweat off my forehead. "That was intense."

"Yes, sir," he murmured, still not looking up.

I reached over and placed my hand on his chin, tilting it up. His eyes were downcast, not meeting mine. "Look at me," I commanded.

"Yes, sir," he whispered, his eyes meeting mine. "I'm yours to do with as you please, Master."

Master.

I liked the way it sounded and felt my cock pulsing.

I stood up and stepped up to him. I slapped his face with my cock.

"Suck me, boy," I commanded.

He opened his mouth and swallowed my cock. His hands reached around and grasped my ass, pulling me closer. His tongue worked the underside of my erection while his hands kneaded my ass. I unsnapped the leash from my collar and let it fall. He kept working on my cock with his tongue and mouth.

It felt incredible.

I reached down and put my hands on the powerful muscles of his shoulders and started applying gentle pressure, massaging. He tilted his head back without stopping the expert work he was doing on my cock, and his eyes were half-closed.

"Mmmmm," he moaned, and the vibration from his throat and tongue pulsed against my cock.

"Oh, fuuuuuuuuuuck," I moaned.

He let my cock slip out of his mouth, licking the tip a few times before he got down on all fours and turned his big hairy muscle ass up to me. "Fuck me, Master," he said, almost begging.

I got down and stuck my tongue in between the two cheeks, tasting his sweaty muskiness. He moaned as I worked his hole with my tongue, going around and around the opening before darting my tongue as deep inside of him as I could get. His body shuddered as I worked him. I reached around with my left hand and grabbed hold of his huge dick, stroking it, running my thumb over the head as moans and gasps from deep inside his diaphragm escaped. I spit on the hole and slid my left index finger inside, wiggling it around. He was tighter than I expected, which got my cock even harder. He went down onto his elbows and ducked his head down as I moved my finger around, lightly tapping on his prostate. His cock was dripping now, the stickiness of his precum getting on my hand.

I wanted to be inside him.

"Fuck me, please," he breathed as I continued massaging his prostate, his body shuddering with delight and pleasure.

I let go of his cock but kept my finger inside him as I slid the condom over my aching cock. I pressed the head against his hole to tease him.

"Oh God," he shuddered again, "I want you inside me, please fuck me."

I smacked his ass with my free hand lightly. "Beg."

"Fuck me!" he roared.

I rubbed the head of my cock against his hole again. "I said *beg*, boy," I snarled. "Beg, or no cock."

"Please," he whimpered, the last bit of defiance gone from his massive body. "Please, sir, please put your cock inside me, I want it so bad I—"

His voice was cut off by a loud grunt as I shoved my cock deep inside him. He went rigid at first, the beautifully sculpted muscles in his back and shoulders leaping out in definition as they flexed.

He was truly magnificent.

I stayed like that, impaling him, shifting my hips from side to side as he moaned. Slowly I began sliding out of him, his tight hole reluctant to let me out, until all that was left inside him was the tip. I smiled as I sat still, not moving, waiting for him to beg me to push back inside him.

It didn't take long before he was whimpering, begging me for it.

I shoved in as fast as I could, and he moaned loud enough for it to echo in the corners of the gym.

I kept it up, coming out bit by bit as slowly as I could, then trying to shove my cock as deep inside as I could go before my balls slapped against him, twisting my hips to make my cock rotate clockwise inside him.

He was whimpering.

There's nothing hotter than a huge muscle stud whimpering and begging for your cock.

I started moving faster, slapping his ass every so often.

His hole tightened on my cock.

The friction was so strong I was surprised sparks didn't fly off my cock.

And I felt it—the telltale slight ache in my balls that meant it wouldn't be long before I came.

For a split second I debated waiting, taking a break, sliding out of him and starting over.

And looking at the beauty of those so perfectly formed muscles, I knew I couldn't.

I shoved inside him again and again, and then—

He moaned, his body convulsing with each shot of cum squirting out of him.

And my entire body went stiff, my mind utterly consumed

with the power of my own orgasm flooding my consciousness. All I was aware of was my cock inside his ass.

And then, it was over.

I sat back on my haunches and peeled the condom off.

He got on his knees and turned around, and in the red light from overhead I could see the puddles on the ring. A long string of clear cum was hanging from the slit in his beautiful cock.

He was smiling. "Damn."

"Damn, indeed," I replied, reaching over and feeling his hairy pecs again.

He pulled me into a bear hug and kissed me on the cheek.

"I hope you're a cuddler," he said, standing up and pulling me to my feet effortlessly.

"I can't think of anything I'd rather do than fall asleep in your arms," I replied.

"All right, then." He scooped me up into his arms and carried me to the locker room.

CHAPTER FOURTEEN

I had his head trapped between my thighs. My legs were crossed at the ankles and I was squeezing them together. His face was turning red. With his hands he was trying to pull my legs apart to relieve the pressure on his head. Like he could pry my legs apart. Like anyone could. I squeezed tighter. He slapped my leg, finally. "Okay, okay, okay!"

I let go, and sat back and smiled at him.

"God damn." Mike sat up, shaking his head. His dark hair was drenched in sweat. Beads of sweat were rolling down the deep valley between his pecs. "You do have the quads of death." He smiled at me, a big grin that deepened the dimples in his cheeks.

I laughed. "You've seen all my matches for BGEast—so you know damned well I get a lot of submissions that way."

"Yeah, I know. It's hot. You know I love watching you make some muscle boy beg for mercy when his head's trapped between your legs." He grinned back at me. He stood up and stretched. All the walls in the wrestling room in his house were covered in mirrors. The floor was covered with wrestling mats. I watched him, watched as the muscles in his back flexed and contracted. Damn if he wasn't one of the sexiest guys I'd ever seen. I loved how broad his shoulders were, the big muscular lats fanning out and narrowing down to his waist. The black wrestling trunks he was wearing clung to his hard, round ass so tightly they dipped into the crack a bit, which was so fucking hot I could hardly stand it. He stood in front of one of the mirrors and made his pecs bounce a little bit. He hadn't shaved his chest in a while.

"You want to give it a try?" I rolled over onto my stomach and smiled at him. "Come on, you know you love having my head in there."

He turned back and grinned at me. "You know I do." He walked back over to me and grabbed a handful of my hair. "Get up, boy."

I got on my hands and knees. "Yeah, punish me, sir." He kicked his left leg up and over my head, bringing it down next to my head. He crossed his ankles and flexed his powerful leg muscles. "Harder," I demanded, placing a hand on each of his legs, stroking his strong muscles. "Come on, sir, punish me!"

He squeezed tighter.

Fuck me. He let up for a minute and I gasped in some air. He squeezed again, and I smacked his leg. "Okay, sir, okay! I give, I give, I give!"

He let me go and I slipped my head out from between his legs, shaking my head and checking my jaw. "Are you okay?" he asked, sounding a little worried.

"Fine." I grinned up at him. "I love your legs, sir."

"I was worried I'd hurt you." He leaned down and kissed me on the forehead. "I know you're tough—it turns me on, how tough you are—but still, I worry."

"Ready to get your ass kicked?" I growl. "I'll show you how tough I am."

He grinned. "Bring it on."

We circled each other. I lunged at his legs and took him down. He fell back onto the mat with me on top. Before he could do anything, I snaked my legs around his and stretched his apart. I locked my arm around his head. My cock pressed against his ripped abs as he struggled. I could feel the tip of his cock against my balls. I stretched his legs farther apart.

"Ouch! Okay! I give!"

I let him go but stayed on top of him. He grinned up at me. "Not much of a fight, huh?"

He reached up and pulled my face down to his. Our lips met. His tongue darted out into my mouth. His hands drifted down to my ass and squeezed. I started to grind against his stomach. He shifted his weight, and we rolled until he was on top of me. Our crotches were together. He rubbed his cock against mine. *Damn but that feels good…*

His legs snaked around mine and pulled them apart. My eyes opened. "Hey—"

His mouth closed down on mine again. His tongue was in my mouth as his legs pulled mine farther apart. It hurt, but I couldn't speak as his tongue explored the inside of my mouth. He yanked again and I moaned. He lifted his head and smiled down at me. "Had enough, boy?"

"Fuck—" The sentence died in a scream as he pulled my legs farther apart. "I give, you bastard! I give!"

He let go and swung his legs around so that he was sitting on my stomach. His trunks had come down a bit, and the head of his cock was pressing out.

"That was a dirty trick," I said.

"Never let your guard down, you know better than that." He was smiling. He lightly punched my pecs.

"I know, I know." I reached up with both hands and put my thumbs underneath his chin. I shoved back. As his head went back, I brought my legs up and wrapped them around his head. The momentum flipped him back and I rolled him over onto his side. His head was now trapped between my legs. I squeezed. His beautiful ass was right there in front of me. I smacked it with one hand.

"Fuck!" he shouted.

I squeezed harder. I smacked his ass again. His head felt great between my thighs. He was completely at my mercy. I yanked at his trunks and pulled them down. I smacked his bare ass again. "Whaddaya say, sir?" Smack.

"No way!"

Squeeze. Smack.

"Okay, okay! I give I give I give!"

I let his head go and grabbed his trunks with both hands and yanked them all the way down to his ankles and off. He was naked, lying on his back on the mat.

"Oh man." He shook his head.

I stood up and slipped my own trunks off. I stood, looking down at him. I put one foot up on his chest and flexed my upper torso. "Yeah," I said. "Still the man." He lay there, beaten. I wasn't done.

I sat on his chest, my legs on either side of his head. I grabbed him by the hair and pulled his head up. "Come on, pretty boy. Suck my dick."

He tried to twist his head away. "No way."

"Suck it or I'll hurt you some more." I grabbed my cock with my free hand and used it to slap his face. "You know you want to."

"No."

Slap. Slap. Slap. "We're gonna stay here all day until you do."

He looked up at me and a smile started to form. He opened his mouth and I slipped my cock into his mouth. He sucked on it, his tongue licking the underside. A low moan escaped my lips. "Yeah, that's it. Suck my cock." I reached over to the side of the mat where my bag sat. I pulled out the bottle of poppers and uncorked it. I took a deep whiff up one nostril and then the other. "Oh, fuck yeah." More blood rushed to my cock, making it stiffer and bigger. I brought the bottle down to his right nostril. He stopped sucking for a moment while he inhaled, then I put it under the other. His head dropped back for a minute, and then his mouth was back on my cock again, bobbing on it, licking it. He grabbed both my nipples with his hands and pinched them both. Hard.

His head fell back. He smiled up at me. "I want you to fuck me."

"How bad do you want it?"

"I said *fuck me!*"

I slowly stood up. "Get up." He obeyed, his big hard cock swinging. I pressed the bottle of poppers to my nose and inhaled again. I passed it back to him, and he took two big hits. I put the top back on and put it back in the bag. "You want me to fuck you, you gotta earn it." I smiled at him as I walked toward him. I made fists with both hands and punched him hard in the pecs. He staggered back a few steps and then jumped on me. I fell back on the mat, and before I knew it his legs were around my head and he was squeezing the fuck out of it. His cock and balls were right in my face.

"Come on, tough guy!" he shouted down at me. "Ain't so tough now, huh?"

My head was pounding. *I'm not going to give in, I won't, I won't...*

"*Aaaaaargh!* Okay, okay, okay, I give, I give, I give."

He let go of my head. He stood up. "Did I earn it?"

"Oh, you earned it all right." I stood up, still a little woozy. My cock and balls were aching. He got the bottle of poppers and took a couple of hits. I got out a condom and slipped it over my cock. I got out the bottle of lube. "Down on all fours."

He smiled at me and got down on his hands and knees and lifted that beautiful, so sweet, white ass up in the air. He wiggled it a little at me. *Oh yeah, you're going to get fucked, boy,* I said to myself. I took the bottle away from him and took a hit. He spread his cheeks wide. I slipped the head of my cock into his ass.

He moaned.

I slapped both ass cheeks with my hands. Hard.

He moaned louder.

I slapped them again.

He tried to move back toward me to get my cock to go in. I moved back. "Oh, no, bitch, I told you to work for it."

"I said *fuck me*!" he roared.

"Demanding little bottom whore, ain't ya?" I started to slowly slide my cock into his tight hole. It started to open for me, willingly taking it in. He moaned. I started to slowly slide it back out, but he tried to move back so it wouldn't come out. I smacked his ass again. "Hold still, bitch, or you won't get nothin'." He obliged. I kept sliding back, bit by bit. He was moaning. When it was almost all the way out, I slammed it back in as hard as I could, clenching my ass to shove it even farther. He screamed.

"Yeah, you like that, don't you?" I started moving back slowly. I reached for a sock and dumped the bottle of poppers into it. When the head of my dick was all that was left inside, I leaned forward and tied the sock around his nose so that he couldn't help but breathe it in. He started writhing. I slammed it in again and started moving faster.

His ass felt good, moist and tight enough. He was breathing hard, faster. "Ohgodohgodohgodohgod—"

I felt it. "I'm gonna come."

"Go ahead, I already have, twice," he moaned out.

I kept pounding, harder and faster. I exploded with enough force that if it wasn't for the condom I'd have blown his head off.

I stayed inside as my cock finished dumping its loads. Then I pulled back out and sat back on the mat. He stood up. There was a puddle of cum on the mat. He untied the sock and threw it aside and sat down next to me. A string of cum was hanging from his big dick. He leaned over and kissed my neck.

"Damn," he said. "That was hot."

"Yeah."

He nuzzled up against me. "I have something to tell you."

I put my arm around his sweaty shoulders and kissed the top of his head. "What's that?"

"I got a great job offer." He licked his lips. "I'm going to be moving to Southern California—Los Angeles, to be exact."

I didn't respond, feeling my heart lurch a little bit. I bit my lower lip and blinked a little bit.

"I've been offered a junior partnership with a great firm out there, with a contract guaranteeing a senior partnership if I make my deliverables."

"But—what about GSWA?" I stammered out, my mind slowly starting to wrap itself around what he was telling me. He was *leaving*. I might not ever see him again.

And I really didn't like that idea. At all.

He laughed. "Well, I won't be doing that anymore. I've already told them I was leaving, so I'm going to be losing my title in a couple of weeks." He put a hand on my leg. "I was—I was actually kind of hoping you might come with me."

"To California?" I responded, not quite comprehending. "I still have school."

He sat up, moving away from me a bit. "I meant after graduation. You're almost done. I know you were thinking about grad school, but there are a lot of schools in Southern California. I'm sure you could get into one of them." He took a deep breath. "I love you, Gary, and I don't want to lose you. But if—"

"I need to think about it." I reached over and put my hand on one of his enormous pecs. "I mean…" My mind was reeling a bit. But *California*? "I do love you, Mike. You know that?"

He smiled back at me. "Gary…I know Bill hurt you, okay? I get it. I know that's why you've not been so…open to a relationship. But we've been together awhile now—I don't see anyone else, and I've not been rushing you into anything. But this"—he smiled at me, a little sadly—"I can't pass this opportunity up. Take as much time as you need." He stood and reached down to give me a hand up.

I put my arms around him and kissed his cheek. "Let me process it, and I'll give you an answer sooner than you think."

"Come on, let's get cleaned up and go out for dinner." He pulled me down the hallway to the bathroom.

And as he lathered up my body in the shower, I cursed myself for being such a fool. He was a great guy, he loved me, and Cali-*fucking*-fornia.

Bill was never going to change his mind, and I needed just to accept that once and for all and move on.

Chapter Fifteen

I've always had a thing for cowboy wrestlers.

To me, there was absolutely nothing sexier than a man in cowboy boots and black trunks climbing through the ring ropes wearing a pair of black leather chaps and a black leather vest open to show a powerful chest. He was always a badass—a tough stud who took apart some pretty boy with ease.

And there was no one sexier than BGEast's Big Cliff Tucker. When I first discovered BGEast's website, the front page had a huge picture of Big Cliff, dressed exactly as my ultimate fantasy man: a tough sneer on his handsome face, a curly mullet dropping out from under his black hat, one black boot up on the lower rope in the corner, in his black trunks and black leather vest. The trunks couldn't hide the huge bulge. I clicked through to see the match write-up and the pictures of him just taking apart a handsome muscle stud named Donnie Brooks, and the smile on his face showed just how much he enjoyed destroying the good-looking young stud. I ordered the DVD, and it was one of the hottest and sexiest matches I'd ever seen—Big Cliff left Donnie crumpled and broken in the middle of the ring, stripped of his trunks, his big muscular bubble butt up in the air just begging to be fucked by the big man. But Big Cliff didn't fuck him. He just tucked Donnie's trunks into the front of his own, growled at him, and then climbed through the ropes and walked out as the camera faded to black. I ordered every DVD that had Big Cliff on it—and there were a lot of them over the next few years. No matter how much I hoped for a money shot, though, there never was one. Big Cliff never took off his own trunks (although he always stripped his beaten foe out of his) and never did anything sexual with the loser. And then there weren't any more DVDs with him. Like so many others, he'd apparently retired. And while BGEast always introduced new studs, there was never another cowboy star.

Apparently, Big Cliff broke the mold.

I'd asked the boss about him, but all I got was a shrug. "Last I heard, he was living in Houston. He was supposed to come up and tape for us, no-showed, and he stopped returning calls or answering e-mails." The boss had shrugged again. "It happens. We were sorry to lose him."

And I'd be passing through Houston on my way to California.

Mike had already gone. I'd somehow managed to keep it together, although I missed him horribly. I notified my private wrestling clients that I was retiring and booked a few last gigs at Blackbeard's for dancing. I'd already been accepted into grad school at UCLA, and so all I had left to do was finish the semester, graduate, and pack my shit and drive cross-country to the house Mike had found for us in West Hollywood. He called every night when he got home from work, and he was loving everything about Southern California. "You're going to love it here," he said every night, "you really are."

But as the moving date came closer, I was getting more than a little sad. I'd miss Phil, and I'd miss being able to drive to Lauderdale to tape—but the boss told me I could still fly in to work if I wanted to.

Mike and I still had a lot to talk about—I didn't know what the rules were, but surely things wouldn't be as loose as they'd been once we moved in together. And I was going to need to do something to make money, to help pay for grad school. My parents were flatly against it—against my moving to California—so they weren't going to help me anymore.

With nothing to lose, I finally came out to them. It went about as well as I could have expected. My dad screamed a lot and slammed down the phone.

A week before I was due to leave Bay City forever, I was checking my e-mails on a wrestling contact site when I noticed I had one from a name I didn't recognize: *bigdallasstud*. I clicked it open.

> *Hey Cage:*
>
> *Just watched your latest match against Nicky Romanov. Nice ass kicking you gave the Russian, boy. Love to take you on and see what you've got, man. I used to wrestle for BGEast years ago when they were getting started—Big Cliff Tucker. Think you can handle one of the original badasses from BGEast?*
>
> *Big Cliff*

I read it twice to be sure I wasn't daydreaming, then I clicked on the link through to his profile. The home city listed for him was Houston. There was only one picture on his profile, and it wasn't very clear—a big man wearing jeans and a black leather vest hoisting a guy in a pair of fight shorts up over his head. I couldn't get a good look at the face, but the body description in the profile sounded about right. But nowhere in the profile was any mention of his glory days with BGEast, which seemed odd. I had it all over my profile that I was a worker for BGEast.

I hit reply and typed quickly:

> *Hey there Big Cliff:*
>
> *Stud, I'd love nothing more than to take you on sometime. You were my absolute favorite wrestler for BGEast, bar none—I still watch some of your*

old matches from time to time. I'm going to be
passing through Houston next week—I'm moving to
California—you up for it?
    Cage

Just thinking about wrestling him made my dick hard. All the rest of that night, I kept checking the site to see if he'd answered me and was disappointed every time. *Ah, it's probably just some freak getting his rocks off on pretending to be Big Cliff,* I consoled myself as I got ready for bed. *I mean, really, what are the odds that it really is him, and that he'd want to wrestle me? Big Cliff would have his choice of guys to take apart whenever he wanted to—what would he want with me?*

But the next morning, there was an answer: a phone number and the words *Call me.* I grabbed my phone and dialed.

And as soon as I heard his voice, I knew it was him. I'd know that voice, that accent, anywhere. I'd heard it so many times taunting his victims, mocking their suffering, belittling their manhood, as he just beat the living crap out of them. "You coming my way, boy?" His voice sounded delighted. "Haven't had a tough fight in a while—you think you can give me one?"

"I know I can," I replied. Just the sound of his voice had gotten me hard as a rock as I sat there in my underwear, drinking my first morning cup of coffee.

He laughed. "Well, son, that's what they all say—then they get in the ring with Big Cliff and it don't take long before I am whipping their ass. When you gonna be here?"

I got out my appointment calendar and figured out what day I'd be passing through Houston. "That date work for you?"

"The only thing wrong with it is it ain't right now, boy." He laughed again. "You ready to give up your ass when I beat you?"

"You going to give up yours when I beat you?" I shot back. It was more bravado than anything else. While I was in pretty good shape at five-eleven and 190 pounds, Big Cliff was six-five and, according to his profile, 240 pounds.

He laughed again. "Check your e-mail, son, and we'll see whose ass is going to get served up. I got to run to work now, boy, but you check your e-mail and let me know if you still want to take on ole Big Cliff." He hung up.

I logged on to the site, and sure enough, there was another e-mail from *bigdallasstud*, with an attachment. I downloaded the JPEG, and when it opened, my jaw dropped.

It was a photo of Big Cliff, with a date stamp on it that showed that morning. He was standing, stark naked other than a white cowboy hat, with both arms raised in a double-biceps pose. His stomach was flat, his chest even bigger and more powerful-looking than his days in the video world, and his biceps looked gigantic. And he was sporting one of the hugest erections I'd ever seen in my life.

Oh yes, I was definitely going to make a stop in Houston.

He e-mailed me directions to the small ranch he lived on just north of town, and we planned on meeting at two in the afternoon.

"When you pull into the driveway, head all the way around the house to the barn," he instructed in that accent that drove me wild. "That's where my ring is set up. I'll be in there, waiting for you."

He'd told me he had about a hundred acres and about twenty head of cattle—he mostly ranched for the fun of it. He'd grown up working on ranches, until when he was about thirty he'd been thrown by a horse and hurt his back. "That was when I stopped wrestling for BGEast," he confided to me over the course of one phone call, "and I just got depressed, stopped working out, and gained a whole bunch of weight. When I finally got my shit together, I figured I was too old for them to want me anymore, and I bought this place." He currently managed a Lowe's in Houston. What I wasn't prepared for was how lovely the ranch was, and when I turned into the driveway the little blue house looked as immaculately kept as the sweeping green lawn. Huge rose bushes bloomed along the front of the porch, and a huge Dodge truck was parked in front of the house. As instructed, I followed the driveway past the house and stopped in front of the barn.

The big barn doors were open, just a little.

I turned off the car and got out, hefting my bag of gear onto my shoulder. I stood there for a moment, breathing in the fresh morning air. *He's in there waiting for me,* I told myself, and a rush of desire went through my body.

I took a deep breath and walked inside the barn doors.

It wasn't a working barn anymore—there were no farm smells inside, no cow or horse shit, no alfalfa or hay smells. There was a ladder leading up to an empty loft to the left, but in the direct center of the cement floor was a wrestling ring, and the only light in the barn came from a single bulb hanging on a long cord over the ring.

And he was standing in the far right corner in full gear.

"Get your gear on, boy!" he roared. "I'm tired of waiting on your ass."

He was wearing a pair of pro wrestling boots with black kneepads just over them. He had on his leather chaps and his leather vest; a black cowboy hat rode low on his forehead so it shadowed his face. But he wasn't wearing pro-style trunks—he was wearing a black jock—and even at that distance, I could see his big cock was hard.

I put my bag down and pulled my T-shirt over my head. I kicked out of my shoes, undid my pants, and slid them down. I turned my back to him as I slid out of my underwear, letting him getting a good look at my ass as I slid a red jock up my legs. "That's a hot ass you got there, boy," he yelled, "and it looks like it's ready to get fucked by a master."

I pulled on my red kneepads and laced up my red leather boots, ignoring him as he kept up a steady stream of insults about what he was going to do to me after he kicked my ass. That's all a part of the game, after all—trying to get inside your opponent's head. I found that ignoring all that bullshit had a tendency to get under my opponent's skin—no one likes being ignored. Once I was finished lacing my boots, I slid a red leather mask on. It was a new one; I'd bought it specifically for this match. It was red to match the rest of the gear, but unlike most of my masks it exposed my mouth and chin.

Now I was ready for him.

I walked over to the ring and climbed up on the side, keeping an eye on him to make sure he didn't pull any bullshit like attacking me when I climbed through the ropes. He didn't—just stood there in the corner rubbing his cock through the cotton of his jock. Once inside the ring, I moved into the opposite corner from where he was standing and just stared at him silently.

He undid the straps of the chaps and tossed them outside the ring, and then he took the vest off. He took a few steps toward the center of the ring and spread his legs wide and flexed both his arms.

I would have been intimidated were I not already in fight mindset.

I stepped forward and flexed my own arms.

He whistled. "You got some nice guns there, boy, but it ain't gonna be enough to take down Big Cliff." He took his hat off and tossed it outside the ring.

"After I am finished fucking you, I am taking that hat as my prize," I growled at him.

He laughed. "My cock is the only prize you're getting, boy."

"Any time you're ready, old man."

We started circling each other in the center of the ring. I was starting to sweat a little—it was a warm day and there was no air circulating in the barn. We locked up collar and elbow, and he started shoving me back into my corner. I resisted, but he was just too strong for me. He backed me into my corner, and I let him go, raising my arms over my head in a show of neutrality. He grinned at me and drove his right knee into my abs with such force I went up onto my toes, all the air driven out of me. I gasped and sucked for air as he slammed his forearm across my chest. "Ain't no such thing as neutral in Big Cliff's ring," he drawled as I collapsed at his feet. He reached down and grabbed the back of my mask, pulling me back up to my feet. Desperately, I drove a fist into his solid midsection, only earning another contemptuous laugh from him. "Nice try, boy, don't you know better men than you have tried to beat down Big Cliff before?" He reached between my legs and lifted me up like I weighed nothing, and body slammed me into the center of the ring.

I lay there, stunned, and before I could move he dropped an elbow into my abs, driving all the air out of me again. I rolled over onto my stomach, both hands clutching my abdomen. My head was swimming, and I was vaguely aware he was dragging me to my feet again. His body was slick with sweat already, and I could smell his armpits as he lifted me up and across his shoulders in a torture rack.

"What do you say, boy?" he taunted as he walked around the ring with me draped helplessly across his shoulders. "Give it up!"

"No fucking way!" I growled through clenched teeth, but I could feel the blood rushing into my head, the pain starting in my lower back as he stood in the center of the ring and began doing squats.

"I work out with more than you weigh, boy," he boasted as his hand snaked up between my legs and grabbed my cock. "And your dick is hard—I think you *like* getting worked over!"

"No way!" My head was pounding. I wasn't going to be able to hold out much longer.

And still, he kept squatting, slowly on the way down, springing back up to increase the pressure on my lower back.

It felt like it was going to break.

"Okay! Okay! Okay!" I screamed, and he rolled me off his

shoulders. I fell, landing with a thud on my back in the center of the ring.

I lay there, aching, trying to catch my breath with my eyes closed. A drop of sweat landed on my chest. I opened my eyes, and he was standing over me, one leg on either side of me, flexing. Another drop of sweat hit me. He reached down and grabbed the waistband of my jock. "Damn, boy, this thing is soaked through." He yanked on it, and it tore in his hands. He pulled until it came free, and I lay there, naked and hard, humiliated as he tossed my torn and soaked jock down at my face.

He stepped back and grabbed at his own, yanking until it, too, tore with a loud rasping sound. He tossed the destroyed jock to one side and let out a howl of triumph, his huge cock engorged and fully erect, a drop of precum resting in the slit. He grabbed it with one of his big hands. "You about ready to suck this big monster?"

If I didn't do something—and soon—I was about to get fucked.

And I didn't think I could handle anything that size.

I looked up at his grinning face.

I brought my right boot up and kicked him in the balls.

The look of triumph on his face turned to one of horror as he fell down to the right of me, clutching his balls and moaning.

I staggered to my feet, took a deep breath, and kicked him over onto his stomach. I planted myself on his back, shoved my feet into his armpits, and reached down and pulled his chin up. I slid his arms over my knees and pulled backward on his chin.

"What do you say, big man?" I gasped out.

"You're gonna pay, boy, that's what I say."

I yanked back harder, flexing every muscle in my aching upper body to intensify the hold.

"All right! I give! I give!"

I let him go and lay down on top of him, sliding my cock into the crack of his big muscled ass. The only way I was going to beat this man was to keep it up, keep up the pressure and the attack, or not only was I going to get the crap kicked out of me, but I was going to get fucked by that huge cock—and I wasn't sure I could handle that. But even knowing all that, his big hard ass felt so nice against my own cock that I couldn't resist rubbing it in a little bit. "Little boy's going to fuck the big man," I whispered into his ear, and he arched his lower back a little so that his ass was pressing up against me.

"Mmmmmm," was all he said in response.

Could it be he *wanted* to get fucked?

I was just digesting that possibility when he rolled over and tossed me aside like I was nothing. I landed against the bottom rope, my head hitting against the mat and scrambling my mind a little bit. My eyes lost focus, but I was aware that he was getting to his feet.

"Little shithead," he growled, but he was smiling. He came over and brought one of his big boots down on my stomach.

I doubled up and rolled over, thinking to get under the ropes and roll out of the ring, but as I went, he grabbed my left boot and dragged me back out into the center of the ring. He grabbed my cock and dragged me to my feet, and I was up in his arms again. I was airborne for just a moment, then I was hitting the mat on my back, and before I could even think of any kind of defensive move, he had me up again. *Slam!* I hit the center of the ring and bounced a bit. I started moving, crawling toward the ropes again, and could hear his laughter through the ringing in my ears. I was just about to slide under the ropes when he grabbed both ankles and dragged me back out into the center again. He grabbed my cock and brought me to my feet that way. He put both of his big arms under my armpits and hoisted me up into the air, then slapped both arms around my lower back as my head lolled over one shoulder.

A bear hug.

My legs hung around his hips as he applied pressure to

my lower back. I could feel the head of his huge cock rubbing against my ass as he walked me around the ring. I swung my arms, pounding on his back, but it was to no avail. The feel of our sweat-soaked bodies against each other, the smell of pure man coming from his armpits, all of these sensory perceptions ran together and collided in my mind as the pain from my lower back intensified...

"I give!" I screamed. "I give!"

Gently he set me down on my feet and peeled my sweaty leather mask off my face, tossing it away. "Damn, boy, that was hot as fuck," he said as he brought his face down to mine.

Our lips came together and he shoved his tongue into my mouth. I sucked on it for a moment, one of my hands coming down and wrapping around that huge mammoth cock, sliding back and forth.

He brought his mouth down to my neck, and my entire body went rigid. I was sore and achy, but I was aroused like I'd never been before. I'd never been with a man like this one before, I'd never been so dominated and controlled...I was his, I wanted him, I wanted to see if I could handle that monster cock. He dropped down to his knees and took my cock into his mouth, moving his head back and forth until I was at the brink of shooting my load...and he stopped.

He walked over to the side of the ring and slid a condom onto his cock, then doused it in lube. "You ready?"

I nodded, licking my lips.

He walked back into the center of the ring and lay down on his back, his cock standing up and ready.

I squatted down over it and slowly felt it invade my body.

After a few inches I had to stop. I reached down and pulled on his big nipples. "Yeah, boy, you like that cock?" he asked with a half smile.

"Uh-huh," I gasped out as I took a deep breath and allowed more of him to fill me up.

I'd never been filled up like that before, but he kept stroking my chest, flicking my nipples, running his thumb over the tip of my aching cock, and slowly but surely I kept sliding down on him until with one last college try, somehow I managed to take it all.

My entire body went stiff as uncontrollable moans escaped from my mouth. I could barely breathe. He was filling me, it was as though his cock was my torso and the rest of me just extended from it, the line between pleasure and pain was crossed and mindless waves of intense pleasure with a bit of pain raced through my entire body as I sat on him, rocking a little back and forth, working it that way because I knew the feeling of sliding him out would be almost too intense for me to bear, I just wanted to stay there, impaled with that monster cock deep inside me forever and ever and I never wanted to let it go, I never wanted that moment to end, and then—

I screamed as my load flew out of me. I shot into his face, past his head, drops flying and landing on his mighty and sweaty chest, and then I felt his body stiffen and jerk, convulsing as he let go of his load inside me…and in that instant, we looked into each other's eyes and it was as though we were one…

And then I felt his cock shrinking inside me, and I rolled off him and just lay there, staring at that single light bulb swinging over the ring.

After a few moments, he said, "Damn, boy, no one's ever gotten me to submit before. Ever."

I smiled over at him. "This is one case where the reality was better than the fantasy." I rolled over on top of him, mingling my sweat and cum with his, and I kissed him long and slow.

When I pulled my head back, he asked, "How long can you stay, boy?"

I grinned. "I don't have to be in LA till Monday."

He smiled. "We're going to have a lot of fun until you leave, Cage."

I winked. "Counting on it, big man."

He got to his feet and swung me up into his arms. "Let's get showered…and figure out what we're going to do next." He kissed my cheek. "I know at some point I want you to fuck me."

"Your wish"—I tweaked his nipples as he carried me out of the ring—"is my command, sir."

CHAPTER SIXTEEN

T he kid wants a rematch."
    "Of course he does," I said carefully into the phone. I glanced around the gym where I worked. Everyone was busy. They all knew I was gay, but they didn't know I had been a gay wrestling video star under the name Cage Thunder. "I'll get back to you, okay?"

I hung up the phone and looked out my appointment book. I'd been working at WeHo Fitness for over a year as a personal trainer. The money was decent, and I was able to work around my class schedule at UCLA. The gym was maybe a ten-minute drive from where Mike and I lived. I hadn't wrestled anyone besides Mike since moving out there, and while that was always great— everything had worked out so much better than I could have hoped—I still missed wrestling other guys. I'd almost managed to put Bill completely out of my mind, too.

And now, Gino Matarese wanted a rematch.

I thought about Gino Matarese and felt my cock stir in my pants. Damn, he'd been a hot one. Lean, defined, sculpted muscle, a pretty face, and an ass to die for. Since that first match, he'd become the company's biggest star. His DVDs sold well, and he had been on a winning streak for two years. I was the only person to beat him.

Of course he wanted a rematch.

Fuck if I didn't want to wrestle him again.

I needed to wrestle again.

Watching the DVDs and beating off wasn't the same as wrestling. I missed the body contact, the sweat, the feel of trapping another man in a hold he couldn't get out of, both of our bodies straining and struggling, muscle against muscle, seeing who was the better man.

My cock was rock hard.

I got up and went into the bathroom, carefully locking the door behind me. I undid my pants and let them fall to the floor, slipping my right hand inside my underwear and stroking my cock. I remembered Gino Matarese, in his purple squarecut that outlined his perfect ass, the bulge in front from his own erection. I remembered my legs around his head, squeezing. I remembered him on his hands and knees, that beautiful bare ass turned up to me, as I slipped my cock inside him and began to ride him hard.

I gasped as I came into the toilet paper I had spread out on the floor, my body shuddering a bit as I squeezed the last drops out of my cock.

I was going to fight him again.

❖

The day of the match finally arrived. I stood in the locker room, wearing only a black jock. Gino had requested we wrestle in jocks only, barefoot. This wasn't unusual; the company made lots of jock-strap wrestling videos. What was unusual was Gino had never done one, and we were also wrestling in the ring. Jock-strap videos were usually made in the mat room, which had walls painted black and wall-to-wall mats. I'd done a couple jock-strap videos early in my video career. I preferred Speedos in the ring, myself, but hey, since I'd won the first match, I was cool with letting Gino pick the setup for the rematch. The rematch itself was unusual; the company didn't see much point in filming rematches. It made sense—the DVDs would compete with each other for sales. Apparently, though, my match with Gino had sold so many copies (and was still selling) they figured it was worthwhile to tape a rematch. Usually, if you wanted a rematch with someone you'd wrestled on tape, you arranged it yourself and it was private.

I stood in front of the mirror and flexed. I'd shaved my torso so the tanned muscles gleamed in the overhead light. When I'd first wrestled Gino I weighed 175 pounds, all lean, defined muscle. I now weighed 195 pounds, adding twenty pounds of muscle. My body fat was still the same. My muscles were thicker, heavier, stronger.

Gino Matarese was going down.

I walked out of the locker room and down the hall to the ring room.

The door on the other side of the room opened and Gino walked through. I glanced over at him. He stood in the door and flexed his biceps, bringing his arms down together in front so every muscle in his upper body flexed, showing the striations of the muscle. He had gotten bigger since I'd last seen him. He stood there, posing for the camera, for a few more moments, then stalked over and jumped up to the ring apron, then jumped over the top rope, springing as he landed, his fists clenched. Stuart started taking pictures of him, and Steve came over to take mine. And once we were finished, Gino walked over to where I was standing, in front of the ropes.

"You're the one who's gonna get fucked this time, old man," he sneered at me.

I turned and faced him. "Once a bottom, always a bottom, boy."

He shoved me back into the ropes, which propelled me back forward at him. I saw him cock his fist for a shot at my abs, so I planted my feet and kicked him square in the six-pack. He doubled over. I turned, grabbed his head, slipped my shoulder underneath it, and dropped to my knees, driving his head into my shoulder with a good deal of force. He bounced off my shoulder and fell backward, landing on his back. I stood up and walked over to him. He was groaning and holding his head. I planted my right foot square into his abs and stomped. Once. Twice. Three times. He rolled over onto his side in a fetal position. I grabbed him by the hair, pulled him up to a sitting position, then put my legs on either side of his head and fell back to the mat. I squeezed his head as hard as I could, and he let out a scream that made my cock stir. I reached down and grabbed his arms by the wrist, pulling them up and inward. He was immobilized. If the pressure on his head didn't get him, the pressure on his shoulders would. I cranked his arms harder and squeezed.

He screamed again.

"Come on, punk," I taunted him. "Give it up, you know you want to, you know you want my cock up your ass again."

"No fucking way! *Fuck you!*"

His words trailed off into a scream as I tightened my legs again and yanked his arms farther up.

"Come on, boy."

"Fuck you! Fuck you!"

"Okay, then." I squeezed again.

"Okay, okay, I give! I give! I give!"

"What did you say? I didn't hear you."

"I give! I give! Come on, man, I give! I give!"

"That's what I thought." I let go of him and got to my feet. He lay there on the mat, groaning and holding his head. I walked back over to the corner and stood there, leaning back into the ropes, watching him. After a few minutes, he got to his knees, shaking his head. He moved his shoulders a bit, trying to loosen them up.

"Take your time, boy," I said. "I got all day to kick your ass."

"Fuck you," he said. He got to his feet. Sweat glistened on his smooth pecs. He walked back to the opposite corner, still shaking his head. He turned his back to me and leaned into the corner, his head down. He appeared to have the body language of someone doubting himself, doubting whether he could win the next two falls and thus the match. I smiled to myself. *Bring it on, boy.*

He turned to face me again. "I'm ready."

We circled each other in the center of the ring, feinting at each other, looking for an opening. Sweat was rolling down from his curly black hair. His brown eyes looked determined. This fall wasn't going to be easy, I realized.

His left leg shot out and kicked me, square in the right knee.

A bolt of pain shot up and my leg buckled. *Fuck,* I thought, and in that instant he was on me. He grabbed my head and pulled me down into a headlock, his muscles tightening around my head, but all I could feel was the pain from my knee. It still wasn't steady, and as he dragged me around the ring by my head, it buckled from time to time. He flipped me over onto my back, still holding my head. I hit the mat with a thud. My knee was throbbing. He let go of my head only to slam it into the mat. My ears starting ringing. I tried to get up, but somehow he had grabbed my right leg and bent it around his. Pain shot up my leg as he twisted. I let out a howl.

"How'd you like that, old man?" he panted with a grin on his face. He twisted it again.

Motherfucker. I was breathing hard, trying to focus my eyes. It hurt, oh God, how it hurt. I raised my left leg and kicked at him, landing my foot square into his abs. He dropped my right leg and fell back. I rolled over and got on my hands and knees. My knee fucking hurt, my God, the little bastard—

He kicked me in the side.

Air exploded out of me as the momentum from the kick rolled me. He kicked me again, and I kept rolling, trying to get away. My shoulders hit the bottom rope. I reached up for it just as he kicked me again. The rope slipped out of my sweating hands and I fell off the ring apron and dropped heavily to the mats outside.

My head was spinning. I grabbed my knee just as I heard

him drop down to the mats outside the ring. He reached down and grabbed my head and pulled me to my feet. He slugged me in the gut, driving me back into the side of the ring. My ass hit it and I fell back into the ropes, grabbing for them for balance. My knee was buckling, it couldn't hold me.

He kicked me in the knee again.

This time I dropped to the mats, and he scooped me up and slammed me back down onto my back. Before I could get my bearings, he had me up again, this time setting me back down on the ring apron. He grabbed my right leg and dragged me to the corner of the ring, pulled my leg out, and slammed my knee into the ring post.

I screamed.

I could hear him laughing as the ropes squeaked as he used them to pull himself back into the ring. He grabbed my arm and dragged me under the ropes, then planted his feet above and below my shoulder and dropped back to the mat.

My shoulder exploded in pain.

Focus, I told myself. Every hold has a counter. Forget the pain.

Ouch! Fuck!

Forget the pain, don't forget, concentrate, focus.

Sweat dripped into my eyes.

He let me go.

I rolled over onto my stomach, holding my shoulder. It was throbbing. My knee was throbbing. Goddammit. I got to my knees. The ropes squeaked. He was standing in the corner opposite me. He was grinning. I shook my head.

Focus.

I got to my feet, and my knee buckled slightly. I looked over at him. His eyes narrowed and he came toward me. I backed up a little, my leg buckling again. Okay, watch for an opening, careful of the knee—

He leaped up into the air and kicked me in the chest with both feet.

I fell back, tucking my head up so the force of the fall was absorbed by my back. Still, I hit the mat with a bone-jarring thud. Before I could move, he had a hold on both of my legs. He held them up, standing in between them, and then planted his right foot hard into my abs. I barely had time to flex them to withstand the stomp, and then he stomped again, twice, three, four times. My ab muscles were screaming, and then he hooked his arms around my knees and lifted me up onto my shoulder blades.

A fucking Boston crab.

I tried to fight it off, but he just grunted and strained until finally I started to turn. He rolled me over onto my stomach, holding my legs, and then sat back, arching my back much farther than it was ever intended to bend.

I screamed.

"What do you say?" he panted, leaning back even farther.

"I give! I give!" I shouted.

He let go, dropping my legs.

I lay there on the mat, unable to move. My abs ached. My knee was throbbing. My lower back hurt. I gasped for air.

He stood over me, flexing his biceps.

"You want some more of this?" he screamed at me. "Huh? Huh?"

The little fuck. His package was just above my face. His cock was hard, straining against the cotton.

I drove my fist up into it.

Gino screamed and fell to the mat, doubled over, both hands on his balls.

I willed myself to get up, to ignore the pain. I limped over to him. I used my right leg to kick him in the abs. He rolled over onto his stomach, that beautiful white hard ass coming up in the air, framed by the straps of his black jock. I reached down and grabbed the top strap, the thicker one running across his lower back. I grabbed it and yanked. There was a brief tearing sound, and then it came free in my hand. I sat down on his back. He was still moaning, and I pulled it tight around his neck, pulling back.

He gagged and choked.

"Come on, boy," I muttered. "How do you like this?"

His hands came up, trying to pull it away from his neck. His face was reddening as he gasped for air. I smiled. *You want free, boy? Okay.* I let go, and he gasped in air. I grabbed his curly hair and drove his forehead down into the mat. Again. Again, until I lost count.

I got off his back. He was moaning. I grabbed him by the hair and dragged him to his feet, pushing him back into a corner. He sagged against the corner, an arm draped over each side. I stood there for a moment, then started punching him in the abs, those beautifully defined abs. Right, left, right, left, the air exploding out of him with each punch, his body sagging more and more with each shot. I climbed through the ropes and dropped down to the mats outside, still favoring my aching right leg. His muscled arms were just hanging there. I grabbed them both, cradling them inside my left arm as I tied his wrists together with the jock behind the ring post. I glanced over at the boss. His hard-on was tenting his sweatpants out. I faced him and flexed for him, then climbed back into the ring.

Gino's big heavy cock was stiffening as he tried to move his arms.

I slapped his face, his head jerking back. "You like this, don't you, boy? You like being worked over."

He muttered, "Fuck you."

I grabbed his cock with my left hand. It became completely hard as I squeezed it. "You can't hide it, boy. You want to get beaten up, and then you want to get fucked."

"Fuck you!"

I slipped my jock off. My own cock was rock hard now. I shoved my jock into his face. "Smell that, boy? That's what a real man's balls smell like." I rubbed it over his face, then stepped back.

What to do with him now, I wondered. His body was slick

with sweat, still sagging somewhat. I climbed up onto the second rope and started slapping his face with my cock. "You wanna suck it, don't you?" I taunted him.

"Fuck you!"

I climbed back down, and then through the ropes again. I untied the jock, and he slid to the mat, clutching his abs. I climbed back into the ring and grabbed his legs, dragging him back to the center of the ring. Turnabout, I decided, was fair play. I lifted him up onto his shoulder blades and turned him over, then sat on his back.

He screamed, "I give! I give! I give!"

"What did you say?"

"I give, sir! I give, sir!"

I let him go and walked over to the ring corner where I'd tied him, pulling on my dick. His ass was up, even sexier and hotter than it had been two years earlier. The boss handed me a bottle of lube and a condom. He was sweating. He nodded at Gino. "Go fuck him now."

I slid the condom over my cock and lubed it up. I was still limping a little, the dull ache still there in my knee.

He had done that.

I knelt down between his legs. "Arch your back, boy."

He didn't move.

I smacked his ass, leaving a handprint on its hard whiteness. "I said, arch your fucking back!"

He whimpered and complied. I pulled his legs farther apart, staring into the musky-smelling hole. I slid a finger into it. He whimpered again, his ass rising higher into the air. He wanted it, all right. I smiled. I moved the finger around, loosening it up, slipping in a second finger. I moved my hips forward, but a bolt of pain shot up from my knee.

There was no way I could fuck him on my knees.

"Get up, boy." He looked back over his shoulder at me. "I said, get up!"

He slowly got to his feet. His eyes were downcast. I lay down on my back, holding on to my cock. "I want you to ride my cock, boy. Get over here."

He straddled me, reaching behind him and grabbing my cock, guiding the tip into his hole. He shuddered a little when it entered him, his breath coming fast, his eyes closing. He slowly slid his ass down my shaft until he reached the bottom, a half smile starting to form on his face. "You have a nice cock, sir," he whispered.

Sweat was rolling down his chest, streaking down his abs. His curls were damp. "Ride it, boy, ride it nice and slow."

He started moving up, his abs flexing as he did, then slowly coming back down. I reached up and grabbed both of his nipples, pinching them. He moaned again. I heard the ring ropes squeak as Stuart climbed through with the camera, squatting down above my head. I ignored him as Gino, my boy, my conquest, my prize, rode my cock.

"Flex them arms for me, boy," I said. He smiled at me, his eyes half-closed, and obliged. "Kiss those biceps, boy." He pursed his thick, beautiful lips and turned his head, kissing one mound of muscle and then the other. "Now flex your pecs." He brought his arms down and the striations in his chest muscles popped out. I punched one, then the other. His eyes closed.

"Yes, sir. Anything you want, sir."

"Stroke your dick, boy. I wanna see you come."

He picked up the bottle of lube and squirted some on his thick cock, never losing a beat as he rode my cock. He started stroking it, slowly at first, and then faster. His ass began riding me faster, and I could feel my own climax coming.

"Come on, boy, shoot your load!" I panted.

His entire body shuddered, and he yelped as ropes of cum started flying out of the slit in his cock, landing on my abs, my chest, my face, my hair. He kept riding my cock as his body convulsed, and I let out a shout as my entire body went rigid with my own orgasm. We both remained there, my cock in his ass, as both our bodies convulsed and shuddered.

Then, he smiled down at me. "Thank you, sir," he said quietly. He reached down and rubbed his cum into my skin. "I've been waiting for that for two years." He slid my cock out of his ass, then got on all fours and kissed me, deep and passionate.

I ran my hands through his damp hair. "You're a good boy, Gino."

He cuddled up against me, throwing his right leg over my abs.

"And that's a wrap," Stuart said, putting the camcorder down.

I smiled at Gino. "You wanna grab a beer or something?"

He smiled at me. "Yes, sir."

"Come on, then." I got up and helped him to his feet. I touched his rock-hard pecs again. "Such a pretty boy."

And we headed for the shower.

CHAPTER SEVENTEEN

I was stretching and warming up in the ring, psyching myself up for this last match. I'd already decided this was my last trip back. Now that business with Gino had been settled last night, I was doing one more match before heading home.

I missed Mike. This trip had been the first time since I'd moved out there we'd been apart, and I now realized that much as I missed the wrestling, I missed him more.

The guy I was scheduled to wrestle was new to BGEast, and I hadn't met him in person. I'd seen pictures of him, though, and he was gorgeous. He was young, twenty-three at most, with ripped abs, muscular legs, and a stunning upper body. As soon as the boss showed me the pictures that morning, my dick had gotten hard, and I'd said, *Hell yeah, I wanna wrestle him!*

And so here I was, back in the ring, waiting.

I glanced at the clock on the wall. It was a quarter after eight. The kid was late.

I dismissed the thought and went back into my mind space, focusing on my stretching. It felt good to stretch. I was always in such a rush, it seemed, to get through my workouts when I managed to squeeze in time at the gym that I never managed to really get a good, regular stretching routine going. I blocked everything out as I reached for my toes, bending at the waist and trying to lower my forehead to my knees. I heard a phone ringing but blocked the sound out. I glanced up as my torso descended and caught a glimpse of myself in the mirror outside the ring. I gave myself a wink. *The twink is going down.*

"The kid canceled," the boss said from outside the ring ropes. "Car trouble, he says."

"Car trouble my ass—chickened out is more like it," I replied as my forehead finally came to rest on my knees. I could feel the stretch in my hamstrings, and I exhaled. It felt great.

"You up for a rematch?" the boss asked me as he tucked his cell phone back into his pocket.

I gestured down at my ring attire. "All geared up with no one to beat on, boss," I replied with a shrug, but my curiosity was piqued. "Who we talking about, boss?"

His eyes glinted, and he raised an eyebrow. "Micah Coleman."

My eyes narrowed.

I fucking *hated* Micah Coleman.

Our original match was taped when we were both new to the company. It was a motel match, and to be honest, he completely kicked my ass.

But it wasn't really a fair fight. While we were about equal in wrestling skill, in a small space like a motel room a bigger guy has a definite advantage. To beat someone bigger in a small space, you either have to be more skilled or quicker than the big guy. I was giving up three inches in height and twenty pounds, and without a lot of room to maneuver, well, I didn't have a chance. The match didn't start out fair, either. He knocked on the door of the room, the cameras were already rolling, and I answered his knock. We were supposed to trash-talk each other and move over to where the mattresses had made a makeshift arena, strip out of our shirts and shorts, and get wrestling.

Instead, the moment the door came open he attacked me. I wasn't expecting it—he had my shirt pulled up over my head, blinding me and tangling up my arms, and then just started working me over. I was never in the fight, and when I was finally beaten down and couldn't continue had to put up with the humiliation of him sitting on my chest while he flexed his massive arms and laughed at me.

"Did you really think you had a chance?" he mocked as he struck a double-biceps pose. "Look at these fucking guns!"

And as if that wasn't enough, he gave my face a playful slap before he got off me and they turned off the camera.

This match was also before I started wearing masks, and drawing from their power.

Ever since then, I'd wanted nothing more than to just totally kick the shit out of him. I'd tried to arrange a private match in the ring, just the two of us—no cameras, no referee—him and me, two hours. Two climb in, one climbs out. He was always evasive. "What do I have to prove?" he'd taunt me in e-mails or on the BGEast message board. "I already kicked your ass once. What would be different this time? Not a fucking thing."

And I would just burn in anger.

I gave Steve a nasty smile and drove my right fist into my gloved left hand. "Yeah, I could handle another shot at Coleman. Will he have the balls to show up?"

I was wearing my black leather gloves with the fingers cut out, a black leather mask with a white facial outline, my black boots and kneepads, and a flattering black pair of trunks with two silver lightning bolts on the front that met over my crotch and formed an arrow pointing down. I walked over to the side of the ring that faced the mirror and struck an all-muscle pose. I had a deep tan and was in great shape. I'd trained really hard and even managed to watch what I ate in the weeks leading up to the trip to Lauderdale. I'd trimmed my thick torso hair down, and I looked great.

"Oh, he's on his way." The boss gave me his wickedest grin. He picked up a digital camera. "Guess we might as well start taking your portraits until he gets here."

We'd just wrapped up my portraits when there was a knock on the gym door, and Stuart, who was going to run the video camera during the match, opened it.

I walked over to the ring ropes closest to the door and stared at the hated Coleman as he walked into the gym.

He was two inches taller than me at six foot one, and he was wearing a pair of sweatpants cut off at the knee and a T-shirt he'd cut the sleeves from so it was open almost to the waist. He didn't look at me as he walked in and shook hands with Stuart. The boss left me standing there, watching, and went to talk to him. Coleman put his gym bag down and pulled the shirt over his head. He was bigger than he was when we'd last wrestled. His big shaved pecs, thick shoulders, and huge biceps were defined, veins popping out as he slid his shorts down. He was wearing a pair of electric blue trunks with a silver lightning bolt across the front. I smirked. *Lightning trunks to wrestle Cage Thunder, huh?* I thought to myself as he pulled on socks and began lacing up his white boots. When he was finished lacing the boots, he headed for the ring.

He was good looking, with his dark blond hair trimmed close to his scalp in an almost military-style cut. His torso and legs were completely hairless, and there was a big bulge in the front of his trunks that I didn't remember from our original match. His skin was tanned a dark golden brown, and as he climbed through the ropes he looked over at me and gave me a big smile. "Hey, man," he said, dimples deepening in his cheeks. One of his bright blue eyes closed in a wink. "Let's put on a good show, huh?"

I just nodded and watched as he started posing for the boss's camera. I could feel my cock starting to stir inside my trunks. The fucker's body was gorgeous. The big strong muscles of his biceps peaked as he flexed them, veins bulging in his forearms and shoulders. I remembered how it felt to be trapped in his vise-like bear hug, those powerful arms putting pressure on my lower back until I thought it would snap, him tossing me around like I weighed nothing.

"All right, let's get some of the two of you together," the boss commanded, and I walked over to the corner where he stood, with one boot up on the lower rope. "Stand chest to chest," he went on, and I stepped in close to Coleman. Our chests were maybe an inch away from each other. "Perfect."

"I'm going to kick your ass again," Coleman whispered, the smile never fading.

I didn't reply. He was just trying to get inside my head, make me doubt myself. Instead, I looked at his big pecs and thought how great it would feel to put a claw hold on them. All of his muscles were big, everything about him was large—and all that really meant to me was a bigger and better target to go after.

We did a couple more shots of the two of us, and then Steve put the camera down. "All right, when we start taping, we're going to start with the camera on you, Micah," he said. "Stand over there in front of the mirror, and just do some flexing shots—you know what to do."

"Yup," he replied.

"Cage, you're going to be in the locker room," the boss went on. "When Micah is through flexing, he'll call you out. You come out, give him the once-over, and then climb in the ring and head over to your corner. We'll ring the bell, and you start."

I nodded and climbed out of the ring and walked through the locker-room door, pulling it shut behind me. My heart was pounding. I'd been waiting for years for another shot at the big muscle head, and now it was here. My traitorous cock was semi-hard, which kind of pissed me off. Sure, he was hot. Sure, he had a great body, one of the best I'd ever seen up close and personal. But he was an asshole, and he was the enemy.

I wasn't going to lose to that son of a bitch again.

It was hot in the locker room, and I could feel sweat starting to run down my head underneath the mask. I stood there, trying to focus on what I had to do to win the match. I took some deep breaths, clearing my mind. *Forget everything, just focus on kicking his ass.*

"Hey, Thunder, what are you doing in there? You afraid to come out and fight me, pussy?"

I grabbed the door handle and shoved it open. It slammed against the wall as I stalked through the doorway and just stood there. I looked into the ring, and there he stood, his arrogant cocky grin mocking me. I pointed at him, and then down at the mat. "You're going down, muscle head," I growled and climbed through the ropes, heading over to my corner as he retreated back to the corner opposite mine.

He flexed his arms. "You sure you want some of this?" he called. He kissed each biceps in turn. "These big guns are gonna shoot you down and break you, little man."

Stay calm, he wants you to lose your temper so you'll lose focus.

The bell rang.

We started circling each other. I walked slowly while he danced around on the balls of his feet. He kept up a steady barrage of trash talk as we circled each other. "I'm gonna break you," he taunted me, the grin I'd learned to hate on his face. "I'm gonna tear you limb from limb."

We locked up in the center of the ring, collar and elbow. We pushed back and forth, and then with a strong push, he began backing me into my own corner. He was so damned strong! I felt the corner against my back, and he pushed my upper torso up and backward until I was on my toes. He was standing in between my legs, and he was forcing my arms up, my entire torso exposed—

And he slapped my face.

It wasn't a hard slap. It was just a pop, it didn't hurt at all, but it was loud and meant to be insulting. He laughed at me and danced backward to the center of the ring, gesturing for me to come forward again. I came forward, my arms outstretched in front of me, and he darted through them, scooped me up, and body slammed me to the center of the ring.

All the air left my lungs, and a bolt of pain shot through

my body from my lower back. And as I started to get to my feet again, he scooped me up and dropped me again. My ears ringing, the pain in my lower back was starting to throb as he grabbed me by the chin and dragged me back up to my feet. Back into the air I went, and this time he dropped my lower back over his knee. My body bent in two as I rolled off, landing on my stomach.

Fuck, that hurts, damn it to fuck...

And as I tried to clear my head, he grabbed my left leg, tucked the foot under his armpit, and sat down on my upper back, my back screaming as he dragged my leg up into a single-leg crab. I tried to push up, to take some of the weight on my free knee and release the pressure on my lower back as he started twisting my foot around.

I don't know...how...much...more...I...can...take...

I was just about to submit when he released my leg.

Gasping, shaking my head, I started crawling to my corner.

He kicked me in the back.

I dropped to the mat and rolled desperately for the corner.

I started pulling myself up by the ropes when his knee slammed into my back again.

The momentum drove me headfirst into the turnbuckle.

Dazed, I climbed up on the ropes. I was on my feet when he grabbed my arm and my chin and hoisted me up in a rack across his shoulders.

"What do you say?" he taunted me as he walked to the center of the ring with me draped limp across his shoulders. My legs hung from one side, my head and arms from the other side, and my back...

He started doing squats. Every time he got down as far as he could, my back screamed in pain.

I struggled, tried to focus, tried not to let the pain get to me.

"I submit! I submit! I submit!"

He shrugged me off his shoulders, and I dropped to the mat, sprawled, dazed, and in extreme pain. I was vaguely aware of him posing over me, flexing those massive muscles, and then he kicked me in the side, rolling me over onto my aching back.

"Look at that!" he sneered, reaching down and touching my hard cock. "You're hard! You *like* getting your ass kicked by a big muscle stud, don't you?"

He hooked his fingers into my trunks, and with a hard yank, tore them off me.

I lay there, exposed.

He laughed and tossed my trunks outside the ring.

"Anytime you're ready for more, pussy." He reached down and smacked my face again. It was just a slap, hurting nothing more than my pride. With a laugh, he walked back over to his corner.

I rolled over to the corner, pulling myself up by the ropes yet again. I stood there, taking deep breaths, stretching my aching back as I stared across the ring at him. He was smiling at me, contempt written all over his handsome face.

Turn the pain to rage.

I kept staring at him, aware that my cock was still hard, willing the pain away, my hatred for him spilling over.

He held his hands out and signaled me to come and get him.

I started walking across the ring. With each step, my anger rose until I reached the other side of the ring. I was standing in front of him, my cock bouncing.

I drove my fist into his ripped abs.

"Is that all?" He laughed. "Come on, give it to me again! Give me your best shot!"

I slammed my fist into him again.

"I think I may have felt that," he mocked and shook his head. "Steel, baby, they're steel. Give it another try."

I pulled my fist back, smiled to myself, and punched him as hard as I could.

Only this time, I connected with his balls.

His face turned red, his eyes bugged out, and I stepped

aside as he collapsed to the mat. He rolled, clutching his balls, moaning.

I walked over, hooked my fingers into his trunks, and yanked them off.

His hard, muscular ass was—well, spectacular.

I sat down on his back and slipped his trunks around his neck. I yanked back.

He started gasping, his legs kicking as I pulled back, leaning to get my weight into it.

"How them muscles working for you now, stud?" I taunted him as he tried to get air into his lungs. "Ain't such a big man now, are you?"

"You…cheating…*fuck*!" he somehow managed to gasp out.

I let go of his trunks and slammed his head down into the mat. I tossed the trunks outside the ring and rolled him over onto his back. His face was red, he was still trying to breathe, and I sat on his meaty pecs. I put one knee on either side of his head, grabbed him by the hair, and pulled his face up into my crotch, rubbing my cock all over his face. "Yeah, you want to suck that big dick, don't you, bitch?"

"Fuck…*you*!"

I jumped to my feet and stomped on his steel abs. He doubled up, gasping and choking. I jumped onto them with both feet, and that was when I noticed his cock was hard.

It was a beautiful cock, long and thick over a set of heavy balls. He had trimmed his golden pubic hair down to fuzz. I reached down and flicked his cock with my right index finger. "Looks like getting your ass kicked turns you on, muscle man." I laughed.

I had him where I wanted him now. I picked up his left leg, spun it so it was wrapped around my left leg, crossed it across his right knee, and then dropped down onto my ass, locking my right ankle over his left foot.

A figure four hurts like a motherfucker, and sure enough, he was screaming his submission out before I could even ask him.

I released the hold and got to my feet. I kicked his left knee—the one the submission hold had tortured—and he screamed and rolled away from me.

I followed him as he crawled to the corner, and as he started climbing the ropes I kicked him square in the small of his back. He dropped back down to his knees, and I planted my right foot in between his shoulder blades while grabbing both wrists and yanking his arms back.

"What do you say, muscles?" I asked. My cock was getting harder. Every muscle in his back was straining as he tried to use his strength to power out of the hold. But no one is that strong—the leverage I had on the hold was too much for even someone as powerful as Micah Coleman. His ass cheeks were clenching as he struggled, and I knew when he submitted this time, he was going to pay for everything.

"I submit! God, I submit!"

"What did you say?" I asked.

"I submit! I submit! I submit!"

I let him go, and he leaned against the ropes. I stuck my right index finger in my mouth and licked it. I pressed up against him, putting my mouth to his ear. "I'm going to fuck you, bitch."

"No, man, no!"

I slid my slick finger into his asshole. He resisted at first, and then I slipped my right arm around his neck and yanked backward. He relaxed and my finger slid in. A moan escaped from his lips.

"Yeah, you know you want it." I stood up, not releasing my hold on his neck, so he had to come up with me. I reached into my boot and got out the condom I'd tucked in there earlier. I tore the package open, spit into it, and slid it over my cock. I pushed on him so he went up on his toes, then kicked his legs apart. I slid the tip of my cock inside him.

His entire body stiffened, then relaxed with a shudder.

"You want the whole thing, don't you?"

"Yes," he whimpered.

I shoved the whole thing inside him.

He screamed—but the scream died into a primal growl.

He arched his back and shoved his ass toward me.

"Give it to me!" he snarled in his deep masculine voice.

Oh, hell yeah. There's nothing hotter than a great big muscle stud that not only likes to get fucked—but wants it hard.

I slapped his hard ass and slid slowly out of him until all that was left inside him was the head. I just stood there as he started to writhe, his huge muscles trembling with need and desire. He tried to push back, to force my cock into him, but I grabbed his right arm and twisted it behind him. I leaned forward and whispered into his ear, "Beg for it."

"You *bastard.*" He spit the words out. Still holding his arm, I reached around with my left hand and grabbed his cock. He moaned as I started stroking him. We stood there, the tip of my cock inside his ass, for a few moments…and then, as I felt his orgasm starting to build, I rammed inside him again. I thrust hard, going up on my toes, trying to shove every bit of my cock into him. He rose up onto his toes with a loud moan, and he came, and I pulled back and started pushing into him harder and faster until I could feel my cum starting to rise, until I shot my entire load, my head going back, and a gasping growl tore out of me.

We froze like that for I don't know how long, his sweat-soaked body and mine, joined.

I dropped his arm and pulled out of him, peeling off the condom and tossing it into the garbage can outside the ring.

He turned around and smiled at me.

"That was *hot,* guys," the boss called out. "Nice job."

And, I figured as I walked to the locker room, not a bad way to write *finis* to my career at BGEast.

EPILOGUE

Mike was in the living room, watching an old recording of Arn Anderson beating the shit out of some muscle stud, when I walked into the house, tossing my backpack on the floor before plopping down on the couch next to him.

"So," he asked, muting the television just as Arn tossed the stud over the ropes and out of the ring, "how was Bill?"

"Thanks for letting me go," I replied, watching the action on the television. The muscle stud was sprawled on the floor outside the ring, unable to get up. "I needed that." I smiled at him. "And now, now I'm done with it all. BGEast, Bill—everything."

Mike put his arm around me, and I rested my head on his shoulder. "I love you, Gary."

"And I love you, Mike." I snuggled in closer to him. "We're going to have a great life, aren't we?"

He kissed the top of my head. "We already do, baby, we already do."

He turned the sound back on.

About the Author

Cage Thunder is a writer and professional wrestler from Louisiana. He has been writing erotic wrestling stories for years, stories that have been published in markets as varied as magazines, websites, and anthologies. He joined the stable of wrestlers at BGEast.com in 2006 and has been wrestling and writing for them ever since. His blog about wrestling and the eroticism of sport can be found at cagethunder.livejournal.com. He is also on Facebook. *Going Down for the Count* is his first novel, and he is currently working on a second, *Muscles*.

Books Available From Bold Strokes Books

The Seventh Pleiade by Andrew J. Peters. When Atlantis is besieged by violent storms, tremors, and a barbarian army, it will be up to a young gay prince to find a way for the kingdom's survival. (978-1-60282-960-2)

Cutie Pie Must Die by R.W. Clinger. Sexy detectives, a muscled quarterback, and the queerest murders…when murder is most cute. (978-1-60282-961-9)

Going Down for the Count by Cage Thunder. Desperately needing money, Gary Harper answers an ad that leads him into the underground world of gay professional wrestling—which leads him on a journey of self-discovery and romance. (978-1-60282-962-6)

Light by 'Nathan Burgoine. Openly gay (and secretly psychokinetic) Kieran Quinn is forced into action when self-styled prophet Wyatt Jackson arrives during Pride Week and things take a violent turn. (978-1-60282-953-4)

Baton Rouge Bingo by Greg Herren. The murder of an animal rights activist involves Scotty and the boys in a decades-old mystery revolving around Huey Long's murder and a missing fortune. (978-1-60282-954-1)

Anything for a Dollar, edited by Todd Gregory. Bodies for hire, bodies for sale—enter the steaming hot world of men who make a living from their bodies—whether they star in porn, model, strip, or hustle—or all of the above. (978-1-60282-955-8)

Mind Fields by Dylan Madrid. When college student Adam Parsh accepts a tutoring position, he finds himself the object of the dangerous desires of one of the most powerful men in the world—his married employer. (978-1-60282-945-9)

Greg Honey by Russ Gregory. Detective Greg Honey is steering his way through new love, business failure, and bruises when all his cases indicate trouble brewing for his wealthy family. (978-1-60282-946-6)

Lake Thirteen by Greg Herren. A visit to an old cemetery seems like fun to a group of five teenagers, who soon learn that sometimes it's best to leave old ghosts alone. (978-1-60282-894-0)

Deadly Cult by Joel Gomez-Dossi. One nation under MY God, or you die. (978-1-60282-895-7)

The Case of the Rising Star: A Derrick Steele Mystery by Zavo. Derrick Steele's next case involves blackmail, revenge, and a new romance as Derrick races to save a young movie star from a dangerous killer. Meanwhile, will a new threat from within destroy him, along with the entire Steele family? (978-1-60282-888-9)

Big Bad Wolf by Logan Zachary. After a wolf attack, Paavo Wolfe begins to suspect one of the victims is turning into a werewolf. Things become hairy as his ex-partner helps him find the killer. Can Paavo solve the mystery before he runs into the Big Bad Wolf? (978-1-60282-890-2)

The Plain of Bitter Honey by Alan Chin. Trapped within the bleak prospect of a society in chaos, twin brothers Aaron and Hayden Swann discover inner strength in the face of tragedy and search for atonement after betraying the one you most love. (978-1-60282-883-4)

The Moon's Deep Circle by David Holly. Tip Trencher wants to find out what happened to his long-lost brothers, but what he finds is a sizzling circle of gay sex and pagan ritual. (978-1-60282-870-4)

Tricks of the Trade: Magical Gay Erotica, edited by Jerry L. Wheeler. Today's hottest erotica writers take you inside the sultry, seductive world of magicians and their tricks—professional and otherwise. (978-1-60282-781-3)

Straight Boy Roommate by Kevin Troughton. Tom isn't expecting much from his first term at University, but a chance encounter with straight boy Dan catapults him into an extraordinary, wild weekend of sex and self-discovery, which turns his life upside down, and leads him into his first love affair. (978-1-60282-782-0)

In His Secret Life by Mel Bossa. The only man Allan wants is the one he can't have. (978-1-60282-875-9)

Promises in Every Star, edited by Todd Gregory. Acclaimed gay erotica author Todd Gregory's definitive collection of short stories, including both classic and new works. (978-1-60282-787-5)

Raising Hell: Demonic Gay Erotica, edited by Todd Gregory. Hot stories of gay erotica featuring demons. (978-1-60282-768-4)

Pursued by Joel Gomez-Dossi. Openly gay college student Jamie Bradford becomes romantically involved with two men at the same time, and his hell begins when one of his boyfriends becomes intent on killing him. (978-1-60282-769-1)

Timothy by Greg Herren. *Timothy* is a romantic suspense thriller from award-winning mystery writer Greg Herren set in the fabulous Hamptons. (978-1-60282-760-8)

In Stone by Jeremy Jordan King. A young New Yorker is rescued from a hate crime by a mysterious someone who turns out to be more of a something. (978-1-60282-761-5)

Combustion by Daniel W. Kelly. Bearish detective Deck Waxer comes to the city of Kremfort Cove to investigate why the hottest men in town are bursting into flames in broad daylight. (978-1-60282-763-9)

Strange Bedfellows by Rob Byrnes. Partners in life and crime, Grant Lambert and Chase LaMarca are hired to make a politician's compromising photo disappear, but what should be an easy job quickly spins out of control. (978-1-60282-746-2)

The Jesus Injection by Eric Andrews-Katz. Murderous statues, demented drag queens, political bombings, ex-gay ministries, espionage, and romance are all in a day's work for a top secret agent. But the gloves are off when Agent Buck 98 comes up against the Jesus Injection. (978-1-60282-762-2)

Night Shadows: Queer Horror edited by Greg Herren and J.M. Redmann. *Night Shadows* features delightfully wicked stories by some of the biggest names in queer publishing. (978-1-60282-751-6)

Secret Societies by William Holden. An outcast hustler, his unlikely "mother," his faithless lovers, and his religious persecutors—all in 1726. (978-1-60282-752-3)

The Jetsetters by David-Matthew Barnes. As rock band the Jetsetters skyrocket from obscurity to superstardom, Justin Holt, a lonely barista, and Diego Delgado, the band's guitarist, fight with everything they have to stay together, despite the chaos and fame. (978-1-60282-745-5)

The Dirty Diner: Gay Erotica on the Menu, edited by Jerry L. Wheeler. Gay erotica set in restaurants, featuring food, sex, and men—could you really ask for anything more? (978-1-60282-677-9)

Sweat: Gay Jock Erotica by Todd Gregory. Sizzling tales of smoking-hot sex with the athletic studs everyone fantasizes about. (978-1-60282-669-4)

The Marrying Kind by Ken O'Neill. Just when successful wedding planner Adam More decides to protest inequality by quitting the business and boycotting marriage entirely, his only sibling announces her engagement. (978-1-60282-670-0)